Praise for
STELLA CAMERON

"If you haven't read Stella Cameron,
you haven't read romantic suspense."
—Elizabeth Lowell

"Her narrative is rich, her style distinct and
her characters wonderfully wicked."
—*Publishers Weekly*

STELLA CAMERON

is the *New York Times*, *USA TODAY* and *Washington Post* bestselling, award-winning author of more than 50 historical and contemporary romantic suspense novels and novellas. Each of her single-title releases has appeared on the Waldenbooks mass market and romance lists, and on the Barnes & Noble list. Stella has won the *Romantic Times* Career Achievement Award for Romantic Suspense, and both Waldenbooks and BookraK sales awards. In 1998 she was the recipient of the Pacific Northwest Writers' Association Achievement Award for distinguished professional achievement and for enhancing the stature of the Northwest literary community. Stella is married and has three children. Her passions are (surprise!) writing, reading (everything), music and drama—anything performed on a stage. Stella's pets, a dog named Spike and a cat named Raven, are her constant buddies. When she's away on trips, buying gifts for the two furry friends is at the top of her list of musts.

STELLA CAMERON

An Angel In Time

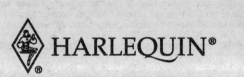

TORONTO • NEW YORK • LONDON
AMSTERDAM • PARIS • SYDNEY • HAMBURG
STOCKHOLM • ATHENS • TOKYO • MILAN • MADRID
PRAGUE • WARSAW • BUDAPEST • AUCKLAND

ISBN 0-373-81075-X

AN ANGEL IN TIME

Copyright © 1991 by Stella Cameron.

All rights reserved. Except for use in any review, the reproduction or
utilization of this work in whole or in part in any form by any electronic,
mechanical or other means, now known or hereafter invented, including
xerography, photocopying and recording, or in any information storage
or retrieval system, is forbidden without the written permission of the
publisher, Harlequin Enterprises Limited, 225 Duncan Mill Road,
Don Mills, Ontario, Canada M3B 3K9.

All characters in this book have no existence outside the imagination of
the author and have no relation whatsoever to anyone bearing the same
name or names. They are not even distantly inspired by any individual
known or unknown to the author, and all incidents are pure invention.

This edition published by arrangement with Harlequin Books S.A.

® and TM are trademarks of the publisher. Trademarks indicated with
® are registered in the United States Patent and Trademark Office, the
Canadian Trade Marks Office and in other countries.

www.eHarlequin.com

Printed in U.S.A.

Chapter One

"Hello! Hannah Bradshaw?"

Hannah heard her name and peered through driving snow. An elderly man waited, smiling, by the front door to her apartment building.

"That's me." Puffing into the scarf she had wrapped around her nose and mouth, she grasped a slippery iron railing and scuffed up the steps.

"A lucky day," the man said, rocking to the square toes of his old-fashioned black boots and back onto his heels. "A very lucky day."

Lucky? So far today she'd lost her secretarial job and been jilted. Well, not exactly jilted. After two years, good old reliable John Norris had told her they shouldn't see each other for a while, that they should date other people to see how strong their bond really was. To Hannah that felt remarkably like a polite way of saying goodbye.

She gained a precarious foothold on the marble top step and took a closer look at her visitor. Clear, kind gray eyes, too young for his face, met her gaze squarely from beneath the rakishly dipped brim of a gray Stetson with a corded band. Hannah thought fleetingly of Confederate uniforms.

"Not the best of days, if I may say so, ma'am." Bushy white brows, a luxuriant mustache and beard covered much of his face.

"It stinks," Hannah said grimly. Usually she loved snow,

particularly in November with the hope of a white Christmas to follow.

"Er, indeed." He bowed slightly. "As you say."

Hannah swept snow from her lashes. There was something about him...

"I've been waiting for you, ma'am," he said, working an envelope from the pocket of the high-buttoned black jacket he wore beneath an oddly long and voluminous gray cape, which looked as if it might be intended for horseback riding in bad weather. A second flap of fabric fell over his shoulders, and Hannah saw with amusement that a stiff collar, held in place by a dark cravat, rose to his jaw. Like a man from another century.

His shaggy brows drew together in a quizzical frown. "Is my arrival inconvenient?"

She realized she'd been staring and pulled the scarf beneath her chin to smile. "Not at all. I've won something, right? Or you're delivering flowers from several admirers. No, no— Miss Universe has been asked to step down and only I can fill her swimsuit."

He shook his head slowly but smiled more broadly. "Does a man a passel of good to hear high spirits from a beautiful young lady." He handed her the envelope and bowed again. "I'm mighty glad I found you. I thought you might be waitin' for this."

Hannah stopped smiling. The accent was soft and unmistakably Georgian, a male echo of her own. And on this "lucky" November day in cold Chicago, the voice from home was enough to drown her in nostalgia. Studying the man, she took the envelope. "You're from Georgia."

He inclined his head. "A long time ago. A very long time ago."

"Where in Georgia?" Hannah ripped open the yellowed envelope and barely caught some sort of ticket that slipped from the folded sheet of paper she pulled out.

"Here and there," the man said, but she'd have sworn he knew her home country, the lush flat land of the state's south, very well. Back there on this early November day, traces of an overnight frost might linger, but chances were the weather was mild enough to make a walk through still-green fields a pleasure.

She unfolded the sheet of paper and read.

> Clarkesville, Georgia
> December 10

My Dearest Hannah,
Mary-Lee Cassidy's baby isn't mine....

Hannah stopped breathing. She raised her face to find the man watching her, unsmiling now, a distant look in his eyes. He reminded her... She made herself continue reading:

I love you, Hannah. There isn't anyone else for me but you. There never could be.

I've tried to find a phone number for you in Chicago. There's no listing. I managed to get the PO Box address from Donna at the post office. Hannah, I can't believe this has happened to us. I got back to Clarkesville a week early, only to find you and your mother had left two days before.

I'm grateful to your mother for the note, but I can't do what she asks. Not trying to contact you is impossible. My father's very ill, and you know how things are here on the farm, otherwise I'd be tearing Chicago apart looking for you. But perhaps it's just as well. We're going to need to be a little careful with money if we're going to try to buy Harmony.

Come home, please. We have a date on Christmas Eve. Four o'clock in the walled garden at Harmony. Remember? I told you I'd have a question to ask then.

Use the bus ticket, Hannah. *Please*. I'll be waiting in the garden.

> I love you,
> Roman.

P.S. Today I thought about us from the beginning, about how we met when you were a scrawny kid with brown eyes that were too big. You had too many freckles and too much shiny brown hair you couldn't braid properly. I thought about how you delivered papers in that awful old truck. Do you remember that, too, Hannah? Those mornings when I waited for you and came along to help out? You were all skinny arms and long tanned legs, but you had a way about you that kept me sneaking out to the road every day. We had to be careful our parents didn't find out because they might say an eighteen-year-old boy had no business spending time with a fifteen-year-old girl. I always told you I was just being kind to a little kid with too much to do, but I loved you then, too. That's something I never did tell you.

The bus ticket's open, so you can come when it's most convenient. Make it real soon. I need you. R.

With shaking fingers, Hannah turned the envelope over again. Her heart pounded, and she blinked to clear her fuzzy vision. The postmark was indistinct, smudged from handling. Scrawled across the bottom in a hand that was unmistakable as her mother's were the words: "Moved. No forwarding address. Return to sender."

And with those words her mother had taken the most important choice of Hannah's life out of her hands. She swallowed acid. A physical blow couldn't have shocked her more. But her mother had been trying to protect her. That was something Hannah mustn't forget, regardless of how wrong the action might have been.

"How…how did you find me from this?"

When she glanced up, the man was at the bottom of the steps. He turned his face up toward her. Failing light and the snow obscured his features. "Like I told you. It's a lucky day." His voice seemed fainter, like the end of an echo. "It's a lucky day. I did a little fancy footwork, put a few things together, and here you were. Enjoy your trip.''

''Mmm?'' Hannah had started rereading. No, she hadn't forgotten the date in the garden, any more than she would ever forget Roman Hunter.

Enjoy your trip? ''How did you know...'' The man had left. Clutching the railing, she went to the bottom of the steps. ''Where did you find this?'' She searched in either direction. Despite the snowfall, she could see to both corners of the short block.

He'd gone. Disappeared. Hannah screwed up her eyes to locate his footsteps. Nothing. As if he'd never existed... Now she was getting fanciful. The snow must have filled in his footprints. But he'd reminded her of someone. She couldn't remember who—not that it mattered. Lots of people looked like other people.

Slowly she let herself into the apartment her mother and new stepfather had insisted on giving her before their departure for Denver a month ago. Hannah had lived here with her mother since they'd left Clarkesville.

She jammed a toe into the heel of one boot and jerked a foot free, then repeated the process with the other foot. In damp socks that left wet marks on worn linoleum tile, she squelched into a crowded room that overlooked the street, shedding outer clothing as she went.

Thoughts of having to find a new job came and slipped away again. She had enough money saved to take her time. At least she could say she'd become redundant rather than been fired. The tiny advertising agency she'd worked for had closed its doors for lack of business.

Blossom, Hannah's oversized black cat, stood up on the back of a lumpy, faded chintz chair and arched her spine until she resembled a pinched croquet wicket.

Hannah sat in the chair and promptly received a bat on top of her head, which she ignored.

She already knew most of the words by heart, but she read the letter again, then closed her eyes. Tall, slim, with thick, slightly wavy black hair and blue eyes; Roman lived in her mind, forever twenty-five as he'd been when they were last together. Now he would be thirty-two, and undoubtedly she'd paled into his past behind whatever life he'd made for himself. Roman's letter had arrived seven years late...too late.

Did he ever think of those early morning meetings now? Hannah rested her head against the chair, breathed in deeply and imagined she smelled sun-dried grass, warm dust and honeysuckle....

"BLAMED TRUCK, anyhow!" Hannah slid from the torn seat of the old, rusted red Chevy truck. "Blamed, rotten mealy-mouthed truck. I'm gonna be late for school and it's all your fault."

She kicked a tire, hopped on one foot and slid to sit on the front fender, clutching a smarting toe. "Darn truck!" If Dad hadn't died and Mom wasn't trying to run the paper without enough money to do more than keep what she called "city sharks" from buying out the *Echo,* then Hannah wouldn't have to get up before the sun did to deliver papers.

"Mealymouthed *truck?*" A soft male voice jolted Hannah. She shot to her feet.

"Can't say I ever heard a truck called mealymouthed before."

She whirled around to face Roman Hunter. His folks owned a peanut farm ten miles or so out of town. He was older than Hannah, but she knew his name because all the girls in class said he was dreamy.

"Anything I can do to help?" He smiled, a slow, one-sided kind of smile. A piece of straw stuck out from between his square white teeth.

"Um...Well..." He was dreamy, all right. Hannah was tall, but he was much taller, with big shoulders and tanned skin. His hair was all ruffled by the breeze, and his eyes were so blue they looked like they'd glow in the dark.

"How come your folks let a kid like you drive around in that big old truck all on your own?"

Pride straightened her back. She wished she wasn't wearing a torn T-shirt and baggy shorts held up by a belt that made the well-washed denim fabric frill around her waist. "The *Clarkesville Echo*'s a family business. We think we should all do something constructive." All two of them as far as actual family went.

"Yeah. That's the way my folks are, too."

Hannah guessed he must not know her dad was dead. "Well, I'd better get on." Please let the truck start. She climbed in and turned the key.

A loud grinding sound made her wince.

She turned the key again.

Nothing.

The door opened beneath her left elbow, almost pitching her out.

"Move over and let me try." Without waiting for her response, Roman climbed up beside her as she slid to the passenger seat. He looked sideways at her and sniffed. "Smell that? You've flooded it."

Hannah frowned. "What does that mean?"

"It means it's gonna take a while before we can get this thing going."

"What am I..." She turned away, scooted close to the door. "Thanks for trying to help. I'll be okay. I'll just have to wait." And be late for school again. Miss Neil made her stand in front of the class and recite a poem last time. And she'd been unable to remember more than every other line. All the kids had laughed.

Roman wasn't saying anything. He wasn't getting out of the truck, either.

Hannah was mortified to feel tears prickle her eyes.

"You're Hannah, aren't you? Hannah Bradshaw?"

"Mmm."

"I'm Roman Hunter. My folks' farm is just back there."

"Mmm."

"Hey! You aren't crying, are you?"

"Nope!" But she dared not turn around. "You go on."

"You gotta deliver all those papers in back?"

She nodded.

"Before school?"

She nodded.

When she felt his gentle tug on one of her braids she held very still. It was very gentle, a kind of friendly tug. Blinking, she turned around and tried a not-too-successful smile. "My dad died last year, and my mom's running the paper. We don't have a whole lot of money to do it with, and so I have to deliver the papers every morning. It's…it's an awful rush…."

Why had she told *him* that? He was years older than her, a senior at the high school when she was only a freshman, and he wasn't interested in her family problems. "I'm sorry."

"Why?"

"For saying all that stuff."

"Listen." He still held the end of her long pigtail. "You start moving all the papers onto the tailgate, okay?"

"Why? I'm already gonna be—"

Roman leaped from the truck, not listening. "Just do it fast. I'll be right back." While she watched, he mounted the bicycle he must have dropped while she was shouting at the Chevy truck and rode off.

Wondering if he was playing a trick on her, Hannah started shifting the bundles of papers from the bed of the truck. Her mother insisted they couldn't afford to hire someone for the rural part of the delivery route. It was up to Hannah to "pull her weight."

Before she'd hefted the last stack, a cloud of dust rose from the track and an even older truck than hers, this one brown with wooden slats along the sides of the bed, roared up. Hannah wished her engine ever sounded as good.

"Right!" It was Roman who jumped out and tossed the papers into the back. "I'll drive, you be the runner. We'll do it in no time."

And they had done it in no time, or so it had seemed to Hannah. Now and then she stole a glance at Roman and felt funny inside. He laughed while he drove, and looked at her as if he liked her, really liked her.

When they'd finished the route he insisted upon dropping her at home to get ready for school and told her he'd get her truck back later. "I do what I say I'll do," he announced when she'd looked dubious and told him she was worried her mother would be mad if she discovered the Chevy truck wasn't around.

Hannah believed Roman. And the truck had been there when she got home from school.

The truck had also started like a dream the next morning, better than it ever had for Hannah before. She'd driven off smiling, wondering what Roman had done to it, and feeling sad that she probably wouldn't ever get to talk to him again. Seniors didn't talk to freshmen.

She'd barely left the last straggling houses of town behind when she saw a tall figure standing in the middle of the road, arms waving overhead.

Roman's smile was something she was never going to forget, she thought, pulling up beside him.

"Mornin'." He rested his tanned forearms on the window rim, grinning up at her. "Could you use some help?"

Hannah's heart had taken off like an automated hammer. "I guess. You don't have to, though."

"I know I don't have to. But people need to stick together. My folks always say that. Move over."

She'd moved over. And morning after morning for the next two years until her mother finally sold the paper, Hannah drove the same road in the seat beside Roman.

When had he said, "You're special to me, Hannah," for the first time? The day when he'd first kissed her she knew by heart: her seventeenth birthday.

"I'm twenty now, Hannah," Roman had said. "Pretty old, huh?"

"Mmm." Seventeen had felt pretty old to her. Roman always seemed the same—grown-up, but like another part of herself, a part she couldn't imagine being without.

"And you're seventeen today. My, are those wrinkles I see around your brown eyes?"

She'd laughed and swatted him. And he'd laughed and caught her shoulders...and stopped laughing.

"You were a kid when we met."

"Yes."

"You aren't a kid now, not really."

"No...I guess not."

"I'm going to look after you, Hannah." His teeth had come down on his lower lip, and he looked at her mouth. "I can't explain it. I just feel we're always going to be together. Do you feel that?"

"Yes," she'd whispered.

Roman's mouth touched hers with such softness, the sensation tickled. But she didn't laugh. Closing her eyes, she waited. He pressed more firmly, parting their lips just a little, until she sighed and slipped her arms around his neck. Roman spanned her waist in wide-splayed, gentle hands, then lifted his head. For a moment he smiled at her, before he held her face against his shoulder and wrapped her tightly to him.

"I love you, Hannah."

HANNAH OPENED HER EYES. So many times Roman had told her he loved her. And so many times she'd echoed him, saying how much she loved him, too.

On Christmas Eve seven years ago she was to have met Roman Hunter in the garden of Harmony House, the beautiful old place they'd planned to buy one day. Roman had been taking a farm management course in Atlanta and had told her he'd be back in time to meet her and ask her something. She'd known the question would be a marriage proposal.

But Mary-Lee Cassidy had blown apart all the years of dreams. Arriving back in Clarkesville from Atlanta, Mary-Lee had sought out Hannah and told her she was carrying Roman's child.

Hannah stood up and slipped the letter into its envelope.

"He didn't want me to be the one to tell you. You know

how kind he is. But this is as much my fault as his.'' Mary-
Lee had put a hand on her stomach. *''You know I was trying
to make it as a model in Atlanta. Roman and I met by accident. I wasn't doing so well. He was lonely.... We met to talk
and... Hannah, we just found we had so much in common.
Now we can't believe it took us so long to realize how much
we've got in common.''*

Hannah would never forget the tearing sensation in her
chest and throat, how she'd turned blindly away and gone to
her mother, who'd insisted they leave Clarkesville immediately.

But Roman's letter of a few days later said Mary-Lee's
child wasn't his. *And Roman didn't lie.* Just as he'd told her
that first day when she'd left the truck on the road near the
Hunter farm: ''You can trust me, Hannah. I don't tell lies. I
do what I say I'll do.'' She'd believed him then.

The phone's raucous jangle made Hannah wince. She
reached past Blossom's disdainful pale blue stare to the table
behind the chair and picked up the receiver.

''Hannah?'' John had a way of sounding frantic. Why
hadn't she noticed that before?

''Hello, John. Are you buried where you are yet?''

''What?''

This was a sign she recognized. When John was nervous
he didn't register enough words to get the gist of a comment.
''The snow, John. Is there a lot of snow over there? It's dump-
ing down here.''

''Oh, yes, yes. Lots of snow. I'm going away for the weekend.''

She didn't recall any agreement to keep each other apprised
of movements. ''Enjoy yourself.''

''Don't be like that. I was just letting you know.''

''I'm not being *like* anything. I hope you enjoy your trip.''
She thought and discarded the notion of telling him she was
back in the job market.

''I'm going with someone.''

Hannah knelt on the seat of the chair, dislodged Blossom

from her perch and rested her own arms on the back. "That was quick. It was only this morning you told me we should date other people, wasn't it? Or did I dream that?"

"Sylvia's someone I met a while ago."

"Long enough to be taking off for a cozy weekend together?"

"Long enough to be considering getting married."

Hannah slowly sank to sit on her heels. "Married?"

"I should have told you earlier."

An understatement. "Possibly, John. Like last weekend when we went out on Saturday night, spent all day Sunday together, and Sunday evening, too. Maybe then?"

"I know this is hurting you. That's why I haven't mentioned it before. I care about you and I wanted to let you down easily."

Suddenly Hannah felt deeply sorry for Sylvia, whoever she was. "Thanks for worrying about my feelings. Have a happy life." John had been fun sometimes, and it was nice to have someone to rely on for company, but he wasn't Mr. Excitement, even if he did see himself in the role.

"You're hurt."

He *wanted* her to be hurt. His ego *needed* her to be hurt. "John, you've enjoyed playing a little game, haven't you?"

"This is typical," he said, sighing. "And I thought you were above the typical possessive female reaction."

Hannah pursed her lips. "This conversation is over. And there won't be any more conversations between us, John. I'm leaving Chicago. And I've got you to thank for helping me make a decision I should have made a long time ago."

"Leaving? But your job. Your apartment."

"I've parted company with my job." He didn't need to know more. "The apartment will sell, and I've never really felt at home in Chicago."

"You're going because of me. You're upset."

Arrogant jerk. She looked at the ceiling. "I'm going because of me. It's time to make a fresh start."

"But where will you go?"

"Home." She removed the receiver from her ear and looked at the mouthpiece. *Home?* Would she really go to Clarkesville?

John was saying something.

"Got to run, John," she said brightly into the phone. "I need to call a real estate broker and start packing. I've got loads to do."

"But I thought we'd get together next week and talk things over."

"Sorry. I'll send you an address when I'm settled. Invite me to the wedding."

"Hannah—"

"Bye, John." She hung up and looked at the envelope in her hands. Why not? She could easily pack up what she cared about, which wasn't a whole lot. Her VW bus was in good shape, and Blossom loved an opportunity to ride shotgun.

Where would she be today if her mother hadn't chosen to take matters into her own hands? Would she have gone back and let Roman say his piece?

Why not go back now?

Head for Georgia, that's all. Visit Clarkesville for a few days and look up a few old friends before she moved on.

Who was she fooling? Seven years late she might be, but she was ready to take the trip Roman had asked her to take so long ago.

Yes. Hannah pulled a phone book out of a drawer in the table and leafed through to the real estate section. She was going home to see Roman Hunter. With luck she'd find the man she remembered so vividly had changed, become dull and ordinary, that it was only distance that made her so sure she still loved him.

Yes, that was the way it would be.

Chapter Two

This was silly, this fluttery, expectant feeling. Coming to Georgia had been silly, a whim she'd almost abandoned many times along the way. She would have been right to give up the idea.

Bypassing Clarkesville and rushing to Harmony House was the silliest thing of all.

But she was here.

Massive holly bushes lined the driveway, their dark, shiny foliage loaded with red berries. Hannah had forgotten how beautiful they were at this time of year. She and Roman used to come here at Christmastime and cut armloads of branches. The gardener had said they could. Then she and Roman would take their hauls home to use as decoration…after they'd crept inside the old house and placed a sprig or two in strategic spots. So Harmony would be ready for Christmas, too.

She and Roman…

They'd been together every spare moment, two people that were like one.

Hannah drove to the side of the house and parked the orange VW bus out of sight. There was no reason to suppose anyone would object to her being here, any more than they ever had.

She got out and looked around. Nothing appeared changed. The two-story house seemed watchful in the pale sunlight of a mild afternoon. Fluted pillars and finely carved friezes shone white against dark red brick.

Just the same. Yet how could it be? When she and Roman used to come here, sneaking into the house with the key they'd found by the sundial, they'd marveled at how beautifully preserved everything was inside. Surely by now there would be signs of decay—not that she expected to find the key still in its hiding place.

Shadowed by the covered porch that circled the house, thick old glass glinted in sash windows.

Could someone have bought Harmony? Hannah and Roman had always been afraid it would happen before they could find a way to own it themselves.

Hannah paused. The only sounds were the shrill call of a lone whippoorwill and the steady rustle of wind in groves of pine and the giant magnolias that crowded the house. *Ring the bell and find out.* Wondering what she would say if someone came, she climbed the steps and pulled the old-fashioned bell.

The ringing echoed and echoed. Then there was silence.

No car stood in the parking area in front of the house. No sign of life showed, except for freshly turned earth in the beds lining the porch. The gardener, the man they'd decided was sent by whoever owned Harmony, must still be keeping his vigil. The gardens, though, were a little overgrown. One man could never do more than touch the surface of the extensive grounds here and there. But there had always been an exotic lushness, even in winter when a promise of chill days hung in the air.

Hannah went back down the steps. The red clay-laced earth sent up a pungent scent like mulched wet leaves. Slowly, her tennis shoes crunching on crushed rock, she circled to the back of the house. Below the porch balusters, hardy russet chrysanthemums nodded between gangly clumps of purple cosmos. Not for the first time this afternoon, she felt her throat tighten. If the doors had been hanging off their hinges and no one had planted flowers, she would have felt sad. Seeing everything as she remembered it brought a storm of nostalgia.

The huge sycamore in the middle of the back lawn stretched naked limbs skyward. Hannah stared at its graceful shape. Winter here was so different from in Chicago, but it felt like her kind of winter. Soon there would be Thanksgiving, then the crisp days before Christmas.

Where would she be for Christmas this year? Not with her mother. Regardless of Emily Bradshaw's motive, Hannah smarted with anger and frustration every time she thought of how her mother had manipulated her. She set her lips firmly together. Wherever she was, she'd make her own happiness.

Behind the sycamore, close to a silver-barked yellowwood tree, the bronze sundial stood on its white stone base. Anxious now, Hannah hurried to stoop and pry up the loose stone at the base.

When she stood, she held a brass key. Automatically she used a toe to push the stone back into place.

Surely someone had bought the house by now. ''I can't just walk in,'' she murmured.

''Hannah Bradshaw, is it?''

She started violently and whirled around, her hand clutching the key against her side. ''Oh! Oh, hello. I didn't hear you coming.'' The gardener, looking exactly as he had on every occasion when she'd seen him over the years, stood only a few feet away.

''How very nice it is to see you, Hannah. It's been far too long.''

Hannah smiled, her breathing returning to normal. ''I've been away. In Chicago. I didn't really expect you to still be here.''

He tilted the wide brim of his straw hat lower. ''I'll be here as long as I'm needed.''

She'd swear the hat was the same one he'd always worn, as was the coarse homespun shirt of dark blue cotton, the old leather suspenders and the loose brown trousers hiked up beneath the knees with string. He looked no older. Not that she could have guessed at his age beyond a vague assessment that he might be in his sixties.

"It's good to see you," Hannah said at last. She'd never known his name, and he hadn't seemed inclined to tell her. "The house looks wonderful. I expect there are new owners."

His gray eyes shifted away. "Nothing has changed, Hannah. It won't until it's time."

Hannah frowned. What an odd thing to say. She shivered. The temperature had dropped. "I don't think I've ever seen so many berries on the holly before."

"Getting ready to show off for Christmas," he commented. His hair, long over the collar he wore buttoned to the throat, was still iron-gray. So was his drooping mustache. "A special Christmas. Welcome home."

A special Christmas. Welcome home. Hannah felt suspended, pulled back in time. "Thank you. I won't be staying long."

"I've no doubt you'll stay as long as you want to," he said.

She wasn't sure what to say. "I expect you're right."

He stood very still. She'd noticed that about him before, the way he didn't seem to move at all until he walked away. She and Roman used to joke that Harmony's gardener just appeared. They never saw him come, only walk away after they'd spoken to him. Hannah realized she was smiling. Talking to him felt comfortable…familiar.

"I'll be on my way," he said. "I oiled the hinges on the back door."

Hannah watched him walk past the yellowwoods and into the dense shrubbery that lined one of the paths leading to the walled garden. She shivered again. The walled garden was one place she wasn't ready to face.

"I oiled the hinges on the back door." The key was hidden in her hand, and he'd never seen either her or Roman retrieve it, as far as she knew. And as far as she knew, no one was aware of their trips into the house.

Fanciful again. Of course he'd seen them—and the key, otherwise he wouldn't mention the door.

"I oiled the hinges..." As if he'd expected her?

Hannah grimaced and hurried toward the back porch. He undoubtedly oiled the hinges regularly.

The screen door creaked on cue, but the key turned easily in the lock, and, as the gardener promised, not a sound came from the smooth hinges.

Then she was inside, walking through the big kitchen lined with glass-fronted cabinets. Iron pots stood atop the black metal stove. Rows of thick crockery jars marched along scrubbed wooden counters each side of steel sinks deep enough to climb inside.

Hannah grinned as she passed into the hall. Nothing had changed. Before she left Clarkesville she'd find out who maintained Harmony. Someone definitely did. She also wanted to know why it had never been put on the market. Roman used to say... Never mind what Roman used to say. The legend of Harmony House was undoubtedly part truth. It was also undoubtedly more fairy story, embellished over the years by locals.

In the wide hallway, with its curving staircase, the jewel-toned glass in the fanlight over the front door cast a colored pattern on polished oak floors.

Someone came and cleaned this house. Why hadn't she ever seen him or her? And why had everyone in Clarkesville always talked as if Harmony was in disrepair? Roman used to say it was because they were all afraid the place was haunted and never came here to see how it looked. And he used to say the two of them should keep quiet so no one else would get the idea they'd like to buy.

Roman used to...

Hannah puffed up her cheeks. One quick look at the windows in the tiny sitting room and she'd leave. And she wouldn't go creeping around town, pretending she was casually passing through, almost by accident, while in truth she searched for a glimpse of Roman. No. One peek in the sitting room and she'd head out of the area.

Head where? She stepped into the little room to the left of the front door. Why not Atlanta? She'd visited there once or twice and liked it.

The blue damask feinting chair stood as it always had, close enough for a reclining lady to have a clear view through the window to the drive. Hannah crossed rose-colored carpet worn soft and thin by the more than a hundred years it had spent on this floor.

Deep blue velvet drapes were caught back from the single window by gold-tasseled ropes. Hannah knew exactly what she was looking for. She lifted the left drape away from the window and touched elegantly scratched words in the glass: *Seth and Esther. December 24, 1875.*

Hannah bowed her head. Had she thought the scratched engraving would be gone? And had she thought that if it had been, the spell of this place would be broken and she'd no longer ache for what might have happened here on another Christmas Eve only seven years ago?

She turned away and her hand went to her throat. On one side of the room stood a fireplace faced with blue-and-rose-colored enameled tiles. Along the molded plaster mantel, someone had arranged sprigs of holly...fresh holly beaded with drops of moisture.

Hannah's heart pounded. That had been one of the spots where she and Roman had put holly for Christmas.

Whoever cleaned the house must have done it.

She shivered. A draft moved across the floor, chilling her ankles. Suddenly she wanted to leave, not to be alone here anymore. Too many memories slept within these walls, waiting to awaken and draw her back. Hannah knew there could be no going back, not to the innocent happiness she'd once thought would last forever.

If she hurried, she'd be more than a hundred miles on her way to Atlanta before nightfall.

HE DIDN'T USUALLY give in to impulse. Not anymore.

Leaving his pickup beside the road, Roman took a side path from the gates of Harmony into the grounds. Funny how that woman in town had started talking about the old house as if she knew it had once been important to him. It still was in a way, not that he'd been out here for years. Not since Christmas Eve of the year when Hannah left.

The heels of his boots sank into spongy turf. All week he'd been unable to get Hannah out of his mind. Maybe it was the season. Christmas wasn't far off, and that had always been their special time of year. But he didn't remember feeling quite the way he did now last year. Now he could see her so clearly he almost expected her to walk around the corner and meet him.

Withered blooms still clung to azalea bushes along the path. That old gardener who used to come years ago must finally have given up...or the owners, whoever they were, had decided to let the place go. From here Roman could see through pine trees to the sloping slate roofs of the house. He never intended to go inside again, not when every inch of the place would remind him of tiptoeing through the rooms with Hannah, the two of them whispering and making plans for when they'd live there themselves.

Roman strolled on, his thoughts now on the present. The farm was doing well. Irrigation had been the best investment he'd ever made. It ensured that he didn't suffer the fate of those farmers who relied on rainfall that sometimes didn't come for months. In a year or two, if things continued as they were, he might even be in a position to think about buying a place like this. Since there must be so much to be done, the price would be bound to be low. Not that any of that mattered anymore.

He came to the tall, ivy-covered wall almost without realizing he'd walked far enough. Red brick showed through the green vines. Roman walked on until he reached the wooden gate with its iron ring handle and hesitated.

Why *had* he come?

"That old Harmony House sure is a lovely place," the woman had said. He'd met her earlier in the afternoon when he was coming out of Cassidy's Dry Goods. She just appeared at his elbow and walked along, talking like they were old friends instead of never having really met before. Donna at the post office had told him the woman's name was Jane Smith and she'd opened a Christmas shop in town—whatever a Christmas shop might be.

Roman threaded his fingers through the handle and turned. Immediately the gate swung inward. This walled garden had fascinated him from the first day he and Hannah had ridden bikes out here and decided to explore.

"I hear tell there's a beautiful walled garden out there."

Jane Smith was right. The lush, almost exotic garden inside the high wall was beautiful. Almond and camellia, draping forsythia and spiky quince, crab apple, hydrangea and myrtle—shrub after shrub vied for attention beneath trailing willow branches. Boxwood billowed in clumps, and clematis vines clung to the inside of the walls.

The garden was beautiful, but he hadn't felt like coming for seven years. Why now?

Roman's feet took him unerringly past beds of roses to the place where a hedge formed a dense screen. He knew where the gap was. Once through, he was faced with the circle of dogwoods, their branches intertwining.

Pushing back his denim jacket, he thrust his hands deep into the pockets of his jeans. Being here still made him feel raw. Damn, and he'd thought he was over it.

Someone had recently painted the white picket fence around the small burial plot amid the dogwoods. Roman shrugged. The place could have been bought, he supposed. In which case he was trespassing. He'd been trespassing when he came with Hannah, but they'd never thought of it that way and the gardener had seemed to encourage them.

Roman opened the gate and walked to the foot of a grave, the only grave in a space that had clearly been intended for several more. If someone came and complained about him being here, he'd apologize and leave. No big deal.

The headstone was of rosy pink Georgia marble. He could recite the inscription by heart, but he read it aloud. "Esther Marie Ashley, born December 24, 1855, died December 24, 1892. Also John Ashley, born and died December 24, 1892. Most beloved wife and son of Seth Ashley. We'll make it grow forever, my angel."

"We'll make it grow forever, my angel." With Hannah, Roman had worried that sentence around and around, coming up with dozens of different meanings. They would never know what Seth Ashley, in his sadness, had really wanted to say.

A sudden strong gust of wind rattled the bare dogwood limbs. Roman shuddered and clamped his elbows to his sides. He should get out to the farm. Tonight he intended to put in some hours on the books. And Adam had asked to talk to him. The thought was troublesome. His brother usually avoided anything approaching a meaningful conversation. This request for a "serious chat" didn't bode well. It probably meant Adam needed another loan against his share of the farm their mother had deeded to them when she'd remarried a neighboring farmer.

Roman turned from the grave and stood still. While he peered through the increasing gloom, he took several sharp breaths through his mouth.

Hell, his mind was playing tricks.

If it wasn't, Hannah Bradshaw was standing a few yards away, talking to someone he couldn't see, someone on the other side of the hedge.

Roman couldn't seem to move. It *was* Hannah. Tall—five foot nine without shoes according to the notches they'd made in a doorjamb out at the farm—she stood just as he'd always seen her in his mind, with her weight on one leg, her slender hips thrust forward.

He swallowed. What the hell was going on? Some strange woman mentioned Harmony and he came rushing out here as if pulled by some invisible string. And here, after seven years, was Hannah, the woman he loved...used to love so much he'd thought he couldn't keep on living without her.

Could Hannah have asked Jane Smith to get Roman to come out here?

Jane hadn't asked him, only sowed the idea. She'd said the place was beautiful, and he'd felt he *had* to come. Coincidence. That was all this was—coincidence.

Hannah's hair was long again, the way it had been when they'd met. He smiled. Those lumpy braids had usually looked as if she'd done them in the dark. Now her chestnut brown hair shone in what was left of this afternoon's light. Straight and blunt-cut, it slipped across her shoulders as she talked.

He couldn't hear what she was saying.

If he moved quickly and carefully, he could leave without her seeing him.

He didn't want to....

Hannah must be twenty-nine. In a bright green sweater with a roll neck, and jeans, her lithe shape didn't appear to have changed. She stood straight, her face tilted up. The sweater emphasized her full breasts, and the jeans reminded him of just how long and shapely her legs were.

His heart thudded in his ears. Was she married? She must be. Did she have children? He raised his chin. They'd talked about the kids they'd have one day. The jolt that passed through him was easily recognizable. He was envious of some faceless, nameless man who had claimed what Roman had assumed for so long would one day be his.

She began to back down the path, and he finally heard her clear voice. "Goodbye. It's been good to see you again. I'll certainly think about what you said."

With that, she turned and hurried toward Roman... "Oh, I'm sorry. I didn't see... Oh, my God!" She almost bumped into him.

Roman thought there was no other face like Hannah's. In summer she used to tan lightly, but evidently she hadn't seen any sun for a long time, and her skin was creamy pale. The smattering of freckles he liked so much showed clearly over the bridge of her tip-tilted nose.

"Roman." It was part statement, part question. Her lips remained slightly parted, and he glanced at their full, softly curved lines.

He still loved her.

SHE HAD ONLY TO LIFT her hands to touch him. "I…" There were no words to say what she felt. She'd been about to leave when the gardener appeared and told her he'd seen Roman out here. Hannah hadn't believed him, but despite her vow not to come to the garden, she'd been unable to resist. Once through the gate in the wall, the gardener had come again— urging her on to the burial plot.

"Hello, Hannah."

"I… Yes." She looked back in the direction she'd come. "The gardener. Well. He was right here." She searched the path. It ran straight through archways of trees, but there was no sign of the man. "You remember him, don't you?"

"Of course."

She might have to touch Roman. Since her legs threatened to buckle, she might have to hold on to him to stop from falling down. "Well, I wasn't sure…. I didn't expect to see him after so long." And where had he gone so quickly?

"Seven years." Roman didn't smile. His firm, serious mouth jerked down at the corners. There were fine lines, squint and laugh lines, at the corners of his eyes. And those eyes were as brilliantly blue and piercing as she remembered.

"Yes, seven years."

"Did you count them, Hannah?"

"Count?"

"The years. I did. For a long time I counted the days. Sometimes the hours."

"Yes," was all she could mutter. He must think she'd received his letter and decided to ignore it. She couldn't bring herself to announce that her mother had sent it back, but that it had gotten lost and showed up only a week ago.

Roman could have put the holly on the mantel in the house. But she wouldn't mention that. And she mustn't read too much into what it might mean if he had.

"How have you been, Hannah?"

She pushed her mouth into a smile. "Fine. Wonderful. You?"

"Fine." He took off the black Stetson he wore low over his brow and ran his long fingers through dark wavy hair. "Wonderful. Just like you."

Although Thanksgiving was barely a week away, his olive skin still bore a marked tan. Beneath his jacket he wore a white cotton shirt open at the neck. Black hair curled there. The heavy muscle in his shoulders and chest filled out his clothes. His shoulders used to feel so solid under her hands, and when he'd held her face to his chest she'd felt safe and so loved.

Hannah looked away.

"What brings you home... I mean...why are you here, Hannah?"

Because, for some reason I don't understand, I wanted to see you. "This is going to sound corny. But I'm just passing through." She laughed and the effort sounded phony. No way would she let him know that the letter he'd probably forgotten sending had had the power to bring her rushing back to try and see him again.

"I see." He kicked at dirt with a scuffed boot. "And you got the feeling you'd like to come out to Harmony."

Exactly. A feeling she'd been helpless to ignore. "Yes. I always liked it here." Her dry throat ached.

"We both did," Roman said softly. "Remember?"

There was no gray in his almost-black hair. "I remember." She glanced the length of him, all the way past his flat stomach to lean hips and long, powerful legs.

"It's nice to see you, Hannah."

She tilted her head to look up at him. "It's nice to see you, too." *And painful, and confusing.*

"You've still got those freckles."

His smile twisted her heart, and she found herself smiling back unreservedly. "Yep. All that rubbing with lemon juice and borax didn't phase 'em, did it?"

"And sugar, too. Wasn't that the other thing old Mrs. Freeman told you to put in that foul concoction?"

"Uh-huh."

"Thought so. Well, it sure didn't help, thank God." He laughed, showing strong white teeth. "I was always crazy about those freckles."

In the same instant, they both stopped laughing.

"When I got back from Atlanta and found you'd gone I thought I'd lose my mind," Roman said quietly.

Hannah put trembling fingers to her throat.

"I finally went to Chicago and searched—" he slapped his hat rhythmically against his thigh "—but I couldn't find you. My God, Hannah. I felt as if I was dying."

His eyes glittered.

Shaking passed through every muscle and nerve in her body. "So did I." It was too late for all this. Too much had happened.

Roman lifted a hand and rested his forefinger on her lips. "I used to wonder what they meant when they said you could exist without really being alive. I don't anymore. I did it for a very long time."

"How—" She cleared her throat and he dropped his hand. "How are your folks?"

"My dad died the year after you left."

"Oh, Roman." Mr. Hunter had been a kind, reserved man who had always made Hannah quietly welcome at the farm. "I'm sorry."

"Me, too. I still miss him."

"How about your mom?"

"Remarried." He smiled, his old lopsided glad smile. "Four years ago to Jed Thomas over the way from us. Mom gave the farm to Adam and me, so now we're neighbors. She seems happy and I'm happy for her. Jed's a nice guy.''

As quickly as he'd smiled, his face became very serious. ''What about your mother, Hannah?''

''Remarried, too. Believe it or not. She married a businessman from Denver and went there to live six months ago.'' *And what about you, Roman? What's happened to you?*

''You're even lovelier than I remember.''

He spoke so softly, Hannah wondered if she'd misheard. The intense gleam in his eyes let her know she'd understood him perfectly well.

''Hannah?''

''Thank you.''

''Your mother's note... When I saw it I didn't think I'd make it through the night.''

He must be referring to the note he'd mentioned in his letter, the one her mother had left for him when they went to Chicago. ''She was trying to look after me.'' Would he deny again that Mary-Lee's baby had been his?

''I know she was.''

He kept looking at her, visually touching every inch of her until she burned.

''I've never stopped wanting you.''

She took a step and stumbled. Roman grasped her arms, and she didn't have the strength to pull away.

''Did you hear what I said?'' Desire was in every tense line of his face. They were older, their lives had taken very different routes, but the raging need that had grown between them was as bright and demanding as ever.

''Say something, Hannah.''

''I wasn't going to come out to the garden.''

''Why?''

She shrugged.

His hands made jerky passes up and down her arms. ''We never... There was so much going on with your mother's problems, and with my folks, too. We both wanted to wait…for everything. It was supposed to be so right when we…'' He closed his eyes and held his bottom lip in his teeth.

Hannah heard the beat of her own heart. ''Don't talk about it, please. It's too late.'' She looked at his left hand. No wedding ring.

''Is it too late?'' His grip on her arms tightened, and he pulled her closer. ''You came here. You must have…you must have thought we might meet.''

She shook her head.

''Yes, Hannah. Yes, you did. Why weren't you going to come out into the garden?''

''Because it would remind me of you.'' There. She'd said it. Her knees weakened. Roman must have felt her start to slump. He gathered her forcefully against him.

''I've got to go.'' She tried to push away.

''Why? You came back. Why do you have to go?''

''It's too late for us, Roman.'' Whatever they felt in this moment was false, an illusion built by the place and the atmosphere—and their shared memories.

''Why does it have to be?''

There was desire in his eyes, and danger…and its power over her.

''I've never stopped hoping you'd come back, Hannah. I never believed that what we'd had together could just disappear.''

''We're older. We've lived separate lives.''

''Are you saying there's someone else?''

''N-no. There's never been anyone too serious.''

He crossed his arms behind her back and pushed his hands into her hair. ''If you wanted to, we could have what we had in the past.''

''No!'' She struggled, but he held on, carefully but firmly. ''That kind of thing happens in movies, not in real life.''

''I love you!''

Hannah opened her mouth. Before she could speak, Roman's lips came down on hers, fierce for an instant, then so very, very gentle. Back and forth he brushed, the tip of his tongue making the barest contact. Deep in his throat he murmured, and she felt him tremble. Hannah let her eyes drift shut.

Magic. Magic had brought her back here, and magic had somehow guided Roman to the same spot at the same time. There was nowhere else she wanted to be.

"I've missed you," he said against her ear. "There hasn't been a day when I haven't wondered where you are and prayed I'd find you again."

"I've missed you, too." The voice she heard barely resembled her own. Joy swelled in her, and passion. She wanted Roman. "There'll be a lot of building to do."

"I know." He nuzzled her jaw up and kissed her neck. His hips pressed into her, and the speed of their response to each other only thrilled Hannah.

"We're not the same."

"Not exactly." Roman raised his head, inclined his face and studied her. "You got even better-looking."

"So did you."

They laughed in unison.

"I knew there was a good reason why I missed you so much. You're the only woman I ever met who said things like that to me."

It would be all right. Roman would make it all right between them again. He'd told the truth in that letter. This was why she'd been compelled to return to Clarkesville. To Harmony.

Slowly he lowered his mouth to hers once more. His hands slipped to her bottom, urging her close, so close she could feel every firm line of him. This couldn't be too fast. They'd been ready to marry seven years ago, even if they had never made love before she left.

Hannah wrapped her arms around his neck and arched her breasts against him. If the surge of pulsing heat she felt was lust, then she hoped she'd feel it again and again with Roman Hunter.

He laughed and rubbed a slightly stubbly cheek against

hers. "When I got up this morning I never dreamed what the day would hold."

"Neither did I." And she didn't intend to question too closely the events that had brought her back to Harmony.

"Kiss me, Hannah. Hold me. Make me believe I'm not dreaming this."

She sighed and parted his lips with her tongue.

"Where are you?" A high-pitched voice shrilled from behind Hannah. "Hello! Are you here?"

At the sound of a childish voice, Roman stepped back so sharply Hannah grabbed his sleeve.

A small girl flew down the path, a froth of blond curls whipping in the wind.

Hannah swallowed and looked at Roman. "Do you know her? Who's she looking for?"

Roman turned up a palm. "You and I need to talk."

"Donna at the post office said she thought you might be here." Arriving at Roman's side, the child smiled up into his face. "We couldn't think why you would be, but we came, anyway. Did you forget the school program?"

He smiled at the girl and sent Hannah a look she couldn't read. "This is Penny. Penny, this is my friend, Hannah."

"Hi, Hannah." She took Roman's hand and pulled. "Come on, Daddy. We're gonna be late. Mommy's waiting in the car."

Chapter Three

"Well, if it isn't little Hannah Bradshaw."

"Hello, Ellie." So much for finding somewhere to grab a quick, anonymous meal before heading north.

By Hannah's figuring, Ellie Sumpter must be closer to eighty than seventy. Sumpter's Drop In had been Clarkesville's only restaurant for as long as Hannah remembered. And Ellie Sumpter had seemed old when Hannah was a kid.

"Hey, Al!" Ellie's cracked voice rose to a shriek. "Come and see who we got here."

Hannah couldn't help smiling. Ellie's thin, deeply seamed face had flushed pink with pleasure. Cool as the evening had become, she wore a sleeveless print blouse and baggy cotton slacks beneath a wraparound apron covered with cavorting teddy bears.

Skinny arms akimbo, gnarled, red-knuckled hands plunked on bony hips, she favored Hannah with a broad grin. She hooked a thumb toward the kitchen. "He don't hear so good anymore. Won't get no hearing aid. *Men.* Vain, the whole passel of 'em."

"Vain," Hannah agreed. Men weren't at the top of her list of favored conversation topics tonight. They probably never would be again. "Um, I was wondering if you still made those world-famous hush puppies? And maybe some chicken stew and strip dumplings?" An hour ago, driving away from Harmony after watching Roman leave with the little girl who was obviously his daughter, food had been the furthest thing from Hannah's mind. She'd leaped into the bus, raising a squall from Blossom, and roared out of the grounds.

Encroaching darkness and a rush of bone-tiredness had made her decide that she ought to at least eat before heading for Atlanta.

Clarkesville was the only choice for a place to eat in a radius of fifty miles.

"What you screamin' for, Ellie?"

With something close to total disbelief, Hannah watched Al Sumpter, Ellie's even more ancient brother, emerge from the purple-beaded curtain that separated the kitchen from the restaurant. He puffed and struggled under the weight of a tattered cardboard box.

"This is Hannah, Al. You remember little Hannah Bradshaw? Will Bradshaw's girl?"

Her father's name sounded unfamiliar in Hannah's ears.

"A'course I remember." Al slid the box onto a table and grinned, driving rippling lines into his round, red face. "She thinks I don't hear, nor see, anything. Or say much of any count, neither." He smoothed down the few white hairs left on his pink scalp.

"Hush puppies. Chicken stew and strip dumplings." Ellie nodded approvingly. "You bin away a long time, girl. I'm glad to see you ain't forgotten what good food is. Git what the girl wants, Al."

"But—"

"You git it, Al. Hannah and me's got some catchin' up to do."

Al scuffed off, muttering as he went.

Hannah was pleased to see Ellie, but she didn't want to "catch up" on anything to do with Clarkesville. Deep burning embarrassment at the way she'd allowed Roman to kiss her, hold her, the way she'd kissed him back, washed over her in hot waves.

How could she have been such a fool? At least she'd ignored his attempts to make her say they'd meet again.

"What sent you and your momma rushing off the way you did?" Ellie asked. "Donna at the post office finally told me you'd headed for Chicago. If she knew anything else, she wasn't talking."

Hannah, seated at a window table overlooking the town square, made much of scooting in her chair and pushing her purse onto the windowsill. "Mom and I had been thinking of moving," she improvised.

"Is that a fact?" Ellie, showing surprising strength, hefted the cardboard box to Hannah's table. "Never heard any mention of it. Thought you and the Hunter boy had been planning on tying the knot."

Hannah laughed and waved a hand dismissively. She was grateful Ellie made no mention of Roman's marriage, or his child. But Ellie had always been kind.

"Will you look at this." Ellie pulled an elf with a foam head from the box. "Got this on a box of chocolates from some trucker. Must have been twenty years ago." She smoothed floppy green satin legs and arms and shook a little brass bell atop a red felt hat. "Been putting him on the tree ever since."

"Are you getting out the decorations already?" Hannah peered into the box. A jumble of glitter, ribbon and tinsel gave off the tang of old pine from forgotten Christmas trees. "Looks as if you could use a few new things."

"Nothing like the old ones," Ellie said stoutly. "I'm just going to sort these out. Got to keep pace with the times. Next week's Thanksgiving, and the day after I'm gonna start gussying the place up. Always did love a bit of gaudy glitter at Christmas."

If Hannah remembered correctly, Aladdin's Awful Cave had been the not-too-kind label given to Sumpter's Christmas decor. She picked up a can of spray-on snow. Although she'd never admitted it, to anyone but Roman, she had loved the crowded sparkle of Ellie Sumpter's seasonal splendor. Sitting amid the fragrant smell of pecan pies, drinking hot cider and looking through the snowflakes Ellie made with her can of phony snow and torn newspaper stencils, Hannah used to feel a warm rush of comfort and anticipation.

You can't go back. How many times had she heard that? She should have listened.

"Order of hush puppies coming up!" Al Sumpter arrived to plop a plate of the golden-fried cornmeal morsels in front of Hannah. "Stew to follow. We're sure glad to have you back with us, Hannah."

"Thank you. But I'm not—"

"Will Emily be joining you in time for Christmas?"

"No. She's remarried and living in Denver. But—"

"My. You hear that, Ellie? Emily Bradshaw's got herself hitched again."

"That's fine," Ellie said, smoothing her apron. "Always said she was widowed too young. Poor woman. Struggling with that paper all on her own. Losing the house. Too much."

"That was a long time ago," Hannah said awkwardly. "She's doing very well now. But I won't be—"

"I'm real glad to hear about your mother," Ellie said. "I know she didn't like the office work for Doc Willis. Not that she didn't do a good job. Always determined, Emily was."

And respected, Hannah thought. But never particularly liked for her seriousness and detached attitude toward the people of Clarkesville. Sooner or later, Hannah had to have a confrontation with her mother. Despite what had just happened with Roman, it had been wrong for her mother to tamper with someone else's life.

Ellie pulled a wadded ball of tinsel strings from the box and frowned while she pried them loose, spreading them, one by one, on a table.

The hush puppies tasted wonderful. But it was dark outside now. Hannah stared at the big spruce in the middle of the square. Lights at the base of the trunk shone up into swaying branches.

How far would she have to drive to find a motel? She'd learned to depend upon herself for everything, but the thought of driving through the night with no set destination unnerved her.

A cool draft and the jangle of the bell over the door snared her attention. She held still, the fork halfway to her mouth.

"Ah, lovely." A small woman had come into the restaurant. "Hello, Ellie. How nice and warm it is in here." She carried a large package wrapped in silver paper with a huge red bow.

Ellie straightened from her task and nodded at the newcomer. "Evenin'. What can we get you?"

"It's not what you can get me." The woman's voice was surprisingly low and musical. "I've brought something for you. But I'll sit over here with Hannah."

Hannah put her fork down, a hush puppy still impaled. Victorian, she thought at last. Beneath a short velvet cape, the woman's full-skirted, floor-length dress was made of palest blue silk trimmed with white lace. Long sleeves belled over puffy, frilled undersleeves, also of white lace, and a snowy muslin chemisette frothed from the neck to the waist of a deep-cut bodice. As she walked, there was a swish of many taffeta petticoats.

"Hello, Hannah."

When she realized her mouth was open, Hannah closed it quickly. The woman knew her name. "Hello." Eyes the same pale blue as the gown glowed softly. Beneath a beribboned silk bonnet, silvery blond hair was drawn back from a central part. Ringlets escaped around the face and at the neck.

"May I sit with you?"

"Ah…yes, yes, of course." Hannah felt gangly and clumsy beside this exquisite person. She also felt weird and disoriented. "How do you know my name?"

"Oh—" a small hand encased in a white kid glove waved airily "—someone mentioned you."

Hannah frowned. "Mentioned me?"

"My name's Jane Smith." The woman smiled, curving a small, softly bowed mouth. "The gardener at Harmony House. I think you know him?"

"Yes."

"Yes, well he told me he'd seen you today and that you'd driven toward town. I was coming here to see Ellie, and when I saw you in the window, I thought, 'That must be Hannah Bradshaw.' After all, we don't get many newcomers in Clarkesville." She laughed as she put her package on the table. "Not that you're really a newcomer. But you know what I mean."

Ellie, one arm folded over her middle, toyed with a tight white curl behind her ear. "What will you have?" she asked.

"Oh, Ellie." Jane Smith smiled up brightly and proffered the parcel. "This is for you."

A wary gleam brightened Ellie's eyes. "For me?"

"A little bird told me Christmas is your favorite season. This is a little something to help you get ready."

Ellie took the package, held it to her ear and shook. Immediately she turned a bright shade of pink. "Well, now. For me? You're sure?"

"Absolutely certain." Slipping into the chair opposite Hannah, Jane arranged the voluminous folds of her skirts and worked a small, beaded purse from her wrist. "Open it now so Hannah and I can see if you like it."

With infuriating care, Ellie peeled away wrappings, slipped off the lid of the box inside and parted layers of red and green tissue paper. "Oh, my." Reverently she lifted out two porcelain figures, a man and a woman. The woman's red satin dress was similar to Jane's, with the addition of a white fur jacket and muff, and white fur lining her bonnet. The gentleman was dashingly dressed in knee-length woolen britches over long socks, a woolen jacket, vest and matching cap. Both figures sported tiny but perfect ice skates.

Jane reached to pat Hannah's hand and their eyes met. The little woman's fingers were cold. "Have my coffee," Hannah offered, pushing her untouched cup across the table. Jane smiled and inclined her head. She could be twenty or thirty, or perhaps even older. Hannah couldn't tell.

"Oh, my." Ellie sounded breathless. From the bottom of

the box she extracted a carved wooden drum topped with mirror and edged with piles of glittery cotton snow.

"This is how it works." Jane set the figures atop the mirrored surface and turned a key in the side of the drum. Music tinkled forth, *The Skaters' Waltz,* and the gentleman and his lady began to sweep over the surface, twirling and swinging in time to the music.

"It's the most beautiful thing I ever saw," Ellie whispered. "I'll keep it on the counter and show it to the kids."

"And the grown-ups," Hannah said, enchanted. "What a beautiful thing."

"It's called *At the Frost Fair.* Like they had in London in winter," Jane said, her blue eyes distant. "Graceful days. Everyone so carefree and happy."

Hannah looked at Ellie's tightly permed white curls and Jane's elegant silk poke bonnet bent over the swirling figures. She ought to leave.

"What do I owe you?" Ellie asked awkwardly.

"Why, it's just a little present from the Christmas Shop," Jane said. "From one Clarkesville business to another."

"I can't let you do—"

"I insist." Jane held up a hand. "Do you suppose we could have another cup of coffee? Hannah's given me hers."

Cradling her new treasure, Ellie turned away without a word.

"Do you have a place to stay?"

Hannah stared. "I beg your pardon?"

"A place? With no hostelry in town, I wondered where you were going to stay."

"Well…" She studied the moonless sky. "No, not yet."

"Then fate sent me. I just knew it had."

Hannah looked at her food and realized she'd lost her appetite again. "Fate?" Al must have forgotten the stew, thank goodness.

"Yes. Now, you know I've got the Christmas Shop over on Oak Street."

"Well—"

"I've only been open a few days. I was here some years ago and fell in love with the place. So when the time seemed right I decided to come back and open a Christmas shop. Old world tradition is my theme."

Hannah nodded slowly. "I see. And that's why you dress like that." Quickly she added, "You look very beautiful."

"Umm. Thank you." Jane spread her arms. "Yes. Exactly. And I'm going to be very busy. I can tell already by all the people who come by the window to look. It's a little early, but you wait until the end of next week when Thanksgiving's over. Everyone's going to want my handmade decorations and my baked goods. I'm going to offer complete sets of matching tree decorations from baubles to bows. Or there'll be country mishmash for those who prefer. And candy apples made while you wait. There'll be hot cider and spiced tea and cookies. I just know you're going to love it there."

"I'm not sure I'll have time—"

"You're really very welcome. There are two bedrooms, and I certainly only need one, don't I?"

Hannah opened and closed her mouth.

"They're over the shop with a lovely view of the square. I wanted that so I could see the tree when they've put up the lights." Jane nodded to the big spruce outside. "You make yourself right at home. Use the kitchen like it was your own and come and go as you please."

"Oh, I couldn't—"

"But you most certainly can. Don't we southern people pride ourselves on hospitality?"

"Yes." Bemused, Hannah glanced up as Ellie set another mug of coffee on the table. "Thank you."

Ellie, still looking pleased, hurried back to the counter to rewind her musical skating rink.

"That's settled then," Jane said happily. "I'll have to go, but you come as soon as you're ready. You can't miss the shop."

"But I was going on to—"

"If you like it there, perhaps I can persuade you to take a

little job with me. I've been planning to have an assistant so I can take an outing when the occasion presents.''

Hannah felt tired. "I won't be staying long enough to need a job, I'm afraid."

"No?" Jane's mouth thrust out in a small, disappointed pout. "Never mind. You make yourself at home for as long as you want to. Who knows, you may change your mind about going on to Atlanta."

Not for the first time today, Hannah felt disoriented. Had she said she intended to go to Atlanta? She couldn't remember what she'd said to anyone anymore. "I really should leave tonight."

Jane got up in a rustle of petticoats. "Nonsense," she said matter-of-factly. "A young lady cannot travel through the night alone. I won't hear of it."

"But—" Hannah scrabbled in her jeans pockets for money to pay Ellie.

"Not another argument." Jane reached the door. "I shall put a warming pan in your bed. The shop door will be open."

With that she left, blue silk swirling behind her.

"Good grief! Ellie, did you hear that?"

"Uh-huh. Nice little body, ain't she?" She wound up the music box yet again. "Might have to forget about Thanksgiving and get right on to Christmas," she said dreamily.

"Good grief," Hannah moaned. She could simply walk out the door, climb into her VW and drive away. But... No, she couldn't. "How much do I owe you, Ellie?"

"Not a thing," Ellie said. "That was a morsel of welcome home. Should a'thought of askin' where you were staying myself. Mrs. Smith will take good care of you, though."

"I give up," Hannah muttered. She got up and collected her purse—and noted that Jane Smith hadn't touched the coffee. *Fate.* Hannah didn't believe in fate, did she? She thought of the old letter hidden in the pocket of one of her suitcases. If "fate" hadn't intervened, she'd undoubtedly have made this trip seven years ago...and it would have been just as much of a mistake then.

"Bye, Ellie," she called, and got no response before she walked out into the cool evening.

The town was as quiet as she remembered. The offices and shops surrounding the square showed unlit windows to the hushed street. To her left stood the town hall, its white-columned entrance and stone steps palely illuminated. In the distance, behind the block that housed the police station and the firehouse, a church spire rose. At night in Clarkesville, people were closeted in their homes, or in the homes of their neighbors, unless there was bingo at the church hall or an event at the century-old schoolhouse.

The schoolhouse was probably where most people were tonight, Hannah decided, attending the program Roman's little girl had been so anxious about.

Hannah sighed. The smarting in her eyes annoyed her, but she couldn't expect not to react to the events of today. Suddenly she was grateful for Jane Smith's invitation. She probably didn't even have enough gas to drive far, and who knew where the next open station would be.

She walked to the curb and began to cross to where she'd parked the VW bus. When she made out the silhouette of a man standing on the opposite curb, she stopped. So did her breathing.

"Hannah?"

It wasn't Roman's voice. "Yes," she said uncertainly. "Who is it?"

He moved to meet her in the middle of the road. "Adam Hunter. I've been looking for you."

"You and a few other people," she said before she had time to regroup.

Adam Hunter was as blond and hazel-eyed as Roman was dark and blue-eyed. In the meager light available, Adam's pale hair glinted. Stockier and shorter than his brother, he had the kind of athletic build and all-American features that might have seemed more appropriate had he been the peanut farmer and Roman the illustrator, rather than the reverse.

Adam held Hannah's elbow and led her to the grass verge near her parked bus. "It's good to see you."

"Thank you." She didn't have to ask how he'd known she was here.

"Roman said you were driving through Clarkesville and decided to stop."

"Yes." What else had Roman shared with his brother? The two had always been fairly close. But Adam had always held himself in artistic aloofness from other people. Hannah had never felt she knew him.

"It's too late for you to go on tonight," he said.

Everyone in this town seemed to think they had a right to tell her what she should and shouldn't do.

"There's plenty of room at the farm."

She stared at him, incredulous. "The farm?"

"Absolutely. You know the way. This is yours, isn't it?" He indicated the VW.

"Yes," she agreed faintly.

"That's my Peugeot at the corner. The old white one. I'll lead the way. We'll have you settled in no time."

Hannah felt like a beached fish gasping for air. "Are you running the farm now?"

He laughed. "Good Lord, no. You know I hate all that. I'm trying to find a way to start my own press. Anyway, Roman wouldn't let me within a mile of one of his precious goober plants."

Hannah digested that. "So Roman still runs the farm?"

"Of course."

"And he lives there?" *With Mary-Lee and their child?*

Adam bowed his head as if trying to see her face more clearly. "You know he wouldn't live anywhere else." He rocked back onto his heels and raised his chin. "Ah, I see. No one's told you."

She was past being tired, but she wanted to be alone somewhere, to think, and to plan what she would do next. "Told me what?" she asked, certain she didn't want to know the answer.

"Roman isn't married to Mary-Lee anymore. Hasn't been for several years."

Hannah dug her hands into her pockets. She was already too emotionally numb to be sure how she felt about the announcement. "Really? Well, I'm sorry things didn't work out. I met Penny. She's sweet. It must be hard on her—having her folks divorced but living so close."

"Er... Yeah, I guess. Anyway, hop in your jalopy and follow me."

"I can't do that!"

Footsteps approached and Adam looked past her.

"What can't you do, Hannah?" a familiar voice asked.

She didn't have to turn around to know that Roman stood close behind her.

"Hello, little brother," Adam said. "How was the extravaganza?"

"Penny made a great tree," Roman said. "You ought to have kids, Adam. You don't know what you're missing. Children's plays are stimulating."

Slowly Hannah stepped aside so that she could see both brothers. "I'll leave you two to talk."

"You'll do no such thing," Adam said. "Roman, persuade this woman to come out to the farm and stay. She reckons she's heading out of here on her own in the dead of night. Only we're not letting her go. Right?"

"Right," Roman said quietly. "See you later, Adam."

Adam gave a mock salute. "Later." He backed away, turned and broke into a jog.

"I'm sorry about this afternoon."

"Forget it." She only wished she could.

"I'm not sorry about what happened...between you and me. That was wonderful and—"

"Please don't." She tried to walk away but he caught her arm. "Someone's expecting me."

"Who?"

"You don't have any right to ask me questions." She could

feel his body, its warmth close to her. "I'm sorry your marriage failed."

"I'm not. It never had a chance."

"Excuse me, please."

"I can't," he said very quietly. "Come out to the farm."

"I told you, someone's expecting me." She looked at his hand on her arm. Instead of pulling away, she put her own hand gently on his. "It was stupid of me to come, Roman. Things haven't been going too well for me, and I suppose I thought I could find some sort of... Oh, I don't know."

"I do. You came here because it was the first place you thought of when you needed a friend.... You thought of Clarkesville and...and me?"

Lying had never been her forte. "Yes. I should have ignored the thought. We've both got other lives."

In the silence that followed, the night seemed to seethe around them. Hannah dropped her hand, but Roman immediately put an arm around her shoulders and turned them both toward the spruce. "Ten days and they'll be lighting it up."

Ten days and she'd be hundreds of miles away.

"Will you watch it with me again?" He rocked her close, and she smelled his familiar clean outdoors scent. "Have you forgotten how we used to do that?"

"You can't pretend it didn't all happen, Roman. All the terrible stuff."

"Would you like to?"

"Yes, of... Oh, what's the point of this? I'm a pragmatist. I was always the pragmatist. You were the dreamer."

"And I was the villain, too, huh?"

"I didn't say that." How easy it would be to turn into his arms and hold on. But there was a chasm between them made of time and events, and Hannah couldn't make herself believe it was possible to cross that division.

He took his arm from her shoulders. "Will you come to the farm?"

"I can't tonight."

"Because you're staying with Jane Smith?"

Hannah blinked. Perhaps she'd simply forgotten how easy it was for everyone to find out everything about everyone else in a small town. He must have talked to Jane on his way from the school. "If you already know, why ask?"

"How about tomorrow? Will you come then?"

"I don't know. I don't think so."

"Then I'll come to you."

"Please don't." But she wanted him to. She wanted all they'd missed. She wanted all the lost years to disappear.

"We should talk, shouldn't we?" Roman said. His sad smile turned her heart. "Shouldn't we, Hannah?"

"What good would it do now?"

"Maybe none. It's all so awkward. But it would mean a lot to me, anyway. I've missed you. And I've never stopped hoping we'd be together again."

Without intending to, Hannah rested a hand on his chest and felt the rapid beat of his heart. He wasn't following her around to play some sort of game. Roman had been hurt, too. Regardless of the mistakes he might have made, he couldn't have changed completely from the boy and the young man she'd known so well…and loved.

Roman pressed her hand to him. "I'll come in the morning. Okay?"

She shrugged. What could it hurt? She already knew the answer, but she wanted to be with him, anyway.

The soft purr of an engine intruded, and Hannah glanced up. Roman's hand, stroking her cheek, brought her attention back to him.

"May I come?"

Before she could respond, a white Cadillac, facing the wrong way on the street, drew to a stop beside them. The driver's window rolled smoothly down.

Hannah felt Roman stiffen, but he didn't remove his hand from her face.

"There you are, Roman. What got into you? Rushing away like that."

Mary-Lee Cassidy's voice hadn't changed. Or should that be Mary-Lee Hunter?

"Penny wanted to know where her daddy had gone."

Roman sighed and turned toward the car. "And what did you tell her?"

"Why, that you'd had an emergency at the farm, of course, and that I was sure you'd be over to see her first thing in the morning. It's bad enough you're never here for her at Christmas. The least you could've done was to make sure you made her feel special tonight."

"Mary-Lee," Roman said tightly, "I think you should go home to Penny. I told her I was leaving. And I will talk to her tomorrow."

Roman was never here for Christmas?

The car door opened and Mary-Lee got out. A statuesque woman, her body had always been the object of male admiration. From what Hannah could see tonight, there was still just as much to admire.

"Well." Mary-Lee moved in close. "Hannah Bradshaw! I don't suppose it is still Bradshaw?"

"I'm not married," Hannah managed to murmur.

"Really? Oh, my. That's a shame. But it's perfectly lovely to see you. Penny mentioned meeting you this afternoon. You should have come out to the car. I was right there."

"There wasn't time." This felt like a predictable scene from the type of movie Hannah tried to avoid.

"What did you think of our little Penny? Isn't she a darling?"

Hannah pushed a hand into her bag and located her car keys. "She's lovely."

"Hannah, about tomorrow—"

"I'll tell Penny you'll call first thing, Roman," Mary-Lee said, cutting him off. "He spoils her rotten, Hannah. You should see the two of them together. Sometimes I have to remind Roman it isn't good for little girls to get everything they want, particularly when they start to get older. She is going to be seven, you know."

Hannah drew in a breath and held it. "I do know, Mary-Lee. I know very well. Goodbye." Making a fist, she tapped Roman's arm and met his troubled eyes. "Let it go. It's for the best. Goodbye, Roman."

Chapter Four

Cinnamon? Hannah sniffed. She opened her eyes. *Cloves?*

She closed her eyes again. The alarm hadn't gone off, but it *felt* time to get up and go to work.

"Blossom?" Withdrawing an arm from the warm bed, she patted around on the quilt, searching for the familiar warmth and the expected lick of a rough tongue.

Cinnamon and cloves.

"Blossom!" Hannah sat up abruptly and blinked. Morning light filtered through a crack in the drapes.

Now she remembered. Jane Smith's apartment. When Hannah had arrived last night, Blossom had shown a puzzling unwillingness to come into the building. Finally Hannah had fed the balking cat on the sidewalk, given her time to skulk disdainfully back and forth for a few minutes and returned her to her bed in the van.

She sank back into snowy white pillows and surveyed the room. Of course Jane would have four-poster beds complete with velvet drapes. Blue velvet—naturally. The wallpaper was heavily flocked, blue and gold in a fleur-de-lis pattern, and soft blue rugs lay on dark, highly polished oak floors. Around the room stood an armoire, wardrobe and dressing table—all of black lacquer inlaid with gold and mother-of-pearl.

Roman.

She still loved him. Hannah rested the back of her hand on her forehead. He still cared about her, too. That was obvious.

But the obstacles that would always keep them apart were also obvious.

Hannah turned to see a tiny enameled clock on a gilt table beside the bed. Eleven! She sat bolt upright again. Poor Blossom.

"Are you awake, my dear?" Tapping, Jane peeked around the door. "Don't worry about your darling cat. She's been fed and allowed to walk."

As if the woman had read her mind. Hannah smiled and yawned. "Thank you. I'm sorry I slept so late."

"Late? Nonsense. It's not even noon. I've brought you some chocolate and cinnamon toast."

Hannah glanced at what showed of her body above the billowy blue quilt. Her fleecy nightshirt, emblazoned with the likeness of Winnie-the-Pooh, didn't fit in...with the room or with chocolate and toast daintily served in bed.

Jane entered carrying a silver tray, which she set on the bedside table. She poured from a delicate yellow chocolate pot into a tiny cup. This morning her dress was of blue-sprigged calico with a high, lace-trimmed collar. Around her tiny waist she'd tied an apron edged with matching lace. A dark net dotted with jet beads restrained the heavy chignon she'd fashioned at her neck. "Here you are." She put the cup and saucer into Hannah's hands and settled herself on a tapestry chair. "A beautiful day. And you have so much to do. But there's no hurry. I've told everyone we'll contact them later."

"Everyone?" The delicate cup rattled alarmingly in its saucer. This period stuff could be carried too far. "Who's everyone?"

"Why, all your old friends, of course. I've had callers for you *all* morning. I told them you have to get rested first, and settled in."

"But I'm not—"

"Did I do wrong?" Jane's eyes became wide and anxious. "I do hope not."

Hannah bit her lip. "I'm sure it'll be fine." She wasn't at

all sure, but she couldn't bring herself to upset this tiny, charming creature. "Don't give it another thought."

"Ah, good." Jane held herself very upright, as if held by a rigid corset. "What I liked so much about this town when I was here before was the way everyone looked out for everyone else."

Not as Hannah remembered. But maybe Jane had known different people.

"And they just loved Christmas. That's what gave me the idea to open my shop." She clapped her hands together.

Roman didn't stay around for Christmas. Was that recent? Or could it be that he hadn't since...

"I'm really going to have to work fast," Jane said. "I always think plenty of stock is what encourages purchases, don't you?"

Hannah focused on Jane. "Umm, yes."

"I'm making these dear little pomanders. All that's left to do is the gold thread for hanging." She made a motion in the air. "You put it through the ball with a needle and make a loop. They're darling on the tree, and after Christmas they pop right into a lady's drawer. They smell like cinnamon or cloves. I've been stuffing the last of them."

When Roman wrote that Penny wasn't his child, he'd lied. Roman had made Hannah believe he would always tell her the truth, yet he'd lied. And once he'd given up on Hannah coming back to Clarkesville and giving him a chance to talk her into accepting what he'd done, he'd married Mary-Lee.

"Would you like to talk about what sent you away from Clarkesville?"

Hannah almost slopped her chocolate. "Why did you ask that?" She could hardly ask if the woman read minds—unless she wanted to be accused of being unstable.

"Oh—" Jane shrugged "—I heard you left without a word to a soul. Right when you were expected to get engaged to that handsome Roman Hunter."

It was inevitable that the facts would have been discussed. She and Roman had been close, then she'd left and Roman married Mary-Lee a few months before Penny was born. Hannah flinched. Everyone must know exactly what happened, how she'd run away after Roman had betrayed her.

"Things aren't always what they seem, are they?" asked Jane.

"What?"

Jane lifted a shoulder. "Sometimes we believe what certain people want us to believe. If that happens, we ought to make sure what the truth is."

The woman spoke in riddles. "I don't know what you mean."

"No? Perhaps not. Hannah, would you do something for me?"

"Yes." She said it without thinking.

"I knew you would." Jane stood up, clasped her hands behind her back and walked to the window. "The gardener out at Harmony was talking about how you and Roman used to go there from when you were children."

"We were teenagers at first. We didn't meet until I was fifteen...not really."

Jane pulled the drapes aside and looped them with their velvet ties. "Why did you go there? So often, I mean."

Hannah put the cup and saucer on the tray. She could see that the day was gray. Rain spattered the window. "At first it was because we found it when we were out riding bikes. Everyone in town and on the farms has always known it was there, but no one ever went out to it."

"Why was that?" Jane asked softly.

Hannah gave an embarrassed shrug. "Who knows. Mostly we heard it was haunted. Roman and I didn't believe in old wives' tales." She reconsidered and smiled. "But I think we wanted to think it *was* haunted, so we went out there and poked around. Eventually we found the walled garden."

"Ah, yes." There was a breathy, distant quality to Jane's voice. "The beautiful walled garden. Roman told me about that, too."

"You know Roman?"

"Oh, yes. Very well."

"So you know all about the Ashleys then?"

"Men don't tell stories like women do. You tell me about the Ashleys."

Hannah looked into Jane's expectant face. Why not tell her? "It's sad in a way." And the story had seemed to belong only to Hannah and Roman. "But not all sad. There was an old lady who used to sit in the square on fine days when Roman and I... She told us the story."

"Who was she?"

"She...I don't know. I remember her telling us she'd be going away again." Hannah frowned. The woman had been visiting relatives. "Anyway, she knew all about the history of the area and about Harmony."

Jane settled her hands in her lap. "I love stories."

"It was on December 24, 1875." She thought of the window in the little sitting room. "That was the day Seth Ashley brought his bride to Harmony House. Her name was Esther and she was very beautiful. And Seth was very handsome and very much in love. They both were."

Jane sighed.

"Seth was a wealthy landowner in the area. He had the house built especially for Esther and he was determined it would be ready to move into on their wedding day, Christmas Eve."

"And it was," Jane said.

"Yes, it was." She couldn't bring herself to mention the inscription. That was hers and Roman's secret, even if he had spoiled the magic they'd shared.

"And that's it? All the story?" Jane leaned forward.

"Oh, no. When Harmony was built, Clarkesville was just a little settlement. People were struggling here."

"I know."

"And—" Hannah frowned. "You know?"

"Oh...oh, yes. I read about how hard things were back then. After the war when there was so much destruction."

"Yes," Hannah said. "But Seth and Esther felt so lucky

to have each other and to have such a good life. They looked after the people of Clarkesville. Whenever they heard about someone in need, they helped out. Esther thought nothing of going to nurse the poor. She made sure the children had clothes and that there was enough food. And Seth was always looking for ways to find work for the men.''

''Mmm.'' Jane looked dreamy. ''People should help one another. That's all we have in the end, one another.''

''At Christmastime, they had all the local people come to Harmony to sing carols. Then they gave them food baskets, and every child got a toy.''

''Wooden fashion dolls for the girls…''

''And carts and horses for the boys…'' Hannah stopped. ''Roman did tell you this story.''

''Not much.'' She fluttered a hand. ''Just a little something about Seth carving the dolls and Esther making the clothes.''

''I thought one of their handymen did the carving.''

''Oh, no!'' Jane shook her head, smiling. ''No… Not according to Roman, anyway. It was Seth.''

Hannah smiled, too. Obviously Jane was warming to the story. ''The only thing that spoiled Seth and Esther's happiness was that they didn't have children. Or not until 1892. Esther got pregnant then. But, of course, she was a little old. Thirty-seven.''

''Not so old.'' Jane straightened her diminutive shoulders. ''I imagine they were very happy.''

''Oh, yes. But thirty-seven was a little old back then because medicine wasn't as advanced. Anyway, they were excited because their biggest dream was that their child would grow up, marry and enjoy Harmony with a husband or wife the way Seth and Esther had.''

''Isn't that sweet?'' A faraway look entered Jane's blue eyes. ''True love is such a gift.''

Hannah was tempted to say she wasn't sure true love existed. ''It would be,'' she said and was instantly grateful when Jane appeared to miss the bitterness in her voice. ''Unfortunately Esther died in childbirth.''

Jane leaped up, her fingers over her mouth.

"I know," Hannah said. "That's how I felt when I first heard. And she died on Christmas Eve, the anniversary of the day she was married. So did her little boy."

"Seth's little boy."

"Of course. He belonged to both of them."

"Poor Seth. How he suffered."

Hannah wished she could get out of bed and check on Blossom. She'd better finish the story quickly. "Yes, he did. He grieved and grieved. Esther was buried in the walled garden...you know, the—"

"I know."

"Yes, well, Seth visited the garden every day throughout his life. He never forgot Esther, but he did return to doing the good deeds they'd done together. He even started giving baskets of food and toys to the children at Christmas again."

"What a wonderful man," Jane whispered.

"Yes. But there's a mystery, too."

"A mystery?"

"In the burial plot there was room for Seth's grave. Only he's not buried there."

"Really?" Jane tilted her head in question.

"Yes. There's no record of a final illness, or even of his death. Roman and I went through the public records. Esther's death is noted, and the baby—his name was John—but not Seth." She paused. "Some people say he wasn't buried because he didn't die, that he's still somewhere around waiting until the dream comes true."

Jane smiled. Her skin was translucent. "Yes? The dream?"

"Seth and Esther's. That one day there would be other lovers to enjoy Harmony." Suddenly self-conscious, Hannah folded her arms. "Just a story."

"Yes."

"Um... Weren't you going to ask me to do something for you?"

"Was I?" Jane moved toward the door. "How odd. You

know I can't remember what it was. I probably will by the time you come downstairs for lunch.''

It was time to leave. ''Thank you, Jane, but I won't need lunch.''

''Nonsense. It's made.''

''I've already let you do too much for me. And I'll... Well, I hope you'll let me pay for staying here.''

''No!''

''But I'm a stranger, and—''

''Of course you're not a stranger....'' She opened the door and smiled brilliantly at Hannah. ''I feel as if I've known you a very long time. And I'm so glad you're here. See you in the kitchen.''

Before Hannah could protest again, Jane had closed the door behind her.

This could not go on. She threw back the covers and got out of bed. A shower, then she'd thank Jane again and leave. Last night she'd been too tired to do more than pull on her sleep shirt and fall asleep.

Within half an hour, her hair still damp, Hannah knelt to finish repacking her suitcase. She paused, then felt in a side pocket for Roman's letter. Letting go was an art she would have to work at. Getting rid of a letter filled with lies would be a good start. The pocket was empty. All the pockets were empty. Hannah sat on her heels. She was certain she'd packed it in this case.

Half the day was already gone. She'd find and destroy the envelope later.

The call Hannah knew she needed to make to her mother weighed heavily. She hadn't felt able to speak to her before leaving Chicago. When they'd left Clarkesville, Mother's thought had been to protect Hannah from the gossip that was sure to flare. And to help her get over Roman. Right or wrong, Hannah couldn't blame her mother for that. She *could* blame her for not allowing a grown woman to decide what to do about a letter from the man she loved.

But she wasn't ready to make the call to Denver.

Following the delicious smell of something hot and savory, Hannah left her suitcase and went downstairs. The building, part of a row of businesses, was three stories tall. Jane had said her bedroom was on the top floor, above the one Hannah had used.

The stairs descended to a room stacked with boxes.

A tinkling sounded. Silvery bells. Hannah regarded a door to her left. Light showed through two glass panels. The shop. Last night, Jane had let her into the shop and led the way past dark shapes, shapes that glistened, and things that rustled or clicked. And there had been the tinkling of bells then, too.

"There you are!" Jane popped from another door, on the opposite side of the storeroom. "Good. Your soup is on the table and I'm taking the bread out of the oven."

The kitchen reminded Hannah of her childhood, and the house her mother had been forced to sell shortly after she was widowed. That kitchen had always been warm and filled with fragrant smells. The man who'd bought the Bradshaw house turned it into apartments. Hannah and her mother had rented one of them…not something pleasant to remember.

"Please, sit down." Jane waved Hannah to a place at a scrubbed, white wooden table. "Eat. Before the soup gets cold."

There was no graceful way to refuse. "Thank you." Wonderful homemade vegetable soup, freshly baked, whole-grain bread, a piece of apricot jam tart with knobby twists of pastry on top…she ate every bite.

"Aren't you having any lunch?" she asked when she realized Jane had sat down, placidly watching, with no meal of her own.

"Me? No. No, I'm not hungry. Have some more tart." She reached for Hannah's empty plate.

"No, thank you." Her mouth would love more. Her tummy, much too tightly pressed against the waistband of her jeans, had definitely had enough.

Hannah got up and took her dishes to the sink. Jane hadn't

eaten a thing. Instead, she sat at the table painting silver-and-gold saddles on miniature wooden horses.

"Are those tree ornaments?"

"Yes. Aren't they sweet? You like handcrafts, don't you?"

"Um…"

"I thought so." She lifted a box from a chair and put it on the table. "How would you like to start gluing the horns on these unicorns?"

Hannah stacked her dishes. She could hardly say no. "Show me what to do."

The unicorns were pink and blue with an iridescent shimmer. Jane showed her how to attach transparent horns in front of each ornament's soft white mane.

Hannah sat on the edge of a chair and worked systematically. Occasionally her eyes met Jane's and the other woman smiled warmly. She should be anxious, Hannah thought, but she wasn't. Peaceful was how she felt. An image of Roman came and she swallowed. She wasn't sorry she'd decided to come and see him one last time. The prickling in her eyes was dangerous. Crying was one luxury she usually avoided, particularly in front of strangers. Not that Jane felt like a stranger to Hannah anymore.

"I had a call from Adam while you were sleeping."

Hannah stopped, a horn pressed to a pale pink head. "Adam Hunter called you?"

"Oh, yes. Donna Jackson from the post office came by, too. She said she'll call back. She wants you to have tea. And Libby Miller wanted to make sure you haven't forgotten the Christmas Fair at the Old Schoolhouse."

"Libby Miller?" Libby had been Libby Graves when they were growing up, and just about Hannah's best friend. She'd married young, at eighteen, to her first and only boyfriend.

"Everyone's so happy you're back. Just in time for the cider supper tonight."

"Jane—"

"Isn't it perfect? You couldn't have picked a better day to get together with everyone. They'll all be there."

The cider supper. Hannah picked up another unicorn. Every year, a few days before Thanksgiving, Clarkesville's cider supper was held at the church hall. "Why did Adam call?"

"Oh, silly me." Jane shook her head. "I do get sidetracked. He's going to take you to the supper. Isn't that a wonderful idea?"

Hannah sat very still and took a deep breath. "I really don't think—"

"Now, you're not to worry about what you'll wear." With a satisfied sigh, Jane set aside the last of the cheerful little horses. "That's those finished. We'll look through your things later. Blossom's in the garden. My cleaning lady put her there."

Not for the first time this morning, Jane's subject-hopping made Hannah feel disoriented. She'd seen a small, neat garden through the window over the sink. "I'd better get her. It's raining."

"She's just outside the door. In a basket under the potting table. I'm sure she's fine where she is."

Hannah fidgeted, glancing at the perky yellow-and-white-striped curtains looped back from the window. A puffy valance of the same fabric adorned a window in the door leading outside. Bright yellow accented the entire kitchen, from a row of pottery canisters, to the table runner and a jug holding dried flowers. Fruit and vegetables crowded a yellow bowl on a counter, and yellow cushions were tied to the seats of ladder-backed chairs around the table.

Blossom wasn't an outside cat.

"You're worried about her."

Hannah jumped, then frowned. "I'll just check."

The moment Hannah appeared, Blossom rose from the fat pillow in an obviously new basket lined with blue check. She glowered accusingly at Hannah and stretched.

"Poor girl. You missed me." Hannah picked the cat up and carried her into the kitchen. "Is it all right if I bring her in? She can sit on my... Oh!"

The cat stiffened in Hannah's arms. Fur rose on her neck and back.

"What is—"

With a yowl, and with claws making a pincushion of Hannah's arms, Blossom scrambled to leap down. Spitting, she shot back outside and leaped into her new bed.

"My goodness." Rubbing her skin gingerly, Hannah frowned at the cat. "She's never like this."

"Poor little cat," Jane said. "Close the door and let her settle down again. She's got food and water."

Reluctantly Hannah did as she was told. "She's always snooty, but not wild like that."

"Stop worrying about it. Cats like to know they're settled. Once she knows Clarkesville is home she'll be all right."

This had gone on long enough.

"Dotty!" Jane bounced to her feet. "Oh, my. I'd quite forgotten Dotty. My cousin. She lives not far from Milledgeville. She hasn't been well, and I'd promised to call today. Excuse me a moment."

With that she hurried from the room in a flurry of swishing skirts. Determined not to dwell on her unhappiness over Roman, and trying to figure out a graceful way to leave, Hannah continued work on the unicorns.

Only minutes passed before Jane returned. "This is terrible." She paced, plucking distractedly at her apron. "Poor Dotty. She's never been strong. But this has been a bad winter." She shook her head. "Her chest, you know. She's got a weak chest."

Hannah made a sympathetic noise.

"I'll have to go and help her. Oh, dear." Now she wrung the apron, twisted it through her fingers. "What am I going to do?"

Hannah bit her lip. "I'm so sorry. Can I do anything to help?"

"Thank you, but no. I'll have to…" Jane spun around, the start of a smile relaxing her worried features. "Oh, yes, yes. It's perfect. You don't have a job right now, do you?"

"Well, not—"

"Good, good. I mean… Not good, of course, except for me. And it will be for you, too. Look after the shop for me, Hannah. Run it while I go to help Dotty."

Hannah realized her mouth was open and closed it, pressing her lips firmly together.

"You won't have a thing to worry about, and I'm sure I won't be gone very long. I'll call the bank to let them know you're in charge and can write any necessary checks. The orders will come in as planned. All you'll have to do is open up in the morning and be yourself." Jane clapped her hands together and spun on a heel. "Oh, what a relief. This is perfect. You can live here and have a job here while you get used to being back in Clarkesville. There's plenty of food. Plenty of everything. You won't have a thing to worry about."

"I've never run a shop. I don't know anything about it." *And I can't stay in this town.*

"Nonsense. You'll do beautifully."

"I'm really not—"

"You're going to love the shop. We Christmas people always do like our magic season, don't we? I think of us…well, almost like angels in a way. We want good things for other people. We like to see them happy, and all of this—" she made a wide gesture "—it makes them happy."

The woman was irresistible. "Well—"

"Oh, good!" Jane took her hands. "Thank you, thank you, thank you. I knew you'd help me. I'm so glad you came when you did."

"I'll do my best." She seemed to be losing control of her own life. But she smiled and squeezed Jane's small, cold hands.

"You'll do very well. And think of it—" bowing over Hannah, she smiled "—now you'll definitely be here for the cider supper. Adam will be along for you at seven."

Chapter Five

Roman ran his eyes down a column of figures on his computer terminal. Looked fine. He stored the data and switched off the screen.

"Good year, huh?"

At the sound of Adam's voice, Roman stood up. "Damn good. Too bad they can't all be winners."

"Yeah." Adam walked to the window. "This still seems like a hell of a lot of work. Not my kind of work, either."

The bedroom that had been their mother's now served as Roman's office. The house was built on a slight rise in the land, and from here there was a clear view over the fields and farm buildings.

Roman smiled at his brother's back. Adam wore his work uniform: tattered, paint-and-ink-smeared T-shirt and shrunken sweatpants that didn't cover his ankles. His feet were bare.

"You don't have to worry about the farm, remember? You're the artist. I'm the farmer." One confused and preoccupied farmer at the moment, but at least here, doing what he loved, he had something to focus on besides Hannah.

"It isn't fair that you do all the work. I do think about that, y'know."

"Don't. We only need one boss around here. I'm grateful you don't interfere." He ran a hand around his neck. Keeping his mind off Hannah was getting tougher by the minute. Every time he thought of last night and the show Mary-Lee had put on, he cringed.

"What's eating you?"

Roman started. He hadn't realized Adam was watching him. "Nothing. Just considering where to go with the chickens. Whether to expand production. The broilers have been a boon in the off-season. We've got plenty of room."

"You need to ease up, Roman. You don't take any time off."

"We'll be glad of the extra income when we hit a lean year." Sometimes Adam, with his keen artist's eye, saw too much.

"If you want to raise more chickens, raise more chickens." There was a tough set to Adam's wide mouth. The crease between his eyes deepened. Mostly Roman felt like the older, rather than the younger, brother. Today, looking at Adam, Roman decided there would be no doubt about who was four years senior.

"Sometimes I feel uncomfortable about not consulting you on the decisions I make around here, Adam."

"Why?" Adam gave a short laugh. "I don't know a damn thing about any of it."

"The place is half yours."

"And I get half the proceeds for doing nothing. Not a bad deal."

Roman didn't feel like another discussion about Adam's guilt over not contributing to the running of the farm. He sat on the edge of the worn leather sofa. "You having problems with the painting?" His knowledge of what Adam did was limited. If he asked about "the painting" he felt safe.

"Sometimes I feel I'm wasting my time. I'm good, but it takes more than that. It's been over a year since I illustrated that last children's book."

"Something's going to break for you again soon. You know it will." Adam's ego was fragile, something Roman had come to understand very early in life. Reassurance was often enough to lift his brother's mood. "You're not just good, Adam. You're outstanding. We all know that."

"Sure... Thanks. But you've changed the subject nicely. We were talking about you and spare time. I've been wondering—"

A subtle change in Adam's tone caught Roman's full attention. He studied his brother's face again. Tension was in every line. "What's wrong?"

"Nothing's wrong." He chewed his lip. "And everything's wrong. I *do* feel guilty about you working so damned hard and only getting half of everything. Maybe we should sell."

Roman stared, amazed.

"I know, I know. Where did that come from? I've been thinking. If we sold, you could get a smaller place that wouldn't take so much effort, and then you *would* have more spare time."

Roman found a voice. "You know I'm never going to sell this place. You love it here and so do I, and I'll continue to manage it just fine. More than fine. And one day you'll find a way to start up your own press."

"But—"

"No buts, Adam. And no more guilt. Subject closed." Roman arranged his length on the couch, stacking his hands behind his head and propping his booted feet. "I don't need spare time. I don't *want* spare time," he added, more ferociously than he'd intended.

"Whoa." Adam spun a chair around until the back faced Roman, swung a leg over the seat and sat down. He layered his arms on top of the chair back and regarded Roman narrowly.

Roman raised his brows. "What's this? You going to paint my picture or something?"

"Nope. But I want to know what's eating you."

"Nothing."

"Okay. Clam up on me. I'll tell you what the problem is."

Roman glared then closed his eyes. "Now you read minds?"

"I read yours pretty well. Hannah. Am I warm?"

"Ah, hell."

"Right, little brother. Ah, hell. But hiding from the obvious isn't going to make it go away."

Roman shifted. The couch was too short. "There isn't a damn thing I can do about Hannah now. Not if she won't let me. And believe me, I'm pretty sure she won't."

"Look at me." A strong finger jabbed into the middle of Roman's chest had the desired effect. "Pretty sure doesn't sound definite."

"You weren't there last night when Mary-Lee rolled up. Damn, but that woman can still make my blood simmer."

"I don't think you want me to get started on Mary-Lee."

"No. As far as I'm concerned, she's history. But she's still what's standing between Hannah and me." Had he really dared to think... Yes, he'd dared to think he and Hannah might suddenly have been handed a miraculous second chance together. Her reaction to him in the garden—and before Mary-Lee turned up last night—had given him a reason to hope.

"When I talked to Hannah—before you showed—I could have sworn she was anything but disinterested in you. You should have seen her trying not to look interested when I said you weren't married to Mary-Lee anymore."

"That's nice."

"Hey!" The finger jabbed again, and Roman swatted Adam's hand. Undaunted, Adam said, "Don't take this out on me. You're the one who made the dumb mistake, and—"

"Adam." Roman shot his brother a warning look. "This subject is closed."

"*Don't* treat me like a kid. I care about you. You never would discuss exactly what happened. Why—"

"I'm not discussing it now." If he could, he'd erase the memory himself.

"Okay, but just one question."

Roman started to get up, then flopped back. "One question."

"Donna Jackson told you Emily and Hannah had gone to Chicago?"

"Yes."

"She gave you an address."

"A post office box address. That's two. You're already one question over."

"You waited six weeks after Hannah left before going to try and find her."

Roman sat up and ran his fingers through his hair. "You're out of questions."

"No. No, Roman. I'm just getting to *the* question. Why didn't you try to find her sooner?" Adam's square jaw jutted. When he was being pugnacious he reminded Roman of their handsome, quietly determined father.

"Why, Roman?"

"I did." He let his wrists flop between his knees. "I wrote a letter to Hannah…to the post office box."

"And she didn't reply?"

"She didn't get it. It was sent back. The note on the envelope said it was undeliverable because she'd moved."

Adam played a tattoo on the chair back with his forefingers. "Crap. You never told me that."

"I wasn't telling anyone much of anything, if you remember. And then things kind of got away from me." And he wasn't going to elaborate on the ensuing mess with Mary-Lee. "I used to look at that envelope every few days. As if I could will it into her hands or something. Finally I stuffed it away. Damn, I've never felt so helpless…until last night."

"I've never thought of you as a quitter."

Roman smiled cynically. He wasn't about to be baited.

"I was talking to that nice woman who runs the new Christmas shop in town," Adam said.

"Uh-huh." Christmas was one of Roman's least favorite topics. "I talked to her yesterday. Friendly. Chattered away as if we'd known each other for years."

"She called me this morning."

Roman frowned.

"Yeah, I know," Adam said. "I was surprised, too. She needs some windows painted. Christmas scenes. You know the kind of thing. Rudolph and gingerbread houses with snow on the roofs. Normally I'd have said she'd come to the wrong man, but, what the hell."

Roman laughed and shook his head. "You agreed to do that? I almost hope she never finds out what you really do. She'd be embarrassed."

"I doubt it. I'm not sure anything would embarrass that lady. Did you know Hannah's staying with her?"

"Yes."

"You didn't tell me."

Roman stood up. "I didn't know until last night. Some woman at Penny's pageant told me. Mrs. Grady, or something. Her husband's a retired minister. They're staying in that old Victorian behind Town Hall."

"I wonder how Hannah knows this Jane Smith."

"No idea." Roman only knew his head was beginning to ache, and he couldn't shake the picture of the way Hannah had looked last night. When she'd said goodbye.

"Jane reminded me about the cider supper at the Old Schoolhouse tonight."

"Yeah." One more of the things he'd cut out of his life since Hannah left.

"She said how nice it would be if someone invited Hannah to go."

Roman looked down at his brother until Adam tilted up his chin.

"I told her I thought it would be nice, too." Adam smiled innocently. "I told her to consider Hannah invited and that you'd pick her up at seven."

"You what?" Roman let out a soundless whistle. "Of course, Jane told Hannah and she said I could go to hell. Damn, I wish you hadn't done that."

"Jane asked. And Hannah said yes."

"She what?"

Adam spread his hands. "Be there, little brother. I'm a persuasive guy."

UNBELIEVABLE. She'd actually agreed to go to the cider supper with him? Roman opened his closet. He probably ought to call and check with her, only he might hear what he didn't want to hear.

The worst that could happen would be that he'd arrive and be told to get lost. He could take that. Couldn't he? If he couldn't, he'd find out when it happened.

One of these days he'd have to go to the city and buy clothes. Jeans were fine for a Clarkesville supper, but if he wanted to take Hannah somewhere... His imagination was getting away from him.

The top shelf in his closet was piled high with things he hadn't touched for years. He ought to throw them all away.

Not the leather box tooled with fading gold, though. That had been his father's. When Roman was a little boy, his dad had given him the box to keep "special bits and pieces" in.

Roman pulled the box down. The letter he'd tried to send to Hannah was inside. He turned the key in the lock and lifted the lid. There was no point in keeping useless scraps of history.

Letters from Hannah were on top. She'd written to him when he'd been in Atlanta...the first time they'd been separated since they met. He picked up the pile and set it aside.

This was where he'd put his own letter, wasn't it? Roman scrabbled through the remaining contents: school dance programs, notes received from Hannah when they were in school, the few photos he had of her, including one taken the summer before...

The letter wasn't there.

He closed the box slowly and frowned, trying to remember the last time he'd looked inside. Several years ago now. He was sure he'd never taken the envelope out.

Shoving the box back, he rooted among his clothes until he found a decent white shirt. Hannah liked white shirts.

How could a letter disappear from a locked box inside his closet?

Chapter Six

The black silk jumpsuit looked too "city" for Clarkesville. Hannah studied herself critically in the gilt-framed mirror on the bathroom wall, threw up her hands and returned to the bedroom. There hadn't been time to look through her baggage for something more festive and less sophisticated. Besides, anything that might be suitable would be creased.

She couldn't go.

Hannah sat on the tapestry chair beside the bed.

What if Roman was there?

Somewhere, she had a pair of crystal snowflake earrings. They would look great with the black jumpsuit.

Roman might not be there?

"Argh!" She got up and paced.

You want him to be there.

Why would Adam decide to invite her to the supper? It had to be because he was acting as intermediary for Roman. She smiled. At least she had the sense to recognize and admit her own shallow reasoning—and desires—to herself.

Blossom reclined on a towel on top of the bed. She'd whisked into the kitchen while Jane was leaving.

Hannah scratched the cat between the ears. "Glad you're over your sulk, cat. Smart move. You might as well make the best of whatever home you can get." A sawing purr rewarded the effort. "Make yourself useful. Share that dark wisdom of yours. What have I gotten myself into? I'm going to get hurt again. D'you know that? And I can't help it. I know I want to see him again.''

She found the earrings and put them on. Their sparkle was gratifying. When Hannah turned her head, facets shot tiny spears of light against soft tawny hair she'd brushed until it gleamed.

Roman used to say he could see red in her hair....

Roman would probably be there.

She *would not* go. If she did, he'd think she was chasing him.

The cuckoo clock at the top of the stairs chimed the half hour. Another half an hour and Adam would be at the kitchen door. As Jane had left—the moment the shop closed at five o'clock, and without changing from her calico dress—she'd informed Hannah that Adam would come to the back door. Then she'd swept away down the garden path and into the street behind the buildings, murmuring something about a waiting taxi. Hannah couldn't help liking the woman, but she was certainly unusual.

If she wore the heels that really streamlined the outfit she'd probably be taller than Adam.

Roman liked her in high heels. She wouldn't be taller than Roman.

Rummaging in a box she'd brought up from the van, Hannah located the shoes and put them on.

Adam had invited her, not Roman. She'd be dancing with Adam.

Hannah took the shoes off again. She wouldn't be dancing at all.

The sound of a rap on the kitchen door almost stopped her heart. She'd propped the bedroom door open, and the door to the kitchen, to make sure she'd hear.

''Blossom! What shall I do?''

The cat jumped daintily from the bed and rubbed against Hannah's legs. Another knock echoed up the stairs.

''Here goes nothing.'' Grimly Hannah shoved her feet into the shoes again. She tucked a lipstick and the door key Jane had given her into her purse and took a calming breath. Arranging a calm expression, she went down to the kitchen and opened the back door.

Her hand went to her chest. Now her heart had definitely stopped.

"Hello." Roman Hunter was, and always would be, the most appealing, the sexiest and most handsome-looking man alive for Hannah.

He held a bunched-up dark jacket in one hand, and the other hand supported his weight against the doorjamb.

He wore a white shirt, open at the neck. White shirts had been a joke between them once. Hannah bowed her head, remembering....

"YOU LOOK DIFFERENT in a white shirt, Roman."

"What does that mean?"

"I don't know." The evening had been warm, and Hannah had felt even warmer. "You make me feel kind of funny."

Roman had leaned closer. "Funny nice, or just funny, funny?" He smelled warm and clean—and the night had been filled with the sweet fragrance of early sweetpeas.

"Funny like I want to hold you."

He'd kissed her then. Under the willows in the gardens at Harmony. She'd been nineteen. Roman was twenty-two.

"I KNEW IT," Roman muttered. "I'm sorry. Wait till I get my hands on Adam."

Hannah jerked her head up. "Why?" She already knew. Adam's fine manipulative hand was very evident. "You're not late. He said seven, and it's almost exactly seven." From Roman's exasperated expression, she guessed he'd seen her surprise before she had managed to mask it and realized that Adam had tricked him into being here.

Shaded by the night's backdrop, Roman's eyes glinted black—and speculative. "It's okay, then?" The shadows slashed beneath his cheekbones and deepened the cleft in his chin. "You do want to go?"

So that's what Adam had done. He'd told Roman this was her idea. She should be embarrassed, or angry, but Hannah could only smile. Roman's reputation had always been for supreme confidence. She'd bet on being one of the few who had ever seen the vulnerable, almost shy, flip side of the man. He wouldn't hear from her that his brother had set the two of them up. That was assuming Roman really hadn't been a party to the scam in the first place.

"Hannah?"

"I want to go." She might regret the decision later. But for a few hours she would try to pretend the last seven years hadn't happened...because she wanted to. "Come in a minute."

She turned away, leaving Roman to close the door. As she moved around the kitchen, putting out fresh water for Blossom, turning down lights, Hannah didn't look at him. But she felt him. His presence surrounded her, making her fingers clumsy.

"Is Jane going to the supper?"

"She's out of town. A relative in Milledgeville is sick, and Jane's gone to be with her."

Making small talk with Roman felt awkward and stilted. "In your bed, Blossom." She arranged the basket in a corner.

"How long will Jane be gone?"

Hannah hesitated. "I'm not sure." She hadn't even thought to make sure there was a number where she could reach Jane. Surely she would have left it somewhere.

"Will you be looking after the shop?" Roman's voice was even, conversational.

"Yes."

"And you get to baby-sit the cat, too, huh?"

"She's mine."

"You really did decide to pack up everything and move on."

Hannah glanced at him. Roman had dropped to one knee

and was stroking the cat, who preened and stretched for his benefit. Hannah was afforded a view of the top of Roman's black wavy hair. He wore it slightly longer than she remembered. She liked it that way.

"I never really felt at home in Chicago." It was so easy to slip back into the habit of telling him exactly what she thought and felt.

"I'm glad."

Surely he knew what she knew, that they'd probably used up all their chances together. "Atlanta's going to be a big improvement." She looked unseeingly through the window, aware that she'd only admitted a probability to herself that there could be nothing more between them, not an inevitability.

"You look wonderful, Hannah."

She hadn't realized he was staring at her. "Thank you." It had been a long time since anyone had told her that. And even if John had been the type to give compliments, they could never have meant what they did coming from Roman.

Hannah finished fussing around the kitchen. She stood, rubbing her palms awkwardly together. Roman and Blossom were becoming great friends. Hannah propped her hips against the edge of the table. The room was silent, yet it seethed in the subdued glow of the one lamp still alight.

Roman had draped his jacket carelessly over a chair. Bent above Blossom, the muscles in his shoulders and back flexed visibly beneath his shirt. Jeans, snug-fitting as ever, made the best of strong legs Hannah could visualize with no effort. The years of physical work had honed him into an even leaner, harder and more incredibly desirable man than she remembered.

"I like your hair like that, Hannah. Soft." He stood up and laughed, his eyes traveling all the way to her toes. "Some of the ladies at the church hall may not be too thrilled to see you."

Another compliment. Hannah smiled again. "Is it just the same—the supper? I remember we usually found ways to slip…" Heat washed over her face. She shook her head, annoyed at her own carelessness.

"We did, didn't we?" Roman said softly. "I don't really know what it's like now, Hannah. I haven't been since the last time I went with you."

Would he talk about it all now? "You never took Mary-Lee?" Hannah asked tentatively.

"No." The softness left his voice—and his face.

"How long were you and Mary-Lee—" If he wanted to tell her the details of his marriage, he would. Hannah lifted her heavy hair from her neck.

"We were divorced three years ago. Is that what you're asking?" He met her eyes squarely.

"It's none of my business." But it was. And what she'd really wanted to know was how long he'd waited before marrying Mary-Lee, and… Hannah sighed. She wanted the impossible, to hear him say it had all been a mistake and that the little blond girl who called him Daddy had been an illusion.

Roman didn't pursue the subject. He picked up his jacket. "Where's your coat?"

Hannah felt panicky. What was she doing here? The past couldn't be erased or changed. Silently she took her red suede jacket from the hook where Jane had hung it.

Roman eased it from her grasp and waited while she turned and slipped her arms into the sleeves.

Beneath his fingers, the heavy satin lining slid over the silk of her jumpsuit. He settled the coat on her shoulders and let his hands rest there. His warmth spread to her skin. Roman was very close.

Hannah's lungs didn't want to expand. She stood still, feeling his breath move her hair. Slowly he turned her to face him.

Her eyes were on a level with his mouth. She glanced up into his eyes, and they narrowed with his slight smile.

"Is it…" Her swallow made a clicking sound. "Is it still raining?"

''No.'' Tilting his head, he touched her hair, wound a lock around his fingers. ''It's nice out there. If you want, we can walk.''

''I'd like that.'' He'd always made her feel tall and graceful...and so feminine, rather than gangly, the way she'd grown up thinking about herself.

Roman lifted the hood of her parka over her head and ran his fingers around the edge. ''Hannah—''

''We should go.'' Her attention flickered back to his mouth. ''I've got to open the shop in the morning. I've never done anything like that before, so I don't want to be out late.''

''Of course.'' He stepped back and opened the door.

Once outside, Hannah flipped the latch, preceded him to the gate and out into the alley. She hadn't come this way before. There was barely room for them to walk side by side.

Roman's hand settled on the back of her neck. ''Did you tell Adam you wouldn't mind if I took you tonight?''

Hannah trod carefully on uneven ground. ''Oh, yes.'' Adam's motives could only be unselfish. And she wouldn't be the cause of friction between brothers.

''Why don't I quite believe you?'' Roman said.

They emerged onto a side street leading toward the square. Hannah used the diversion of crossing the road to avoid answering. Fifteen almost silent minutes later she walked ahead of Roman into the church hall. The uncanny sensation of being in a backward time warp paralyzed her on the threshold.

''Tickets?'' A round-faced woman dressed in something resembling a square dance costume stood just inside the door. She'd chosen an unlikely black-and-orange-check fabric for the homemade creation. ''We can sell 'em to you right here. Right on the spot. If you don't have 'em, that is. Newcomers always welcome.''

Why should she be recognized? ''Yes. Just a minute.'' She started to open her purse, but Roman's hand settled on hers.

''Don't you know who this is, Donna?'' He pressed money into the woman's hand.

Donna Jackson? Removed from the counter at the post office…and from the saggy gray cardigan, cream blouse and cameo brooch that were her work uniform…she was barely recognizable.

"Hannah Bradshaw!" Donna beamed. Her hair used to be iron-gray. It was still pulled back into a severe bun but had turned white. She raised her face to Hannah. "Little Hannah."

Roman chuckled. "That's right. She's back, Donna, so we persuaded her to come to the supper and get reacquainted."

"Oh, this is wonderful," Donna crowed. "I did hear because Mrs. Grady said you were staying with Jane. I called over there to invite you to tea, and Jane said you weren't quite settled. Nobody told me you were coming tonight."

Nobody knew but wily Adam Hunter.

"You go on in and get something to eat and drink. We'll talk later," Donna said. "This is a wonderful night. Just wonderful. I'll expect you over to help me make the post office look like Christmas, mind. Hasn't been the same since you left."

Hannah frowned, then remembered. "I'm not sure—"

"Oh, none of your talking about how I do just as well without you. You always used to come arrange the paper chains. No one arranges paper chains like Hannah does, Roman."

"I'll bet."

Not daring to look at him, Hannah smiled as he placed a hand at her waist and urged her on. He pulled her hood down, but she still kept her eyes ahead. *"Little Hannah,"* he whispered.

"Shh. Don't be smart. She wasn't talking about my size. Donna remembers me as a kid and probably still thinks of me that way."

"Sometimes I do, too." He kept his voice at conspiracy pitch. "Pigtails and freckles and long, long bare legs."

His voice had slowed as he dragged out the last words. Hannah shot him a sideways glance and he grinned.

"You know something else, Hannah?"

"I've got a feeling you'll enlighten me, anyway."

His hand slid to her side until they walked hip to hip. "I've always loved you being tall. In those heels, all it takes is an inch, one little inch."

She glanced again, questioningly. "Yes, an inch and what?"

"And we're—" His attention was on her mouth. "Eye to eye. What else?"

Hannah opened her mouth to say this was ludicrous, that they were playing foolish games. A hand on her arm stopped her.

"Hannah?" The blue eyes that had been the model for Roman's smiled up at Hannah. "Roman Hunter, why didn't you *tell* me Hannah was back?"

Back, back, back. When would they understand that she was only passing through?

"Sorry, Mom," Roman said, sounding anything but contrite. "I've been busy. I would have gotten around to it."

"I'm so isolated these days. Always the last to hear everything. Never mind. I'm so happy to see you. You'll sit with us. Roman, take Hannah's coat. When did you get here? You should have called me at once. Oh, I always knew you'd get over it all and—" Lenore paused, her pretty face flushed. She fiddled with the belt on her red woolen dress. "Well...I always did talk too much."

Hannah smiled. Roman helped her out of her coat and left to hang it up.

"You remember Jed?" Lenore indicated Jed Thomas, a ruggedly appealing man in his early sixties who bore the stamp of the outdoorsman.

By the time Roman returned, Hannah had been introduced to the party at the Thomas's table and extra chairs had been brought.

Roman held one of the chairs for Hannah, and she took advantage of the opportunity to quietly ask, "Where's Adam?"

Roman made a wry face. "He never comes. You know that."

She did once, but she appeared to have forgotten.

People thronged the small hall. Pumpkins and wheat sheaves decorated corners, and a bowl of wintry foliage graced each table. Jed Thomas brought cups of orange-colored punch for Roman and Hannah. "Watch out with this stuff. It's Davis Murray's secret kicker."

Hannah peered into the murky substance. "What's in it?"

"No one knows," Lenore said, wrinkling her dainty nose. "Probably rubbing alcohol for all we know." Her hair was still as black as Roman's, but with silvery threads in the soft curls around her pretty face. She dropped her voice and leaned near. "Some say Davis has his own still."

"Who's Davis Murray?" Hannah asked, smiling. She didn't recall hearing the name before.

A short silence followed before Lenore, with an inscrutable look at Roman, said, "He's the manager at Clarkesville Trust. Took over from Ted Yates about four years ago."

Clarkesville Trust was the bank most locals used. Hannah sipped the brew and could taste whatever bitter additive comprised the "kicker."

"Davis is married to Mary-Lee," Roman said tonelessly. "Has been for three years."

The surge of relief Hannah felt was out of proportion and inappropriate, but she felt it nevertheless. She touched Roman's arm lightly and said quietly, "Is it all right? Or do you feel badly about...well, about losing her?"

"I feel relieved." When he turned his face, the thin and rigid line of his lips startled Hannah. This subject went deep enough to make him angry. "The marriage—mine—should never have happened."

"What about Penny?" She held her breath and felt the blood drain from her face.

Roman picked up his punch cup and swallowed the contents. "They'll start the music soon. Remember Billy-Bob and the Broilers?"

Hannah swallowed. "Yes, of course."

"Believe it or not, they're still broiling along, so we're in for a treat."

In other words, the subject of Penny was off limits. And his silence said as much as any words could.

Donna Jackson joined the group at the table, bubbling as Hannah had never known her to bubble. She realized, almost sadly, that these people were genuinely glad to see her.

"The sign-up's tonight," Donna told Hannah. "For the Christmas Fair?"

Hannah nodded and smiled.

"Oh, the Gradys," Donna cried, waving. "Have you met the Gradys?"

No answer was necessary as all faces turned toward the handsome couple who walked directly toward the Thomas's table.

The woman, diminutive, with hair that might have been silvery or simply very light blond, appeared to be about the age of Lenore...although she might have been much younger. She held her tall husband's arm and glanced repeatedly and adoringly up at him through gold-rimmed glasses. The two laughed together as if sharing a private and delightful joke.

"There you are," Jed Thomas boomed. "We were talking about you earlier and wondering what was keeping you."

The man took his wife's hand in one of his and slipped an arm around her waist. "We newly retired folks tend to get a bit lazy. Mrs. Grady and I sit around talking and forget the time."

Retired? Hannah studied the man's face. She supposed he could have retired very young. Clean-shaven, his features were strong and clear with none of the blurring of middle age. His dark brown hair waved slightly. She met his eyes and almost caught her breath. They were gentle and humorous, the kindest gray eyes she ever remembered seeing.

"Who's this?" he said of Hannah.

Lenore was quick to make the introductions. Hannah learned that Mr. Grady was Reverend Grady, a retired minister. He and his wife had moved into a Victorian house near the post office and planned to stay indefinitely.

"I feel as if I know you," Mrs. Grady said, laying a hand on Hannah's. "Jane's been helping me redecorate the house, and she's told me all about you. It's so nice of you to look after the shop while she's away. What a worry, having to leave in a hurry like that. Thank goodness you were back."

Hannah nodded, smiling over gritted teeth. There might almost be a conspiracy to convince her she was "back" and staying.

Mrs. Grady, who seemed to have difficulty keeping her attention on anyone but her husband, turned bright blue eyes on Hannah again. "Whenever you feel like it, just drop in. I'll be there. We'll have tea and talk. You can tell me everything you know about Clarkesville, and I'll tell you everything I've found out. I just *know* we'll have fun together."

From anyone else, the river of words would be effusive. From Mrs. Grady it was charming. Hannah inclined her head. "I'll try to come by."

Billy-Bob and his aging Broilers had been warming up. Now they swung into a boot-stomping rendition of something that brought a chorus of approval across the room.

Mrs. Grady clapped her hands and bent close to Hannah. "Doesn't it warm your heart to see good people having so much fun?"

Hannah smelled lavender water. "Yes," she said loudly. There was a warmth here, a feeling of being accepted into the fold as if she'd never left.

Men and women got into formation for the line-dancing Hannah hadn't seen since she left Georgia. Back and forth, hands on hips, upper bodies unmoving, the lines moved in heel-clicking formation. Hannah caught Roman's eye and he grinned. She smiled and looked away…straight at Lenore, who radiated worry in the few seconds it took her to paste on a smile.

Lenore Thomas was worried? That Hannah wouldn't become part of Roman's life again? Or that she would? Or simply that she'd manage to cause difficulties just by being in Clarkesville.

The rhythm of the music changed abruptly to a soothing slow piece. The Reverend and Mrs. Grady moved gracefully into each other's arms and onto the floor, followed by Jed and Lenore.

Roman stood, his face solemn, and offered Hannah his hand. She felt other eyes upon her and joined him.

"Would you dance with me, Hannah?"

Rather than answer, she walked on the floor and turned to face him.

Roman drew her against him, and they moved into the dance. Hannah had no idea what steps they did. Her brain seemed to cease functioning.

"Thank you," Roman said, close to her brow. He made no attempt to rest his jaw at her cheekbone as he would once have done.

They circled, circled again, and swayed together.

"Aren't you talking to me anymore?"

"Of course." Where was this leading? Where did she want it to lead?

"Good. You didn't really expect me to show up tonight, did you?"

She raised her chin. There were lines etched at the corners of his mouth. They hadn't been there when she last saw him. "No. But don't blame Adam." From here, his eyes were indigo. As he turned her toward a spotlight she saw again the piercing, sun-bleached blue that had held her captive from that first day on the dusty road by his farm.

"What are you thinking?" he asked.

Hannah caught her bottom lip in her teeth and shrugged.

"Tell me." He ran a hand around her neck beneath her hair.

"You'll laugh. I was thinking about the day you first helped me with those rotten papers. I thought you had the bluest eyes I'd ever seen."

His lips parted as he assimilated what she'd said. "You never told me that."

"You were already big-headed enough."

He pressed her face against his shoulder in a reflexive and spontaneous motion that turned her heart. "I thought you were the most beautiful girl *I'd* ever seen."

Hannah raised her head. She didn't smile.

"I still do," Roman said. A muscle in his cheek twitched and he stared into the distance. "Did Adam say he wanted to bring you here himself?"

"Uh-huh." She wanted to touch his face. "But forgive him, please. He thought he was doing us both a favor."

"Was he?"

Hannah made a fist on his chest.

"Hannah?" He leaned away to see her face.

"Let's just dance and not think." Discarding caution, she looped her arms around his neck and rested her forehead on his shoulder.

Roman spread one hand wide on her back and smoothed gently back and forth. The knuckles of his other hand moved against her neck.

Softness ran like a warm river through Hannah. Softness tinged with longing. *Don't think.* But even if she could stop thinking, feeling was something over which she had no control. Roman felt familiar, wonderfully familiar, and at every point of contact with his solid body a point of desire burned in Hannah.

He hummed. She'd forgotten how he did that. How could she have forgotten? A rumbly noise that sometimes skated up to falsetto on the high notes. Hannah had never mentioned the habit for fear he'd be embarrassed and stop. Hannah squeezed her eyes shut, enjoying being in Roman's arms.

"You feel so fine," Roman sang, very low with the old song. And his hands stroked in time to the words and the swaying rhythm. "I'm calling you my own." And he hummed as they moved.

They weren't kids anymore. They weren't even twenty-two

and twenty-five and innocent by many people's standards, as they had been at that age. The heat intensifying in Hannah reminded her sharply that they were a man and a woman who could never be just friends. What would it be like to make love with Roman? Hannah felt her face flame.

The number ended.

For seconds Roman continued to hold her. Hannah didn't try to move. She couldn't.

Billy-Bob said something she didn't hear, and the music started again.

"Why, there you two are."

Hannah snapped her head up, although she didn't have to look to know who had spoken. Roman stiffened. His eyes narrowed before he turned slowly toward his ex-wife.

Mary-Lee's red mouth formed a coy moue. She moved between Hannah and Roman to slip her arm around his waist. "I don't think there's any point, but I'm going to keep right on trying to train you to have some good manners, Roman. You are so naughty."

"Mary-Lee—"

"Shh." Her finger, placed familiarly on his lips, silenced him. She leaned against him so that he either had to make a scene or rest his arm across her back. "Hannah understands propriety, don't you, Hannah?"

Roman, muscles twitching in his jaw, settled a hand on his ex-wife's back.

"There. That's nice. You go and have some more of Davis's rotgut punch, Hannah." Mary-Lee gazed sweetly up at Roman. "It's only right for me to have at least one dance with my little girl's daddy."

Chapter Seven

This woman was still messing with his life. Roman set his teeth and didn't move. Mary-Lee made to slip her arms around his neck, but he caught her wrists and held them. He kept his eyes on Hannah's. Who knew what she was thinking?

"Hannah—" Mary-Lee peeked coquettishly over her shoulder "—you look el-e-gant. Doesn't she, Roman? You surely did outgrow our little town."

Mary-Lee wasn't worth hating, but what he felt for her came close.

Hannah's already creamy pale skin had taken on a chalky tinge. She seemed rooted in place, and Roman longed to shove Mary-Lee aside, grab Hannah and leave. There were reasons why he had to control that urge.

"I don't think I'll every outgrow Clarkesville." Hannah's tawny eyes glittered, and Roman felt a surge of pride. She'd always been too feisty to be put down. "In fact, I can honestly say that I wouldn't like myself if I thought I didn't belong here anymore."

Did she know how badly he'd needed to hear those words? Were they, at least in part, for his benefit? Roman prayed they might be.

"Isn't that sweet," Mary-Lee said. She smiled coyly up at him. "Dance with me, sweetie. No one dances like you do. Aren't I right, Hannah?"

"You two go right ahead." She backed away. "Enjoy yourselves. I've got a lot of catching up to do."

Shoving Mary-Lee aside, as he longed to do, would cause repercussions. Swallowing acid, Roman danced, holding Mary-Lee off despite her efforts to wrap herself around him. He smelled alcohol on her breath and averted his face.

"Still can't give up on the notion that she's your virginal little childhood sweetheart, can you?" Mary-Lee crooned, smiling for anyone who cared to look. And many people in the room did care to look at Roman Hunter dancing with his ex-wife. He was mightily sick of providing gossip for the town. "Well, you'd better give it up, honey. Anyone can see from looking at her that she's been around."

"Shut up," he said, emphasizing each word. "And when this dance is over walk away with that phony grin in place and don't come near me again tonight. If you do, I won't bother to try keeping up this charade."

Mary-Lee tutted. "Now you know that's an empty threat, darlin'. And you know what would happen if you did do anything... Well, anything unwise. But we don't want to waste time arguing, do we?" She stroked two fingers along his jaw and down his neck. "You've been avoiding my calls. That isn't very nice. We're good together, Roman."

"Mary-Lee, I'm warning you."

She made a face. "You're such a puritan, Roman. Nobody has to know. I'll take care of everything."

For months, Mary-Lee had been trying to entice him into a sexual liaison, and she wasn't above using the threat of withholding his visits with Penny as a lever.

"Spend some of your overdeveloped libido on your husband, Mary-Lee."

"Ssh!" She swiveled her head in all directions, teetered on impossibly high-heeled red shoes and steadied herself by grabbing Roman's sleeve. "Someone might hear."

The music ended and he stepped away. "Have a nice evening, Mary-Lee. Be good to Davis. He's giving you what you wanted. A big house and lots of money. A little fidelity would be a nice gift in return.''

Her face darkened. The smile slipped. "I've been faithful to Davis. But there's only one man I'm interested in—and that's you. And—"

"Be quiet," he told her, low and urgently. "Lay off the bottle, Mary-Lee. Clean up your mouth. Stop chasing after what you can't have, and be good to Penny. By God, if I ever find out you aren't—"

"You'll what, Roman?"

Disgust rose in a choking wave. "Later, Mary-Lee." He turned, searching for a glimpse of Hannah in the crowd.

"Most definitely," Mary-Lee said silkily. "Later, darlin'" She slid a hand down his arm as she glided, a little unsteadily, past.

"Roman, come on!" Donna Jackson bounced beside him. Donna was famous for the change in her normally reserved personality that occurred during the Christmas season. "We're having sign-ups for jobs at the Christmas Fair. This year, you aren't getting off lightly. This year, we're insisting you come."

He tucked Donna's hand through his elbow and threaded a path toward his mother's table. All the time he searched for one face. When he finally located Hannah—sitting beside Lenore—she was staring sightlessly into the distance.

Hell. Just how much did she know about the history of the Bradshaws and the Hunters? Years ago, he'd planned to explain what her mother didn't appear to have told her. Somehow he'd never gotten around to it, and he knew why: he'd been afraid of her reaction and of his own inability to make her see things from what he believed to be the true point of view.

"Hi, there," he said, dropping into the seat beside her. "Are you hungry? Can I get you something to eat?"

She shook her head. The vaguely agitated expression on her face wounded him. He might not have any control over

Mary-Lee, but it was his fault that she had the power to hurt Hannah in the first place.

The band was gearing up again. "How about another dance?"

"No, thank you," she said politely. "I'm enjoying sitting here and catching up with old friends."

Did she include him as an old friend? At this moment he doubted it.

"Here's the sign-up sheet." Donna slapped a clipboard on the table. "Lenore, I've already got you and Jed down for the cake walk. And Reverend and Mrs. Grady are going to provide Christmas food baskets for the raffle. Isn't that wonderful?"

There was a chorus of assent.

Roman glanced at the Gradys. They were unusual, and he wasn't sure what to make of them. Certainly they'd made every effort to fit into life in a small, close-knit rural community. Grady was absorbed in his wife, leaning toward her to catch every word she spoke as if no one else in the room existed.

Courtly. The word came to mind, and it suited the man. In his immaculate, but outdated black suit, with a large black bow tie flopping loosely at the soft and oversized collar of his white shirt, he resembled a nineteenth-century poet rather than a retired minister.

"So you and Hannah will do it?"

Roman looked sharply at Donna Jackson. "I beg your pardon?"

"Pin the nose on Santa? You and Hannah always used to run that for the children at the fair. It hasn't been done since… Not since Hannah left," she ended in a flurry. "It would be so lovely to see the two of you working together on something again. Wouldn't it, Lenore?"

"It certainly would."

His mother's eager smile held longing. Roman made fists on his knees. His mother had never stopped dreaming that he and Hannah would get together again. Last night he'd had to beg her not to go to Hannah on his behalf.

"Can we put you down, Hannah?" Donna asked.

Hannah looked, not at Donna but at Roman. He could almost see her thoughts, the questions she must long to ask. She thought he was a liar and that he'd betrayed her. Hannah was fair. She'd want to ask him if those things were true. If she did, what would he say?

"Give that to me." He grinned and took the clipboard from Donna. "Of course Hannah and I will stage a return performance of our Christmas spectacular. We wouldn't miss the opportunity, would we Hannah?"

She stared back mutely.

Damn it. He wasn't giving her up without a fight. With a flourish, he signed both of their names on the sheet. "Trusty Helper, check that blindfold," he bellowed. "Make sure this kid didn't cheat. No one gets that close to the target without being able to see!"

At least Hannah smiled at that. "Target, sir?" she said. "What target? Since when has the object of this very scientific game been to pin Santa's nose in his ear?"

A laugh went up around the table.

"How long is Jane going to be gone?" Lenore asked Hannah.

"I'm not sure when she'll be back."

"How lucky she is to have you," Mrs. Grady said. "Jane is just so fortunate."

Roman would swear Hannah looked…panicky?

"Well, regardless of when she comes back, we'll be expecting you for Thanksgiving dinner, Hannah," Roman's mother said. "Jed and I already talked about it. Didn't we Jed?"

"Certainly did." Jed Thomas sounded hearty, but Roman didn't miss the wary reserve in his eyes. Jed had always been intuitive about people, and if he was judging Hannah as less than enthusiastic about Lenore's invitation, he was probably right.

Roman pretended to study the list of events for the Christmas Fair. Hannah's silence spoke for itself.

"You will come, Hannah?"

"Thank you, Lenore. But I'm not sure I'll still be in Clarkesville on Thursday."

"Hannah!" The distress in his mother's voice smote at Roman. "You've only just got here. Surely you can't be leaving Clarkesville already. You could at least stay through the week."

"If Jane gets back I'll be moving on."

Roman rested his brow on a fist and jabbed the pencil tip into the paper. He wouldn't let her go again. He damn well wouldn't. Somehow he was going to find a way to keep her with him...or at least near him.

Someone came to stand at his elbow, but he couldn't bring himself to look up.

"Hello, Hannah. We heard you were in town. We thought you'd come by and see us."

Roman closed his eyes. Beaulah Cassidy. Mary-Lee's mother would make the perfect last straw for an already-disastrous evening.

"How are you, Mrs. Cassidy?" Hannah was as polite as always.

"Did I just hear you say you'd be moving on soon?"

Tapping the pencil against his teeth, Roman raised his face and found Beaulah looking directly at him. The malevolence he'd come to expect was firmly in place.

"I said I wasn't sure I'd be here on Thursday," Hannah said in a deceptively soft voice Roman recognized. It was that tone he knew as a warning not to push too far.

"Didn't I also hear you were thinking of settling in Atlanta?" Color rose in Beaulah's flat cheeks. As usual, her dark hair was securely pinned into a bun at her nape.

"You may have heard that," Hannah said.

Beaulah's pale eyes made a swift journey between Roman and Hannah. "You should do just fine there." Without attempting to be discreet, she looked Hannah over. "Yes, I'd say you're a whole lot better suited to Atlanta than our little town.''

A pool of silence formed around the table. Donna crossed her arms tightly, and Lenore glared at Beaulah. Roman stood slowly. After all this time, Beaulah Cassidy still behaved as if he'd sullied her daughter and deserted her. There were a few truths he'd like to voice…only he couldn't, for Penny's sake.

Hannah got up so abruptly she had to grab her chair to stop it from tipping. ''This has been lovely,'' she said—too loudly. ''I've got a busy day tomorrow. First day as a shopkeeper.'' Her laugh was forced.

''You'll be very good at it,'' Mrs. Grady said. Roman had forgotten the Gradys' presence.

''Yes. Thank you. Well, I'm going home now.'' Hannah laughed again. ''Wherever that is. I guess I don't really have one, do I? I mean… Good night.''

Lenore stepped into Hannah's path and caught her hand. ''Will you come on Thursday?''

''I don't know. I'll probably be—''

''Yes. But if you *are* still here?''

''I—''

''She'll come, won't you?'' Reverend Grady said in his deep, clear voice. ''The poor girl's just too tired to think. Take her home, Roman, and make sure she's all right.''

The man's request surprised Roman, but he smiled gratefully. '''Night all.'' He nodded in the direction of Beaulah's stare. For Penny's sake and none other, he'd continue trying to maintain peace.

Hannah was already speeding away from the table, her head held high. She'd stand out in any crowd, he decided. Just seeing her brought the old longing flooding back.

''Slow down.'' Drawing level, he grasped her elbow. ''I'm sorry, Hannah. That woman's poison. She always was.''

''She's your mother-in-law.''

He winced. ''My *ex*-mother-in-law.''

''She hates me.''

They reached the vestibule. "She hates you because she knows you're everything her daughter never could be."

Hannah swung toward him. "Then why did you—" She paused, lips parted, then pulled her arm away. "Excuse me."

He let her get her jacket and pull it on. The more energy she spent, the more rage, the better. She'd be over her anger that much more quickly.

In the street, she set off with long, rapid strides, her high heels clicking on the sidewalk.

Roman let her get ahead, took a deep breath and jogged to catch up. She turned sharply and crossed to the square.

"Hannah."

Before he guessed her intention, she veered from the sidewalk to a path running between plantings in the park.

Roman caught up just as she reached the old spruce tree. "Hannah, stop. Please."

"I've got to get back."

"Some things never change!" He clamped a hand on her shoulder. "Stay right where you are and *cool down*."

"I *am* cool." But she kept her face averted, and he felt the tension in her body. Wind tossed her hair.

"No, you're not," he told her quietly. "This is me, Hannah. Roman. I know you, remember?"

"You used to know me."

When he turned her toward him she made no effort to resist. "Do you really believe I'm not the same man I was?" he asked her.

Hannah shook her head. "Don't ask me that." Her eyes were closed, shutting him out. Spruce branches blew back and forth across a spotlight, sending ripples of light and shadow across her face.

Roman pulled her closer, slipping his hand behind her neck. "Answer the question." Using his fingers, he urged Hannah nearer yet. Only inches separated them. He could smell the light perfume she wore and feel her warmth beneath his hand, see the faint flicker beneath her closed eyelids.

Leaning, bending his head, he touched his lips to her cold cheek.

And she shuddered.

"Hannah?"

She opened her eyes and he saw her confusion.

"Oh, Hannah." Light wavered again, scintillated in prisms from the sparkling earrings she wore…glinted on her parted lips.

The kiss happened. There was no decision. Carefully, slowly, with the conviction that if he didn't move very carefully she'd whirl away and be gone, Roman brushed her mouth with his own.

An aching jolt pressed his gut, closed his eyes, tightened muscles in his jaw, his back, his legs. He fought a silent battle against crushing her to him and kissing her with the pent-up need of too many years of waiting.

He heard Hannah's tiny moan and felt her soften. She rested her hands lightly on his chest beneath the jacket.

Drawing back a fraction, he looked at her face. Hannah opened her eyes and stared up at him.

It was her cold finger, outlining his mouth, that undid Roman. The resolve fled. But Hannah met him with her own urgent, reaching lips. All he heard were the small keening sounds she made and the mingling of their short breaths.

His body quickened. The need sent his hips against her, but she didn't pull away.

Hannah's hands went around his neck, tangled in his hair. Her breasts were a softly insistent pressure on his chest. Roman tasted her, opened her mouth wide beneath his own, filled his hands with her hair and rocked her face with the force of his lips and tongue.

"No!" Hannah gasped the word and tore her mouth from his. As quickly, she fell against him, burying her face in his shoulder and clinging.

"Shh," he whispered. "Shh, sweetheart. It's okay. We won't go too quickly. We don't have to go too quickly. We've got as long as it takes."

She trembled. Roman rested his cheek on her hair and stroked her back. "Hannah, Hannah. We can work it out, my darling. We were meant to be here tonight, on this spot, starting again." If he said it firmly enough he'd make himself believe it. Could he make her believe, too?

The sound he heard was a dry sob, and he held on tighter. "Don't cry. Please don't cry."

Hannah lifted her face. Tears glistened in her eyes and shone on her cheeks. "We're not the same, Roman." She fumbled in her pocket.

"Couldn't we build back what we had?" He kissed her cheek again and tasted salt. "We could."

"I don't know about that. They say you can't go back. And some things... Some things don't go away, do they?"

She was talking about the fiasco with Mary-Lee and about Penny. *Penny.* He had to talk to Hannah about his daughter, but he wasn't ready yet—there hadn't been time to decide what to do and say about his gentle little girl.

"Please. Just let me go, Roman." Producing a wadded tissue from her pocket, she wiped her eyes and blew her nose. He almost smiled at the vigorous snort and thorough rubbing her pert nose got. One more little habit that used to be a joke between them.

He made up his mind. "Come on. I'll walk you back. You're tired out and so am I." But he wasn't out of patience or determination.

They walked side by side. Hannah let him thread her arm through his. On the other side of the gardens, he paused and pulled her hood over her hair. "Keep you warm." He smiled down into her face. So vulnerable and open. She twisted everything vital within him.

Too soon they approached the Christmas Shop. Roman halted and turned around, pulling Hannah with him. "I forgot. Back door."

"No." Hannah looked at the key in her hand. "This is for the front door. You don't need to come any farther."

"Yes, I do."

"No, really."

He laughed. "Yes, I *do*. And I'm coming in to make sure there's nobody under the... I'd prefer to make sure you're safe. Is that okay?"

Hannah smiled. "Okay, okay."

He hadn't really noticed the shop before. In fact, he didn't remember looking at the place at all. They'd reached the bowed front window. Surely that had been added. And the square leaded panes. Inside, wintry blue-white light illuminated an animated scene.

Hannah stood beside him, and he glanced down at her. She stared into the window, visibly fascinated.

"I must be more preoccupied than I realized," she said.

He frowned and draped an arm around her shoulders. "Why do you say that?" Touching her, feeling her near, seemed completely natural.

She shrugged. "Oh, no reason. I just hadn't noticed this window scene, is all. Must be the lighting that makes it look different. Look at the angels!"

Miniature fir trees sprouted from a mounded layer of glistening snow. More snow sparkled on the branches. A cottage stood at the edge of the forest, its door open. Two figures, a girl and a boy muffled against cold, moved toward the clearing.

"I've never seen anything like it," Roman said. "The figures move so smoothly. There must be tracks we can't see."

"Yes. But the *angels,* Roman. Aren't they lovely?"

"Mmm." The boy and girl slid away from the cottage as if they hadn't seen it. Every few seconds they halted and turned this way and that as if searching. "The girl's got braids like you used to have."

Hannah giggled, the same giggle he remembered and had never expected to hear again. *"Angels,"* she said. "Look."

Seeming to flit, two white-clad figures darted from tree to tree, stopping, tilting as if to peek at the children, then gliding on. "It's all very pretty," Roman said finally. "I like the sky."

Stars twinkled in a black backdrop.

"Aren't they going to find the cottage?" Hannah rested her forehead on a pane. Her breath misted the glass. "They'll get lost in the woods."

"Hannah!" Roman laughed again. "It's just an animated scene."

"I know." She hunched her shoulders and continued to stare. "There. Look at that."

He bent close. "Ah, the guys in white save the day. Cute."

Hannah elbowed him. "The angels are showing them the way." The figures in white had met the children who turned and headed for the cottage. When they disappeared inside, colored lights came on around the door and in little bushes laden with snow. Hannah sighed. "I love it. And don't pull the macho act on me. I know you too well."

Roman pretended to concentrate on the scene, but he hadn't missed the significance of her comment. Just then, minute colored signs flashed the message Merry Christmas! in each window of the cottage, and the door swung shut. "Corny, Hannah. Corny."

She swung to face him, hands on hips. "It is not. It's beautiful."

He held up his palms. "Right, it's beautiful."

"Roman."

"I mean it. It's…magical." And he was enjoying every lighthearted second he could snatch with this woman.

"We'd better say good-night."

"I'm seeing you inside."

"It's all right. I… Oh, well, thank you." The key was slapped into his hand and he unlocked the door.

Hannah passed him and he shut them in.

"I'll be…" Roman followed Hannah through the subdued glow that pervaded the shop. "This is… It's really something."

"Jane's very clever," Hannah said. "She makes a lot of the things she sells."

"She doesn't make those?" He indicated a row of oval

recesses into each wall. More animated scenes. An old-fashioned Santa Claus admonished a wayward Rudolph, who repeatedly climbed a red pole and slid down again. "What's with the reindeer and the pole?"

"It's the North Pole, of course," Hannah said, sounding disgusted. "Rudolph's still a youngster and getting into mischief. And Santa's telling him off."

"I see," Roman said, struggling to keep humor out of his voice.

"And there's Santa's workshop with all the elves. And Frosty marching across the street with the children." She walked from one animation to another. "Roman! The Grinch. Jane must have decided he's a classic now. He's my favorite."

He did laugh then. "Really. I'm learning all kinds of things about you."

"Isn't his green face adorable? And that's Cindy-Lou Who."

"Who?" He heard his voice wobble.

"Cindy-Lou Who. See, the Grinch is stealing her candy cane while she's asleep."

"And he's your favorite?"

"Well, he'll give it back later." She sounded peeved.

Roman bowed his head. "You always did go nutty over Christmas. I've loved that about you, Hannah. The sweetness. The special part that's still a lovely child." He sounded like someone else, someone he used to know.

"Thank you."

He reached for her hands, and she let him thread their fingers together. "Would you like us to try to make it again, Hannah? There's nothing stopping us."

"Isn't there?"

Nothing that she could possibly guess at. "I don't think so." He'd have to open up to her soon. She deserved that much and more from him.

"I'll be all right here now. You've still got a drive ahead of you."

"Don't avoid this, Hannah. We were always honest with each other."

"Honest? I—" Her hair whipped over her shoulder as she turned her head. "This isn't getting us anywhere."

Roman raised a hand, let it hover inches from her head, then hesitantly stroked her hair. "You already admitted that you didn't just drive by and decide to look in on Clarkesville...and Harmony. We both know you deliberately came here. And we know why."

"I'm not denying any of that." Her voice cracked. "But I made a mistake. You know why I say that. Don't pretend I'm wrong."

"You are wrong—"

With enough force to make him step backward, Hannah swung around and flung herself against him. "Just hold me. Just for a little while." Her hands slid beneath his arms, and she hugged his body in trembling arms. "Then leave me. And don't look back."

He heard the low crooning of his own voice while he cradled her and rocked. She turned her head sideways to rest a cheek on his shoulder.

Colored lights twinkled on a tree in one corner. Dim shapes took on clearer form: a rocking horse with a silver mane, a Victorian dollhouse lighted inside to show rooms decorated for the season and filled with perfect miniatures, heaps of pungently scented wreaths encrusted with silvery packages and satin bows.

Hannah's rapid breathing settled down. She raised her head to look at him. "This place makes me feel peaceful."

"Mmm." He felt anything but peaceful. His need for her was a pulsing thing he couldn't ignore. And he couldn't ignore the blossoming fear that she was right, that it might be too late for them. Only he could make sure they had a chance, but at what cost?

Tinkling sounded, like hundreds of crystal bells ringing in the quiet of a snow-blanketed night. A frosted breeze seemed to brush his face. He was getting caught up in all this Christmas mumbo jumbo.

"I really hated living in Chicago," Hannah said. "It's fine for people who like cities. I don't. I never felt at home there."

"And you won't in Atlanta. You belong here."

She shook her head slightly. "I'd lost my job. And the man I'd been going out with…"

"Who was he?" He winced at the sharpness in his own voice.

"John Norris. I don't hide things, Roman. But John and I were never meant to be anything more than friends."

He had no right to press her with the questions he longed to ask about John Norris—damn him, whoever he was.

"John met someone else. They're going to get married."

Swallowing hurt his throat. "And you miss him?"

She slid her hands up his back and massaged slowly. "No."

Roman's concentration was slipping. "You didn't want to marry him?"

"I thought I did once. It would have been a mistake." Hannah turned her face toward his neck, and he felt her breath on his skin. "Then Mother got married and moved away. So I decided I was going to pack up and move on, too. Then…" Her brow pressed against his jaw. She shifted her hands to his chest. "Then I just wanted to see you. I can't pretend there was any other motive for coming here. I needed to see you."

His heart did wild things. "And you have. And you can stay and keep on seeing me."

Hannah straightened, her hands resting on his shoulders. "I'm not going to pretend I don't wish that was true. I do."

"Then *do* it." He held her face in his hands. "Just *do* it."

She evaded his kiss. "Please go now, Roman."

"You don't want that."

"Yes, I do," she said very softly. "This is some sort of dream. Sugarplum fairies and letters to Santa. He's too busy already, Roman. He isn't going to have time to deal with the kind of wish you're sending his way.''

''How will we know if we don't ask?''

The tinkling sound intensified until the air around them tingled with the peal of tiny bells.

''What makes that noise?'' he asked, distracted.

''I don't know. Probably a record or tape that didn't get turned off.'' She passed him and opened the door. He had no real choice but to go outside.

''Hannah, let's just forget everything but us. Let's make this the new start. The beginning of what we lost.''

''That's a lovely wish, Roman. But some wishes can't come true.''

He could tell her everything. Right now. It would either draw them together...or be the end. ''Hannah, I'd like to talk some more.''

''No. Please. Good night, Roman. Thank you for taking me to supper.''

He glanced at the shop window where the angels were turning the children back toward the warm cottage again. What should he do? ''We need an angel,'' he murmured. ''Someone to guide us.''

''Do you think any angel would be dumb enough to take us on?'' Hannah laughed bitterly. ''I don't.'' She closed the door.

Chapter Eight

Blossom followed Hannah into the shop. Nine o'clock was opening time. It was only eight-thirty, but Hannah was nervous. She must at least familiarize herself with the cash register and try to figure out what was where in the mass of stock Jane carried.

The vintage, brass-trimmed cash register fitted perfectly with the old-world theme. Not a very functional piece of equipment, but pretty. And there was already money for change inside. "I guess we're in business, Blossom. Shopkeepers. For a day, anyway."

She looked around for the cat and laughed. Blossom had arranged herself artfully on a red-and-green rag rug before a black, pot-bellied stove that stood in a corner close to the Christmas tree.

Hannah strolled around the shop. Crowded shelves, heaped baskets standing on the oak-planked floor, toys used as display props and a ceiling-high tree that showcased many of the ornaments on sale. Lovely. She raised her shoulders. The ache of indecision about Roman would probably never go away, but this room held a magical atmosphere that was too powerful to be completely overshadowed.

Roman had said the window scene was magical.

She'd forgotten to turn it off last night. The figures still moved, and so did the small animated scenes in the walls. She'd leave them all on for customers now.

Humming, she rearranged a group of soft gray mice on a round table covered with a poinsettia-emblazoned, floor-length cloth. Mr. Santa Mouse, Mrs. Santa Mouse and a bevy of Santa's mouse helpers—and a sleigh pulled by mouse reindeer. Next she moved a collection of German nutcrackers shaped like soldiers, placing them in marching order along the front of the counter. A brightly painted wooden train stood on a circular track around the base of the tree. Hannah wound up a key in the engine and it chugged off with a satisfying clatter.

She rubbed her hands together and noticed logs beside the stove. When she opened the glass screen, she discovered Jane must light a fire each day. The strike of a match sent flames crackling up the stove pipe and brought a pleased purr from Blossom.

Playing shop, Hannah thought. But why not?

A tap on the glass in the front door startled her. Suddenly insecure, she glanced around. If this was an early customer, she supposed she was ready.

With her heart fluttering, she went to shoot back the bolt and sweep the door wide. "Good—" There was no one there.

Frowning, she peered outside.

No one.

"Kids!" Some things never changed. She could imagine some little imp, or imps, hiding around a corner laughing.

It was the color that pulled her attention to the mat outside the door. "Oh, how beautiful." A big bunch of snapdragons, their stems captured in a white paper sack, lay at her feet. Hannah picked them up and touched a fingertip to a velvety yellow bloom. Snapdragons had always been her favorite. Once she'd told John about them and he'd laughed. She had *plebeian* tastes, he'd said. And he'd found it hard to believe that in Georgia they bloomed late into winter.

She shut the door and hurried to the kitchen. *Roman.* She turned on the faucet to fill a vase. Of course. Who else around here but Roman would bring her flowers, these particular flowers? ''Darn!'' The water overflowed and splattered the counter.

Hannah arranged the flowers and set them in the middle of the table. When she stood back to survey her efforts, tears stung her eyes. Closing the door on him the night before had devastated her. Sleep, when it finally came, had been fitful, and she'd awakened with a clear image of his troubled face.

But the facts hadn't changed. It no longer mattered when his letter was delivered. He obviously believed she'd received it on time and chosen not to reply. That meant that he assumed she'd read his lies. Now he thought that because he was no longer married to Mary-Lee, he could expect Hannah to fall into his arms again and forget the past.

Slowly she returned to the shop. Forgetting the past was what she'd like to do more than anything else in the world. But she couldn't, especially when he persisted in avoiding honest discussion with her.

When she'd brought in the rest of her belongings from the van, a search had failed to produce Roman's letter. She'd packed to leave Chicago in such a hurry, who knew when she'd find everything.

Hannah opened a cardboard box that contained blown glass tree ornaments: icicles, snowflakes, hummingbirds—all impossibly fragile. She began to hang examples of them on the tree. More would be hung from the tinsel garlands looped along the shelves.

Just as Hannah reached for a high branch, the phone rang. Still holding a snowflake, she scrambled off the stool she was using and snatched up the earpiece from an antique instrument on one end of the counter. ''Hello. The Christmas Shop.''

She took a few moments to recognize Jane's clear voice.

''Jane! Hello. How are things there?''

''Not good,'' Jane said. ''Not good at all. My cousin's condition has worsened, I'm afraid.''

Protecting the glass ornament, Hannah leaned over the base of the phone to talk. ''I'm sorry.'' She didn't know what else she could say without sounding insincere.

"Yes. So am I." There was a pause. "Hannah, is everything all right there?"

Hannah glanced at the storybook shop. "Everything's beautiful."

"I knew it would be. You won't mind staying on for a few days will you?"

"Oh." Hannah puffed up her cheeks. Her emotions warred. The desire to run as far and as fast as possible from Clarkesville—and Roman—was very strong. So was the overwhelming longing to see him again.

"You don't mind?"

Just once more. That's what had brought her here in the first place. She'd already seen him "once more" on three occasions, and each time the result had been personally disastrous.

"Hannah?"

"Of course I'll stay. When do you think you might be back?"

"Oh, thank you, thank you." Jane's voice trilled happily. "I'm so grateful. I just knew I could count on you."

Hannah had to smile. "Thank you. But when—"

"I've got to go, dear. Don't forget. If you need more money you can get it from my account at the bank. I made the necessary arrangements. Talk to you soon."

"Jane—"

"Oh, dear. I hear my cousin calling. Bye, dear."

The line went dead. Hannah looked at the earpiece. "Just like that." And she'd forgotten to ask for a telephone number in case she needed to make contact.

The distant sound of the cuckoo clock chiming nine sounded from the top of the stairs. As if someone had been watching the clock, the shop door flew open. Donna Jackson marched in, clomping in her sensible brown lace-up shoes.

"Hannah." Donna beamed. The woolen cardigan and skirt, cream-colored blouse and cameo brooch were back where they belonged. "It was so wonderful to see you and Roman together again last night. I hardly have a moment. I'm going to be late as it is. But I had to stop by and tell you how glad I am you're back.''

And so it started again. "Thank you, Donna."

"This Friday afternoon—as soon as the post office closes—I'd like to get the paper chains up. Would that be convenient?''

Hannah remembered the snowflake and used it to gain thinking time. "Excuse me for a moment." She climbed up to hang the ornament on a high branch. Today was Tuesday. Jane had said a few days. She was bound to stay with her cousin over Thanksgiving on Thursday. Hannah stepped to the floor again. "I'll probably be able to come."

"I need to know if I should wait," Donna said, sounding anxious.

Hannah made up her mind. "I'll be there."

"Good!" Donna clapped her hands together, then seemed to remember her dignity. She cleared her throat. "The old paper chains are really in poor condition. If you have the papers in stock, I'd like to buy them now. I can get started in the next few evenings. Mother would enjoy that, too."

With a smile, Hannah located a drawer marked Paper Chains and Streamers and selected several packets of multicolored strips with gummed ends. "Tell your mother I'll be by to see her," she said before realizing she was unlikely to have an opportunity. Old Mrs. Jackson was very old, so old that people speculated on the subject.

"I'll do that," Donna said happily, handing money to Hannah before leaving with a cheerful wave.

Hannah looked at her watch. The entire encounter had taken only ten minutes. This could be a long day.

After another hour had passed, Hannah changed her mind about the potential for boredom. Her old school friend Libby Miller, plumper and holding hands with two toddlers, had rushed in on her way to the town's only preschool. She bought each little girl a snow scene, one that wound up to play "Jingle Bell Rock" while white flakes drifted down on a guitar-playing elf, the other a demure, tinkling rendition of the Sugarplum Fairy with an appropriate ballerina twirling. Libby then dashed away with Hannah's promise to talk on the phone that evening.

Ellie Sumpter and Mrs. Grady arrived neck-and-neck.

"Pies," Ellie announced, plunking two cloth-draped tins on the counter. "One pumpkin and one apple. Still warm. Where's Jane?"

"She's gone to help her cousin in Milledgeville," Mrs. Grady said while Hannah was still opening her mouth to reply. "Her cousin's got a weak chest. Hannah's running the shop while Jane's gone, aren't you dear?"

Hannah nodded.

"Well, that's wonderful," Ellie said. "Any night you feel like it, you just run on over to Al and me. Dinner'll be on the house. We don't get half enough young company. Not half enough."

Hannah smiled and mumbled thanks…and felt the net tightening around her.

"How're you and the Reverend?" Ellie asked Mrs. Grady. "How's that old barn of a house coming along?"

"Just beautifully," Mrs. Grady said, apparently unperturbed by the description of her present home. "You know Jane's been helping with the redecorating."

"I bet she's good at that," Hannah said, finally finding her voice. "Look at this shop. Isn't it beautiful?"

The other women made approving noises while they surveyed the room.

"Got to get back," Ellie said. She wore an apron under her raincoat. "More pies in the oven. See you later, maybe."

As soon as Ellie left, Mrs. Grady began inspecting merchandise, and Hannah watched her covertly. The woman was small. Her silvery hair was pulled into a roll around her head, a style that was vaguely reminiscent of the forties. A blue wool coat trimmed with black braid hung open over a soft gray dress. Again the style was unusual, as if the wearer had somehow become suspended in a bygone time, then discovered the clothes of the era suited her and decided not to catch up with everyone else.

A yowl startled Hannah. "Blossom!" Fur bristling, the cat leaped from her place by the stove and bounded toward the door to the rest of the house. "That's the second time she's done that," Hannah said apologetically. She let the wide-eyed cat out. "She must be unsettled here."

"Give her time," Mrs. Grady said. Behind the incongruous wire-rimmed glasses, her pale blue eyes also held a smile. "I have to buy new decorations. Did the garlands I ordered come in?"

Hannah frowned, feeling her first rush of insecurity. "Which garlands are those, Mrs. Grady? Jane didn't mention them, I'm afraid."

"Evergreen, my dear. I'm going to wind them around the banisters. Such beautiful, carved banisters. Jane wrote the order down in her red book. She said something about how she matches the numbers to numbers on boxes when they're delivered—so she can locate the right order."

"Red book." Hannah began opening drawers beneath the counter. Ornaments and more ornaments. There was a business checkbook in one drawer, but nothing else relating to the running of the business. "No red book."

"It's her order book. That's what she said."

Hannah glanced at Mrs. Grady's smooth face. She had to be at least in her fifties, didn't she? Yet she could easily have passed for no more than thirty. Hannah closed the drawer. Clarkesville air must be some sort of elixir of youth, although she hadn't noticed it having such wonderful effects on a lot of people around here.

"Oh, dear. I expect you wanted to pick up the garlands."

"Don't you worry, Hannah," Mrs. Grady said. "I'll check back later in the day. You're sure to find the book somewhere in the house."

"Yes." Hannah wasn't at all sure where to look. "I don't suppose Jane left you a phone number? For her cousin's home?"

"No, dear. She didn't." Mrs. Grady was pulling supple black leather gloves onto her smooth hands.

"Do you think there's anyone else in town who might know?"

"I doubt it. I certainly wouldn't know who to suggest. Jane can be quite private, you know. Goodbye."

Hannah waited until the door closed behind Mrs. Grady before searching the drawers again. No red book. No record books of any description. Mrs. Grady was right; going around town asking questions about Jane wouldn't be appropriate.

The kitchen yielded nothing, or the storeroom. Hannah went back into the shop, hoping to find that Jane had left a phone number after all. She hadn't.

If she propped open the door to the storeroom, she'd be able to go upstairs and still hear the shop bell.

Hannah darted up one flight of stairs and peered into the shadows on the flight leading up to Jane's floor. She climbed more slowly to a landing with two open doors. One showed the bottom of some stairs running to yet another floor. The second door revealed what must be Jane's bedroom.

Reluctantly Hannah stepped inside. The furniture surprised her; an exact replica of that in the bedroom she was using, with identical colors and fabrics. The one difference was exactly what she'd been hoping to find—a desk. Not a desk exactly, but a writing table with raised cubbyholes at the back and a leather top tooled with gold scrollwork around the edges. Narrow drawers were tucked beneath the top.

She couldn't look through someone else's desk.

But if she was to run the shop efficiently, she had to know what stock had come in and when other shipments were expected.

A glance showed that the cubbyholes contained nothing but writing supplies. The top of the desk was bare.

"Wonderful," Hannah growled to herself. "I wonder how many more customers I'm going to have to turn away because I can't tell them what they want to know."

A chirrup that slid into a purr heralded Blossom's arrival.

She slithered around Hannah's legs and followed her happily to the wardrobe. Hesitantly Hannah opened it and peeked inside.

"Good grief." She swung the door wide. No clothes hung on the rail. The shelf was empty, and nothing was stacked on the bottom. Could Jane have taken everything she owned in the one small suitcase she'd carried?

Hannah shook her head and turned back to the desk. Standing at a distance, she leaned to pull one drawer out a fraction, and a fraction more. Empty. The next drawer was also empty. And so were the other two.

Odd.

Dropping to sit on her heels, Hannah stroked Blossom. "Nothing here, girl. It's almost as if no one ever used the room." She straightened and went back into the hallway.

Before Hannah could reach back for the door handle, Blossom, her fur sprouting from her back like a spiked crew cut, shot from the bedroom. Spitting, she hit the rug with claws extended and rushed down the passageway.

Hannah's hair rose on the nape of her neck. Twice in one morning? Blossom might be cool on occasions, but she was even-tempered. Fear was the only thing likely to send that cat into a frenzy.

Rising to her toes, Hannah reentered Jane's bedroom. She peered quickly behind the door, but found no sinister figure lurking there.

A skirt on the four-poster bed touched the floor. Moving soundlessly, Hannah took a few more steps and dropped to her knees. Her heart hammered so loudly her ears hummed.

Using a finger and thumb, she caught a fold in the bedskirt, edged it gradually higher and bent to peer under the mattress. Light from the window shone through the fabric on the other side of the bed.

No murderous villain skulked there, either. Of course not. Blossom had done the same thing in the shop.

Faint with relief, Hannah stood again and pressed a hand to her stomach—and glanced across the room.

She screwed up her eyes and advanced on the writing table once more. A book bound in red leather lay on one side. She must need glasses. It had to have been there all the time.

A glance inside revealed the order book she was looking for. Mrs. Grady's garlands were noted, together with the fact that they had been delivered. Hannah smiled with relief. Now she'd be able to track them down by matching the number in the book with that on one of the stored boxes.

She hurried out...and stopped. Looking over her shoulder, she took in the room again. So unused. And she'd have sworn the book hadn't been... It was the shop. And the season. She was getting caught up with the make-believe feeling that pervaded everything here.

A screeching yowl, Blossom's, grabbed Hannah's attention. The noise came from somewhere above.

"Blossom," she called. "Blossom. Come here." Calling the cat was useless if she didn't want to come. After several minutes of waiting, Hannah decided this was one of those times.

The only route upward from here was via the second door with its dark stairway. Hannah bent and looked up. Dim light showed at the top.

"Blossom!" She started up. "Will you come? Now!"

The answer was another wailing meow.

Tutting, Hannah took the steps two at a time until she emerged through a door at the top into a cobweb-festooned attic crowded with what appeared to be antique nursery furniture and toys.

"There you are, you wretched cat." Blossom sat stiffly on a couch covered with a dustcover. "Come on. Now! I probably wouldn't hear the shop bell from here."

Blossom stood and arched her back. She showed no sign of being impressed by Hannah's urgency. Above her, a dusty skylight cast eerily filtered daylight over the stored treasures.

With a sigh, Hannah advanced. "You can really be a pain. I don't know why I put up with you." She loved the ornery animal. That's why.

She leaned to pick up the cat and stumbled over a hobby horse lying on the floor.

Blossom leaped over Hannah, whipped through the attic door and disappeared.

"Ungrateful feline!" Picking herself up, Hannah dusted off her gray slacks and straightened the matching silk blouse she wore.

A slam brought her to attention. The door had closed. That rushing animal must have created quite a breeze.

Smiling ruefully, Hannah went to the door and grasped the handle. The book was what she needed and she had it. Time to get downstairs and find Mrs. Grady's garlands.

She rattled the resistant handle and tried turning it the other way. Then she pulled, and pulled again. With a foot braced against the jamb she used all her weight to tug.

The door was locked.

Chapter Nine

Hannah's angels still made their gliding circuit around the window display.

Roman shoved his hands into his jeans pockets and stared until the glittering snow became a blur. She wouldn't want to see him.

He faced the street, trying to decide what to do. Why Jane Smith had chosen to call him was a puzzle, but she had. And she'd sounded concerned about Hannah because she wasn't answering the phone.

She could have overslept. They'd both been upset last night, and if she'd stayed up late after he'd left... He wanted Hannah. If such a thing were possible, he wanted her even more than before she'd disappeared from his life.

The phone was probably out of order.

Hannah could have had an accident and be unable to reach the phone.

Roman pushed open the door. Overhead a bell jangled loudly. He walked into the shop and closed the door again. He smelled cinnamon, cloves and pine. Then he heard the tinkling sound that had caught his attention last night.

"Hello?" He threaded a path through brightly colored displays to the counter. Another bell, brass this time, stood near an antique telephone. Roman tapped the plunger and winced at its tinny ring.

He waited. Nearby, a few embers glowed inside a black wood stove.

A hurdy-gurdy fairground noise startled him. He twisted around, searching. The noise stopped for a moment, then started again. He located a miniature wooden carousel on a low shelf. White, with gold-and-green stripes on the roof, its cargo of garish circus animals revolved as the music played.

Roman wiped his palms on his jeans. The door to the back of the shop stood open. "Hannah!" More seconds passed, then minutes. He was aware of feeling vaguely sick.

Enough pussy-footing around. Quickly he covered the distance into some sort of storeroom piled high with boxes. The kitchen was open to his left. There was no one inside. To his right, were stairs. He climbed several of them and shouted again, "Hannah! Are you up there?"

Jane was out of town, and the shop was open and supposedly in Hannah's charge. She *had* to be here.

At the top of the flight he paused. Straight ahead lay a bedroom decorated with loads of blue. The furnishings looked antique. "Hannah?"

Holy hell. Where was she? "Hannah, where—?" Something black shot along the hallway and landed at his feet. Hannah's cat. Roman bent, absently stroking the animal while he looked in the direction the cat had come from.

More stairs.

With Blossom at his heels, he went up once more. He felt like the intruder he was. Another bedroom, a twin of the one below, opened before him. Again there was no sign of life.

The cat made little, high-pitched purring sounds. "What is it, girl?" Roman said. Promptly Blossom ran to another door and disappeared. Roman followed up yet more stairs.

Another door. This one closed.

He tried the handle but it didn't turn. He knocked.

The responding silence sent his heart plummeting. Hannah must have gone out for something and forgotten to lock the shop door. She certainly wouldn't be hiding out in the attic.

He turned to leave, then frowned, concentrating. Had he

heard a scuffle on the other side of the door? Leaning on the wood, he placed an ear against a panel. Someone could have brought Hannah up here.

All caution disappeared. With a grunt, he drove his shoulder against the door and it shot inward.

Blossom immediately sauntered past and went to leap on a painted leather chest already occupied by several Raggedy Ann and Andy dolls. Roman took a step forward, screwing up his eyes against the poor light afforded by the single skylight.

A scraping sound preceded the violent slam of the door into its frame. An instant later something shiny and blue narrowly missed his head on its way to crash and break on the floor.

Roman swung around in time to see Hannah fall to her knees, the neck of a ceramic vase still in her hands. She stared up into his face, then down at the pottery—and let it drop.

"Hannah?"

"I thought you were some maniac come to murder me." Her expression was stricken. "I might have killed you."

Roman struggled for the sober reaction the moment demanded—and failed. He hauled her to her feet...and laughed. Leading her across to a couch covered with a dustcover, he eased her down. Crossing his arms, he rubbed a hand over his face and chuckled.

"It's *not* funny," Hannah said, but her voice wobbled. "I've been locked in for ages. I was beginning to think I'd die here in the end. Then you came crashing in, and I thought you were someone who'd captured me and come back to hurt me. I really might have killed you if that vase had hit your head."

"But it didn't," Roman managed.

Hannah frowned. "*Why* didn't it? I aimed carefully."

Roman's laughter exploded afresh. Hannah in an outrage was wonderful to behold. "I don't know why, my love. And I'm very sorry you're disappointed." He picked up a wooden tennis racquet with broken strings. "Here. Try again. I'll hold still this time."

Hannah took the racquet and tossed it aside. "You always did enjoy making fun of me." Slowly her lopsided, self-derisive grin dissolved and she laughed with him. When she could speak, she said, "I don't know why you're here but I'm glad you came."

"I came to find you," he told her. "Do I get to sit down, too?"

She got up to tug the dustcover from the couch. Yellow-and-umber chintz covered the lumpy old piece. "Sit down and rest. Rescuing must be tiring work." She sat and waved Roman down beside her.

He deliberately made sure there was space between them, then turned, hooking one knee sideways on the seat so that he could watch her face.

"I didn't sleep last night." He hadn't intended to say that, not that he seemed to have much control over what he said around Hannah.

She tilted her head. Her shiny hair slipped forward around her shoulders. A soft gray silk shirt and gray wool pants fitted her beautiful body perfectly. Pewter earrings shone dully at her ears. His Hannah had grown into a fascinating woman.

Roman swallowed and tugged at the already-unbuttoned collar of his denim shirt. "I expect it was that punch that kept me awake. I never was much of a drinker."

"The Roman I remember quite enjoyed an occasional drink." She held up a hand to stop his response. "I didn't sleep much last night, either. And when I woke up this morning, the first thing I thought about was your face when I closed the door on you last night. I want you to be happy."

Hannah always said what she was thinking. One of the many things he loved about her was her honesty. He wanted to hold her hand, to hold her, but he propped an elbow on the back of the couch and laced his fingers together instead. "You can make me happy, Hannah."

She looked at him sharply.

"I didn't mean—"

"I *know* what you mean. But I think you know what's getting in the way of that...of us being together."

He knew, too. "Things get complicated. They get out of hand. Do you know what I mean?"

"I think so."

"Then time goes by and you aren't sure what you ought to do about any of it anymore. Does that make sense?"

"Perfect sense."

He aimed a thumb in the direction of the door. "It wasn't locked."

"Are you sure?" She drew her brows together. "I couldn't make it budge."

"Uh-uh. Just stuck. You gave up too easily."

"Maybe I didn't try. Maybe what I really wanted was to stay up here forever. Did you think of that?" Hannah stuck out her bottom lip in a way that made him smile. "What are you laughing at?"

"I'm not. I'm smiling. You used to pout like that when you were a kid."

She didn't reply. And she didn't smile in response. Seconds dragged by before she said, "Tell me about it, Roman. About what happened. Penny and everything."

He felt his skin tighten, and a chill passed down his spine. He straightened his back. "I thought you'd already decided you knew everything. Isn't that the way it is?"

"Is it? I guess I'd just like to hear you say the words. Yes, I definitely would. I need to."

And he needed to tell her, but he'd never been less certain of the wisdom of an idea than he was of this one. "I married Mary-Lee three months after you left Clarkesville."

The light went out of her lovely brown eyes. She looked at her hands, clasped in her lap. "You didn't take long to get over losing me."

"I still haven't gotten over it," he murmured.

"You should have thought of that before—" She dropped

her head back against the couch and stared up at the skylight. "I promised myself I'd never say anything like that to you."

"I deserve it."

"If you'd found me in Chicago, what would you have said? That Penny wasn't yours?"

His stomach felt like a steel coil. "That was a long time ago."

"There's never an excuse for lies, least of all to someone you say you love."

"I did love you, Hannah. I still do."

She rolled her face toward him. "You think you do. You're in love with something elusive. Some sort of old dream." A pulse beat visibly in her pale, arched neck.

He glanced at the thrust of her breasts, her flat stomach, the curve of her hips. "I know what I want."

She did smile then, a tight little smile. "Want is an interesting word, Roman. Let's not confuse it with anything else."

An unaccustomed warmth rose to his face. He felt caught out, and cornered. "I was taking that course on farm management."

"I don't want to go back to that."

"In Atlanta."

"It's history."

He shifted closer. "And *I* need to talk about it. Mary-Lee was trying to become a model and not having any luck. Wrong kind of figure, or something."

Hannah rolled her eyes. "I'd have thought that would depend on the type of modeling she wanted." She bit her lip. "That wasn't nice. But Mary-Lee makes it hard to be nice sometimes."

"I know. She does have some good points, though."

"You should know."

"I guess I deserve that, too." Did he? Perhaps. "She was living not far from the motel where I stayed. We got together a few times and had a drink." He shrugged.

"And the rest is history?" Hannah wasn't doing a good job of hiding her unhappiness. "Penny's a lovely little girl."

''She certainly is.'' He breathed slowly, filling his lungs, making a decision. ''Penny isn't mine.''

He saw Hannah's pupils dilate. She ran her tongue over her lips.

''The birth certificate says she is. Everyone in this town thinks she is—except for the Cassidys and Mary-Lee. They *know* she isn't.''

Hannah pushed herself upright and turned toward him. ''Why are you saying this now?''

''Because I want you and I'm going to fight for you. Mary-Lee came to me and told me she was pregnant. She said she didn't even know who the child's father was. It happened at some party or other when she was drunk. Evidently she was drowning her sorrows over the latest job failure, and the guy took advantage of her.''

She took a while to answer. ''So you decided to throw away everything we had by offering to marry her?''

''No. It wasn't like that.''

Hannah bowed her head and her hair fell forward. ''This is unbelievable. Every bad line I ever heard.''

He couldn't blame her for sneering. ''Hannah, she came to me because she had nowhere else to go. She told me that if she went home pregnant and unmarried her parents would turn her away.''

In a sudden, almost violent move, Hannah grasped his thigh with both hands. She brought her face close to his. ''You told me you never lie.'' Her voice rose. ''I trusted you from the day we met. Do you expect me to believe that you loved me, but that you decided to throw away all our plans so that you could save Mary-Lee? Why didn't you tell me what happened and ask me to help figure out what to do?''

''I would have!'' His temper began to slip. ''You left without giving me a chance.''

''Mary-Lee told me her baby was yours and you were going to marry her. My mother knew I couldn't stay here and watch the two of you together, so we left. Do you blame me for wanting to get away?''

"*Yes,* damn it. Yes…" He covered her hands on his leg. The pressure of her nails, digging into his flesh, felt good. "You should have waited and talked to me."

"Why? What would it have changed?"

"*Everything.*" He searched her face. "Everything, Hannah. I tried to get a message to you and couldn't. Then I couldn't find you. God, it was awful."

She parted her lips, clamped her teeth together. "Is… Is it true? Isn't Penny your child?"

"No!" He fought to calm down. "No, Hannah. And I hadn't said I'd marry Mary-Lee. She gambled to get you out of the way and it worked. Later—when I came back and found you'd left—she finally told me what had happened. That's what I meant when I said she wasn't all bad. She regretted what she'd done."

Tears welled in Hannah's eyes and glistened along her lower lashes. "That was big of her. No wonder you felt you had to be noble and marry her."

"Sarcasm doesn't suit you." And he couldn't deal with much more of what he was feeling: anger, frustration, overpowering need.

Hannah blinked and the tears coursed down her cheeks. "I believe everything you've told me. And I don't feel like being nice anymore." A jerky breath expanded her chest. "I want to scream, dammit."

"Then do it." Roman framed her face with his. "Do it for both of us. I've hated these years…except for Penny. I love that little girl."

More tears slid from Hannah's eyes and she began to shake. "Seven years. That woman took seven years away from us."

At this moment he understood what an aching heart felt like. "Try not to hate Mary-Lee. She's a good mother to Penny."

"She should be. That's the way it's *supposed* to be. Why did you get divorced?"

"She had an affair with good old Davis. Then she told me

she wanted out…because Davis had all the things she wanted most. He had money, a big house and 'prospects.'''

''Had you—'' She tried to turn away, but Roman wouldn't let her. ''Did you love her?''

He laughed and hated the harsh sound. ''No. How could you even ask? In the beginning I thought I could make a life for the three of us. I thought it would fill the gap you left—help me get over you. Then—'' he shrugged ''—then the whole thing started to crumble, and the best I could do was protect Penny.''

''Oh, Roman. I should have known. I should have kept right on trusting you.''

With his thumbs, he smoothed the tears from her cheeks. He looked at her lips and felt his own part. Hannah closed her eyes. and he kissed her. Her soft skin tasted of salt. She made small, choked sounds.

Her fingers spread on his thigh. He willed his mind to ignore his body's reaction to her touch. But she kneaded the muscle…and stroked.

Roman slipped his hands down to circle her neck. With the tips of his thumbs on her chin, he pushed his tongue just inside her mouth and along moist skin from tilted corner to tilted corner. Hannah leaned into him and their tongues met.

The kiss was passionate, yet searingly tender. And it wouldn't be enough.

He raised his head and looked down at her. ''If anything's changed for me, Hannah—about the way I feel—it's that I love you even more.''

Her shakiness increased and more tears welled. ''I never cry.'' She tried to smile but failed. ''I'm tough, Roman. You know I am.''

He brushed the backs of his fingers across her cheek. ''Sure you are. Just be quiet.''

Hesitantly, he unbuttoned the top button on her blouse, and the second, and another.

Hannah didn't try to stop him. Her eyes were huge and luminous.

Roman pushed the blouse gently from her shoulders. Her full breasts barely stopped it from falling to her waist. First one, then the other, he plucked down her bra straps and smoothed his hands over the pale skin he'd exposed.

"I've wanted to kiss you here." He pressed his lips to her jaw, her neck, the hollow above a collarbone…a shoulder tip. "And here." Beneath his mouth, the satiny swell of her breasts rose and fell with every ragged breath she took. The edge of a nipple showed. Raising his face to watch her once more, Roman slowly eased his hand inside flimsy lace to support the weight of her breast. Just as slowly, he bent again and took her nipple between his teeth.

Hannah fell back against the couch. She held his head and he heard her soft moan. They both needed so much more. They needed everything they'd been denied.

But not here. Not now. He sighed against her skin and rested his cheek on her breast. "We're going to work it out now, aren't we?"

Instead of responding, Hannah urged him up. She kissed his mouth sweetly, took his lower lip in her teeth and sucked lightly. Her eyes moved beneath lowered lids. Dark lashes flickered against her cheeks.

She massaged his neck beneath his open collar, slipped buttons undone and flattened her hands on his chest. His blood pumped harder. The beat of his pulse thundered in his ears.

"Hannah," he whispered when she let him catch his breath. "I want you. But not here."

Passion shone in her eyes. She nodded, her lips moist and parted. "We're going to have to work things through carefully."

"Yes." She didn't know how carefully. But it would be all right now. "Mary-Lee can be difficult. When she's upset— which is most of the time—she threatens not to let me see Penny. That scares me sometimes, but I don't think she'd really do it."

"She can't, can she?" Hannah eased her bra cup over her breast.

Roman felt himself tighten even more inside his jeans. "Not very easily." He pulled up her straps, then trailed his fingers along the silken skin to the deep shadow between her breasts. Raw throbbing pushed deep into his groin.

Hannah buttoned her blouse. "Davis didn't adopt Penny, did he?"

"No."

"So she's still legally your daughter?"

"Yes. And I don't intend for her ever to suspect she isn't mine in every sense of the word."

Hannah paused in the act of tucking her blouse into her waistband. "Do you mean…? Roman, Penny's seven. Surely she knows by now that you only adopted her."

He stared. "I told you my name's on her birth certificate."

She shook her head slowly. "No…I guess I didn't understand. Are you telling me you've allowed Penny to believe she's really your biological daughter?"

"As far as I'm concerned, she is."

"But she's not. And it's wrong to let her get any older without explaining that. She's already long past the age when it would have been an easy thing to explain."

He passed a hand over his face. "Why would she ever have to know?"

"Because she's going to find out some way eventually. And when she does, if you haven't told her, she's going to hate you. You're forcing her to live a lie. Maybe it doesn't matter so much now, but it's going to."

"No, it's not." The uncertainty he hated crept to the surface and he tried to ignore it. "When I put my name down the day she was born I said she was mine."

"And you thought that meant she would never have the right to know the truth? Don't you know anything?"

"I know I can't hurt her." And he knew, as he had for years, that he was going to face the time when Penny must be told. Would he lose her then? Hannah's words rang true. He'd already waited too long. "Mary-Lee was so determined that Penny shouldn't find out. She said it would make her feel…like dirt, dammit.''

''She really tied you to her, didn't she?'' Hannah said, almost to herself. ''And now you're afraid you'll lose Penny if she finds out the truth.''

He stared at her. ''You always had an uncanny habit of reading my mind. I can't take the chance, Hannah. I won't.''

She seemed about to speak, but closed her mouth again. ''It's not my place to tell you what you ought to do. In the end it has to be your decision.''

What mattered most now was making sure he never had to be without Hannah again. ''Can I see you tonight?''

Their eyes met and he read her thoughts. They were headed in only one direction. Sometime soon they would make love. Every muscle in his body tensed.

''Hannah?''

''Not tonight. I want to spend some time getting more familiar with the stock and the shop.''

''When's Jane coming back?''

''Not for a few days.''

He felt warmer, warmer and full of hope. ''I see.''

''I'm not making any long-range plans, Roman. Give me time, okay? And you need to do some thinking yourself. Right now you're only reacting.''

''Wrong.'' His gaze centered on her mouth once more. ''Reacting, maybe. But feeling, too.''

''The shop!'' Hannah shot to her feet. ''Oh, no. What am I thinking about? It's probably full of people.''

Roman followed her downstairs. ''If they've come, they've probably given up and left again.'' He laughed. When she glared over her shoulder at him, he quickly turned the corners of his mouth down. ''Sorry… Oh, hell. I forgot to say Jane called me. Evidently she tried to reach you by phone and there was no answer. That's why I came looking for you.''

''Great,'' Hannah muttered. ''She'll be even more worried by now.''

They arrived in the storeroom.

"Poor Jane," Hannah said. "I hope there hasn't been so much stuff stolen that I can't pay her back."

"This isn't the big city," Roman said. "There's a good chance nothing's been taken."

The shop was deserted.

"Oh, dear." Hannah began ranging between baskets and displays, bending to check the stock. "I'd better call Jane."

Roman glanced at the door. "Yeah. I really should have told you she was trying to get in touch."

"Now she'll be sorry she ever trusted me here."

He began to smile. "Maybe not." Taking her hand in his, he led her to the shop door and tried the handle.

"Locked?" Hannah turned puzzled eyes up to his.

Roman inclined his head.

A sign hung from a hook in the window. Facing them was the word Open. To the world outside, the shop was closed.

"You did that," Hannah accused him. "Why didn't you tell me? I was worried to death."

"I didn't do it." Roman smothered a chuckle, then sobered completely. "Hannah, do you think I'd tell you any lies? After what just... After..."

"No," she said hastily, turning wonderfully pink. "But I don't get it."

Neither did Roman. He turned the sign over and unlocked the door. "Must have been the wind when I closed the door. Flipped the sign."

"And the lock?"

"I wasn't thinking. I was worried about you. Probably slammed the thing too hard."

Hannah's frown faded. "You must have."

Chapter Ten

"Daddy!" Roman heard scrabbling and turned his head to look into Penny's pointed face. "Watcha doin'?" she asked.

Lying on his back beneath a combine, he grinned at her. He began working his way out. "Checking things out here," he told her when they were almost nose to nose. He planted a kiss on her cheek before rolling from his back and sitting up on the dirt. "What are *you* doing?"

"Don't josh me, Daddy. Mommy dropped me off. You know it's Thanksgiving." Penny's eyes were dark, a striking contrast to her blond curls. No one had ever commented on a brown-eyed child with two blue-eyed parents. Hadn't anyone ever wondered about that?

"I know it's Thanksgiving, sweetie. And we're going to Grandma and Grandpa Thomases'."

"And Grandma Thomas said she's making me a little cherry pie all of my own." Penny didn't like pumpkin, pecan or mincemeat. "Is Uncle Adam coming?"

"Yes. In fact, he already left."

"Why aren't you ready?" Despite her pristine brown velvet dress and black patent shoes, Penny plopped down on an up-turned crate. She studied Roman very seriously. "Don't you *want* to go to Grandma and Grandpa's? You don't look as if you do."

He had to be careful with this small and very precious girl of his. "Of course I want to go. It won't take me long to get cleaned up.'' Penny invariably sensed when he wasn't in a great mood.

"We don't *have* to go. You and me could just stay here. I could keep you company, couldn't I?"

Roman blinked rapidly. "That would be great. That's what I really like best. Just you and me. But Grandma and Grandpa would be disappointed, wouldn't they?" How he loved this kid.

"Yeah. We'd better go." She folded her hands on her knees and rested her chin on top. "Mommy's grinchy today."

He looked at her sharply. Penny didn't tend to say negative things about Mary-Lee. "I expect she wishes this wasn't your year for Thanksgiving with me." He hated this tug-of-war over an innocent child.

Penny shrugged. "Dunno." She wrinkled her nose. "Davis told me not to mind her. He said she has P…M… Something with a P and an M."

Roman laughed and hopped to his feet. "PMS, I expect. Don't worry about it." He began packing tools into his box.

"Why're you doin' that stuff today?"

He stared over the acres of graying earth. Pale shreds from the harvested crop littered furrows awaiting next year's planting.

"You know I have to make the best of the months when we aren't planting or harvesting to keep up the equipment. Today seemed as good as any other day for checking out a combine."

"Yeah. I see what you mean."

Roman turned to look at her and laughed. "Sometimes you sound more like twenty-seven than seven, young lady. And I think you see too much." He would not think about Hannah's insistence that he should tell Penny the truth about her real father—not today.

"You're dirty, Daddy."

"And you're right. As usual." Roman wiped his hands on a rag, put the toolbox in the back of his pickup and opened the door for Penny. "Climb in. I've got oil on my hands. I don't want to get your dress dirty."

She scrambled into the cab and he closed her in.

Within minutes he pulled to a stop at the back of the house. "You go watch TV while I change."

Penny raced ahead showing flashes of white cotton petticoats. One thing Roman would never be able to fault Mary-Lee for was the way she looked after Penny.

By the time he passed through the kitchen, Penny was already disappearing into the den. "Don't be long, Daddy," she called. While he climbed the stairs he heard the TV come on.

In the shower, he raised his face and let the water beat down. The heat felt good on his shoulders. He'd spoken to Hannah on the phone yesterday, but she'd said she wasn't ready to see him again yet. At least she wasn't telling him there was no hope.

He turned the water off and slicked back his hair. Tonight he'd try calling her again.

As usual, he'd forgotten to turn on the bathroom fan. Rubbing moisture from his eyes, Roman slid open the shower door and reached for a towel.

"Some things never change, do they, honey?"

Roman dropped his hand from his face and looked down into Mary-Lee's eyes. She leaned against the wall outside the shower, his towel dangling from her hand.

"Mary-Lee—"

"Tut, tut. You're going to have to tie a string on one of those beautiful, talented fingers of yours every time you take a shower. Maybe it'll remind you to put on the fan." She dropped her head back and breathed in deeply. "Although I always did like being in a *steamy* bathroom with you, Roman."

He reached for the towel, but she flipped it out of his range.

"What are you doing here?"

"I brought Penny. You know that. I came in the house to wait while she went to find you."

"She didn't mention that you hadn't left."

"I guess she thought I had. I was going to. Then I remembered there were a few things I wanted to say to you, so I waited in your office. I always liked the view from that window."

She'd always hated everything to do with the farm. What she'd needed was a vantage point from which she'd be able to see him coming.

He was conscious of her indolent appraisal of him. Head tilted, she deliberately ran her gaze over every naked inch.

"Mmm, nice. You've got a beautiful body, Roman. But you know that, don't you?"

"Give me the towel."

"Ah, ah, ah." She stepped away and put the towel behind her back. "It's a shame for a man to keep his best assets hidden so much of the time. I'll bet Hannah thinks so, too."

Roman was conscious of Penny downstairs. "Do you think this is a good time for playing games, Mary-Lee? Our little girl is downstairs and she's expecting me."

"The bedroom door's locked. And I think this is a perfect time for playing games." She expanded her lungs. The bodice of her white wool dress, cut to a deep V between her breasts, expanded, too. "Roman, be patient with me today. *Please.*"

"Give me the towel."

She dropped it to the floor, advanced and ran her hands up his chest. "I'm not happy with Davis."

"Don't behave like this, Mary-Lee. You'll be sorry you did later."

With her hands around his neck, she gave a little pull and he stepped reluctantly from the shower. "I'm not going to be one bit sorry. I know what I want and you want it, too. I made a mistake four years ago. Do we both have to keep on suffering for it?"

There was no smell of alcohol on her breath. Her pretty mouth was slightly open, and she gazed imploringly into his eyes.

Roman removed her hands from his neck. She immediately

slid them around his waist, layered herself against him and rested her face on his chest.

"Mary-Lee, stop this." Her fingernails made circles over the small of his back. "What's gotten into you?"

She began to kiss his chest, to work a path downward to his belly with her lips.

Roman jerked her upright and held her off. "That's enough. Get back to your husband. I'll make sure Penny's home by nine."

"I can make you happy, Roman. You know how well I can do that. Can't we try again? For Penny's sake?"

He felt sickened and embarrassed. "For God's sake get out of here. Forget you ever said any of this. I'll do the same."

"Roman—"

"Stop it!" He grabbed another towel and anchored it around his waist. "We never had anything worth hanging on to. I won't say marrying you was a mistake, because it brought me Penny. But that's all of it. I want you out of here."

"It's Hannah, isn't it." She followed him into the bedroom. "You think the two of you are going to get back together."

"Don't talk about Hannah. I don't even want to hear her name coming from your mouth."

"No man tells me what I can say. She's back and she's flaunting herself in front of you. But don't forget she walked out seven years ago without giving you a chance to explain."

He tossed the towel on the bed, flexed his shoulders and advanced on her. "If she left, it was because of you. I wouldn't have thought you'd raise that to me again."

For the first time her eyes showed a hint of uncertainty, a hint of…fear? "I said I was sorry. But she didn't let you—"

"Hannah didn't let me explain? Well, I've explained everything to her now. Get out."

She moved as if to touch him, then dropped her hand. "You told her about Penny?"

He pulled on clean jeans.

"She won't believe you, Roman."

"Hannah does believe me." He unlocked the bedroom door. "It might be wise if Penny didn't see you leave."

"You know nothing can be allowed to change, don't you?"

He narrowed his eyes. "What do you mean?"

"Penny must never know the truth. Never, Roman. *Never!*"

"Don't shout."

"If you tell that little girl, you'll break her heart." Mary-Lee's face had paled. "And then I'll make sure you never see her again."

He swallowed and forced a laugh. Inside he felt hollow and afraid. "You wouldn't do that." Opening the door, he waved her out. Showing any sign of weakness would be the worst mistake he could make now.

"Tell Penny, and I'll make sure she learns to hate you."

"You wouldn't do that."

She flounced past him. "Watch me."

HANNAH TOOK THE GLASS of white wine Adam Hunter gave her. "Thank you." She hadn't wanted to come to the Thomases' for dinner, but Adam had persuaded her that she'd be hurting their feelings if she didn't.

Lenore Thomas came into the glassed-in porch where Adam had taken Hannah to relax.

"Do you have everything you want?" Lenore put a plate of shrimp and a bowl of spicy-smelling sauce on a wrought-iron table. "I've got all kinds of pickles. And there's cheese and crackers. And chicken livers and bacon. What can I bring you?"

Hannah smiled into Lenore's lovely blue eyes. "Not a thing. Adam tells me I should have started fasting at least a week before one of your Thanksgiving dinners."

Lenore turned and flapped a hand at Adam. "No such thing."

Adam smiled indulgently. "Exactly. No such thing, Hannah. All mother serves is a tiny snack." Wearing dark slacks and a white shirt, Adam didn't look his usual unconventional self. Even his hair appeared to have been deliberately tamed for the occasion.

"He loves to make fun of me," Lenore said to Hannah. "We're so glad you could come. Thanksgiving isn't Thanksgiving without a crowd. I can hardly wait—"

"Mother!" Adam interrupted.

Lenore gaped. "What?"

"Er... Jed told me to tell you to check the bird and I forgot."

"He did?" Lenore frowned, but hurried back into the house.

"She's such a dear." Hannah sipped her wine and stood looking out over wintry pale grass. Leafless maple and white oak trees surrounded a small area where a picnic table and benches had been covered with plastic to protect them until spring.

The Thomas's farm wasn't as big as Roman's.... She had to ask, "Why did Roman decide not to come?" Adam had arrived at the shop an hour earlier to "pry her loose." When she'd haltingly explained that she didn't feel she wanted to see Roman today, Adam told her that his brother wouldn't be at their mother's farm for the holiday meal.

"Adam?"

He didn't answer. Instead, he drank deeply of his bourbon and looked past her.

Hannah twisted to see what held his attention.

"Hello, Hannah." Roman stood in the doorway.

She almost dropped her wine. Her reproachful glance at Adam was wasted. He appeared fascinated by the bottom of his own glass.

"Adam?" she said quietly.

He aimed a brilliant smile in her direction and edged past. "Better go see if Mom needs some help. Take care of our guest, Roman."

"My pleasure." His dark hair was damp, as if he'd just got out of the shower. The pale blue shirt he wore, sleeves rolled up over muscular forearms, did marvelous things for his tan. "I thought you didn't want to see me today."

Hannah puffed up her cheeks and slowly expelled the air. "I said I thought it would be better if we gave ourselves time to think."

He approached until he stood close enough for her to see the black flecks in his blue eyes. "But you changed your mind. I'm glad."

"Don't be. Your brother played Cupid again."

Roman inclined his head.

"He told me you wouldn't be here and insisted I shouldn't be alone on Thanksgiving."

"I see. I'm sorry he interfered."

The subtle downward turn of Roman's mouth filled Hannah with guilt. "I'm not sorry," she told him. Impulsively she touched his jaw. "I'm glad he fibbed. Are you okay?"

Before she could withdraw her hand, Roman trapped it and pressed his lips to the palm. "I'm okay now. Hannah, I needed to see you."

Hannah closed her hand over the sensation of his kiss. "I need you, Roman. But it isn't simple between us. We both know that."

"Yes." He dropped his voice and spoke urgently. "But we'll work it all out. We've got to."

"Not now, Roman." Hannah deliberately made herself smile. "Where's Penny? Adam did say she'd be here."

"Penny's in the kitchen." His old broad smile broke out. "Her grandma always makes her special little cherry pies for Thanksgiving. Penny's checking up on the progress in that department."

The love he had for his... Hannah's jaw tightened. Roman loved Penny. Whatever happened, she knew his relationship with the child must be kept intact. If it wasn't, there would be no hope for her own happiness with him.

"Hannah?"

She started and met Roman's eyes.

"It *will* be all right. Trust me, huh?"

Trust him. "I remember the first time you asked me to do that."

"And did you?"

She spread a hand questioningly.

"Did you trust me when I told you I'd get that beast of a truck back on time?"

"Yes. And you did. And I trust you now." But he wasn't infallible. And he couldn't control what everyone else did around them. "Mary-Lee won't make it easy, Roman. I don't know why I feel so convinced of that, or so threatened, but I do."

He was silent. His eyes lost focus. Hannah took a deep breath and fiddled with the gold watch she wore on a chain under the collar of her rust-colored silk dress. "You're worried about that, too," she told him.

Before he could answer, hard-bottomed shoes clipped on the tiled floor in the hallway outside the porch. "Daddy? Grandma says dinner's in ten minutes."

Roman turned around and his wonderful happy smile was in place again. "Penny, do you remember Hannah? You met her in the garden at Harmony House."

The little girl's hair fell from a brown velvet bow on top of her head to curl around her face. Her expression was open, but Hannah saw a hint of reserve in her brown eyes. "Hi," she said. "Are you having dinner, too?"

"Yes. Your grandma invited me."

Penny's white lace collar was echoed by petticoats peeping from the hem of her brown velvet dress. The child looked charming. "Are you feeling better now?" she asked Hannah.

"Better?"

"You didn't feel so good in the garden. You had to go quickly."

"Yes." Hannah's eyes met Roman's. "But I'm fine now."

"Didn't your grandma need any help?" Roman asked.

The girl looked from him to Hannah. "I'll go ask."

"Just a minute." Hannah took her purse from one of the metal chairs by the table. "Your Uncle Adam told me you were going to be here today, and I brought you something. If you don't like it, I can get you something else instead."

Penny looked at the small, green-foil-wrapped box Hannah placed in her hands. Then she looked at Roman as if asking permission to open the package.

He nodded and smiled.

"I don't know too much about children," Hannah said and realized she was babbling. "But I remember liking these when I was a little girl."

Penny tore off the paper and opened the lid of the box. Inside were layers of red tissue, which she carefully unfolded. Her mouth formed an O as she took out a miniature tree formed of green glass scales. Jewel-toned ornaments, also fashioned from glass, were scattered randomly over the surface.

While Hannah and Roman watched, Penny pressed a button in the base of the tree. The branches lifted and the whole tree twirled, sparkling with reflected light as it revolved.

"A Christmas tree," Penny breathed. "It's beautiful."

"The ones I remember were made of painted tin," Roman said, grinning at Hannah. "How about you?"

"Yes—tin. Jane has such lovely things in that shop. I'm having a wonderful time playing there."

Penny moved to her side, her attention riveted on her gift. "Grandma said you work in the Christmas Shop. I haven't been there."

"Would you like to?"

Penny continued to watch the glint of light on spinning green glass. "Yes. I love Christmas."

"So do I," Hannah said. "Maybe your... Maybe your daddy will bring you to the shop. I'm looking after it while the owner's away. It's full of stuff for Christmas lovers."

Immediately she glanced at Roman. His mouth was set. Muscles in his jaw flicked. In his eyes she read longing. They had intended to seal their love on that other Christmas.

"Can we go, Daddy?" Penny asked Roman.

"We'll go tomorrow.... No. It'll have to be next week. One

day after school." Using a toothpick, he speared a shrimp and ate it. "Hannah and I used to go out to that garden at Harmony House when we were teenagers. Around this time of year we'd cut holly and bring it home to decorate with. Remember that, Hannah?"

"Yes," she said. He spoke more to himself than to her or Penny.

Adam stuck his head into the room. "I hate to interrupt, but dinner's ready."

Hannah moved through the beautiful meal, not really tasting anything, not really aware of the happy chatter swirling around the Thomas's table. Only Roman held the center of her mind.

She was eating brandied peaches and pears when more visitors arrived. The Gradys, Lenore quickly explained, had been invited to dinner but couldn't accept. She was pleased they were able to drop by.

"This is so lovely," Mrs. Grady said, sighing, when they all sat around the fire. She wore the same dress Hannah had seen at the cider supper. Reverend Grady was again resplendent in his poetic outfit complete with floppy black bow tie.

When Hannah sat on the couch, Roman immediately planted himself beside her. Penny flanked the other side and repeatedly whirled her tree. Warm satisfaction at the success of her gift for the girl made Hannah relax.

"You look so nice together," Mrs. Grady said suddenly. "Don't they, Reverend?"

Hannah had noticed the couple didn't use first names. The custom sounded quaint.

"Who looks nice together?" Adam asked, meeting Hannah's pointed stare with an innocent smile.

"Why Roman and Hannah—and Penny," Mrs. Grady said. "Don't you think so, Lenore? Jed?"

The Thomases chorused assent. Lenore positively beamed, while Jed appeared vaguely uncomfortable.

"I cannot tell a lie," Reverend Grady said in his clear, deep voice. "Mrs. Grady and I did have an ulterior motive for taking advantage of you good people's hospitality today."

Mrs. Grady smoothed the shining roll of hair around her head and surveyed the ring of expectant faces by the fire. "Reverend Grady always has such very good ideas." Her spectacles shone.

"They may not think it's so good, my dear."

"Of course they will." She shifted to the front of her seat and centered on Roman and Hannah. "Won't you?"

Roman laughed. "Perhaps you'd better give us a chance to decide."

Hannah's hand rested on the couch between them. Roman's fingers were splayed on his thigh. He moved them a fraction, the fraction it took to bring a finger in contact with her knuckles.

She made herself keep smiling at Mrs. Grady. But all she felt was his skin on hers.

"My idea was that something could be done to benefit two causes at once," Reverend Grady said. "It's always nice if—"

"Oh, let me tell them." Mrs. Grady smiled into her husband's adoring face. "The idea is that The Christmas Shop would be the perfect place to sell Christmas trees. Don't you think so, Hannah?"

"Well—"

"Of course you do. Fresh cut trees straight from the mountains. They'd be a wonderful addition to your...to Jane's stock, and part of the proceeds could go to charity. We know how to get the trees donated, you see. Reverend Grady can make arrangements."

Hannah chewed her lip. "Jane's not here. I couldn't do anything like that without asking her." And she still didn't have Jane's phone number.

"Oh, you don't have to worry about that." Mrs. Grady wrapped her arms around her slim body. "Jane told me she knows you'll do all sorts of innovative things while she's away. She said she'd told you to take charge and make all the decisions.''

''She didn't tell me,'' Hannah said slowly.

Mrs. Grady tutted. ''Jane's such an addle-brain sometimes. She meant to. Don't worry about a thing. The next time I talk to her I'll explain that I let you know you could sell the trees. It'll be all right. Take it from me.''

''Well—''

''It does sound like a great idea,'' Roman said.

She turned and he smiled into her eyes. Either they were heading for something wonderful or she would end up more devastated than she cared to imagine.

''I wouldn't know how to go about getting live Christmas trees,'' Hannah said. ''I'd have to contact people and arrange delivery. I don't know.''

''No, no,'' Mrs. Grady said, wiggling excitedly now. ''Everything's arranged. Give them the map, dear. It'll be a lovely drive. And this is your quiet time of year, isn't it, Roman? You can take one of your trucks and...well, I just know you understand all about things like cutting down trees. You can do that and load them. And then when you and Hannah get back you could set them up on the sidewalk outside the store.''

Hannah stared and swallowed. ''I really don't think we'd be allowed to block the—''

''Oh, that's going to be fine,'' Mrs. Grady said. ''The Reverend talked to...to whoever says you can do those things. Since part of the money will go toward the Christmas baskets and part of it to the children's club, it's fine to put the trees on the sidewalk.''

Adam sat opposite Hannah. He smiled broadly and settled more comfortably in his chair.

''Isn't it a lovely idea?'' Mrs. Grady asked.

''Yes.'' Hannah looked from one face to another, searching for inspiration. ''But I don't think I could take off from the shop until Jane gets back.''

''You don't have to worry about that. I don't have a thing

to do. I'll be glad to watch over that lovely little shop." The Gradys appeared to have thought of everything.

Roman shifted and rested a booted ankle on his knee. "It is a quiet time at the farm," he said. "But I do have things to oversee."

"Don't give it another thought," Adam said. "Even I can check temperature gauges in the chicken sheds. And you do hire Gil to take care of the small stuff, remember?"

"Yes, I guess I do." Roman turned his face toward Hannah and raised a brow. "Hannah—"

"It's all decided then," Mrs. Grady said. "Roman will pick you up first thing tomorrow morning."

HANNAH STOOD at the counter in the closed shop. Roman had dropped her off a few minutes earlier, promising to come for her at seven the following morning.

She picked up the phone and dialed. This call was long overdue. Hannah heard ringing in her mother's Denver home, then a click. "Hello."

"Hello, Mother. It's Hannah. Happy Thanksgiving."

"Hannah? At last! Where are you? You haven't been answering your phone, and there's no reply at your office. I've been worried to death about you."

Hannah allowed her mother to talk, something she did extremely well and with very little prompting.

"I'm in Clarkesville," Hannah said when there was finally an opportunity.

The ensuing silence stretched and stretched.

"A letter came. The one Roman sent after we left for Chicago."

"It couldn't have. I…"

Hannah smiled tightly. "I know. You sent it back. But it never got there. Somehow it floated around and finally ended up in my hands a few weeks ago." Had it only been such a short time since that day in the snow?

"I did what I thought was right. You'd been hurt. Terribly hurt. No parent can bear to see that and not try to help. I knew afterward that I was probably wrong about the letter. By then it was too late, and I decided to forget the whole thing.''

"It *was* wrong, Mother. Completely wrong.'' It was an act that had changed the course of lives. "You had no right to decide what I could handle.''

After a short silence, her mother said, "I wasn't going to allow the Hunters to interfere in our lives anymore.''

"*Our* lives? My life, Mother—not yours.''

"I don't want to discuss this.'' Emily had never been a woman to apologize. "What are you doing in Georgia?''

"I came home to see Roman,'' Hannah said. How could she have forgotten how intractable her mother could be? "He's explained everything to me.''

Her mother said nothing.

"The baby wasn't his, Mother.''

Hannah told Roman's story, compressing the details, allowing her hope to lift her voice.

"I see,'' her mother said at last. "Why did you decide to go back to Clarkesville after so long?''

"John and I had decided to part ways, plus my job was over. And I wanted to see Roman and have him tell me his story himself. I may be getting a fresh start. It could work out for Roman and me. Aren't you happy about that?''

"I want to be.'' The sound Hannah heard was her mother's long, indrawn breath. "There's a lot you don't know about the Bradshaws and the Hunters, Hannah. When we went to Chicago I'd decided Clarkesville wasn't the place for us. I'm still not sure it's the place for you.''

Hannah wound the telephone cord tightly between her fingers. The tiny colored lights around the shop window twinkled cheerily. The angels swept their path through the snow with the two children. "You're wrong, Mother. This is the place for me. Why do you still think it might not be?''

She heard what sounded like a sniff before Emily said,

"I've done all the interfering I intend to do. The decisions have to be yours now. But don't be deceived by a handsome face and all that Hunter charm. Call if you need me, darling. Goodbye."

Chapter Eleven

Roman grinned at Hannah over his shoulder and yelled, "What's that? A new dance?" She hopped from foot to foot in tennis shoes threaded with silver laces. A multicolored scarf swathed her head beneath the hood of her red suede jacket.

"It's *cold* Roman. Aren't you cold?" Her arms flailed in time with her feet.

Roman flipped off the chain saw and stood straight, flexing his shoulders. "No, Hannah. I'm not cold." He mopped his brow with the sleeve of his old plaid wool parka. "I'm hot. And I'm going to get hotter before we finish here."

"Let me do some," she offered for the dozenth time. "I can lift the saw. I know I can."

"I know you can't," Roman muttered and pulled the starter on the saw again before she could answer. "Haul that bail of twine out of the truck."

Before attacking the next trunk, he paused and watched her jog away over the uneven ground. Hannah was a gracefully exuberant woman in everything she did. She made him so happy.

Following Reverend Grady's hand-drawn map, they'd set off at dawn and arrived at this area within three hours. Roman surveyed the rows of pines, of varying heights, growing on a slope in an elevated wilderness spot he hadn't even known existed.

Roman bent to his task. They'd figured that about twenty-five trees would be ample. What didn't sell could be donated to folks who might not otherwise have a Christmas tree. The last was another of Reverend and Mrs. Grady's ideas.

The trunk cracked. Roman adjusted his position and cut through the last inches. He loved it up here. Or rather he loved being up here with Hannah.

He heard her send up an off-key, out-of-control yodel. Her red jacket soon became a moving banner dodging past the trunks of big trees between Roman and the gravel road where Jed's truck was parked. Jed, unfailingly helpful and good-natured, had insisted that although Roman had a new vehicle the same size, Jed's was already beaten up and would be more suitable. Roman hoped the old green monster wouldn't decide to break down on the way back.

On the other hand...

He smiled. A man couldn't be blamed for his wayward thoughts.

That red flag was coming more slowly. "Hannah! You okay?"

"Sure." She puffed into the clearing. The bail of twine probably weighed thirty pounds, Roman thought guiltily.

"Let me get that."

"You'll do no such thing." She drew closer, and he saw that her cheeks closely matched the color of her jacket. "What do you think I am? A wimp?" When she dropped the bail it bounced, then thudded.

"What we're going to do is cut long lengths of that and—"

"And wind them around the trees before loading," Hannah said. "Yeah, I know. I'll get started."

He quelled the impulse to say she should wait for his help.

Hannah pushed down her hood, unwound the scarf and tossed it on a stump. Her wonderful hair shimmered in the clear, pale sunlight of a crystal afternoon.

"I love it up here," she called to him. "I haven't felt this good in years."

Neither had he, Roman thought reflectively. Glittering particles seemed to dance against a glaringly blue sky. There was the scent of fallen leaves and needles, and fresh pine sap. And there was Hannah here with him. Somehow he had to overcome the sensation that he should grab and bottle every second of this day in case there should never be another like it.

He cut another tree, and another, before looking up again… and setting the saw on the ground. Tongue held between her teeth, Hannah rolled the bail backward, trailing a length of twine. Other precisely spaced pieces already lay on the ground. When the fresh piece was as long as the others, she picked up a hatchet, raised it above her head, and brought it down with a resounding *thwack,* to cut through the fibers.

Roman closed his eyes for an instant, took a slow breath and kicked off the saw motor again. He approached Hannah quickly and removed the hatchet from her gloved hands. "*What* are you doing?"

"Cutting twine," she said, sounding indignant. "You told me to."

"Not with a hatchet, Hannah. You'll kill yourself. You'll miss and chop off one of those gorgeous legs of yours. That would make us both very unhappy." He picked up the shears he'd brought for the purpose. "Use these."

"Not as much fun." She pursed her lips.

Roman had an irreverent urge to laugh. "Nope. I suppose not. But that's the way we're going to do it."

She produced an apple from one pocket, then a second apple from the other. "Eat. You're working too hard." She pressed one piece of fruit into his hand while she sank her even teeth into her own.

Roman took a bite and studied her face. With her lashes lowered and peachy color whipped into her cheeks, she didn't look so different from the fifteen-year-old he'd found he couldn't do without.

She munched in silence, met his eyes and smiled, turned to look across the tree-covered rise then up at the sky. "Isn't this something?"

"Yes. Something." He dropped to sit on a fallen tree limb,

let his hands hang between his knees…and watched her up-
turned face.

"I've always been a sky person," Hannah said.

He swallowed the bite of apple. "Sometimes that was all
that kept me going."

Hannah swung toward him. "What do you mean?"

"You won't laugh?"

She approached and rolled another fallen length of wood
closer to his. "You're funny sometimes, Roman. I like you
that way. But I don't laugh at you when I know you're serious." Hannah sat on her log and regarded him intently.

Roman picked up a stick and made shallow squiggles in
the hard dirt. "I've always had the feeling that there's no
beginning and no end to things. Like the ocean…and the sky.
When I was a kid and my folks took me to Savannah, I'd sit
looking at the water running in and out. I'd think that the
water I saw that day would sooner or later be washing against
a shore somewhere else in the world and another kid would
be watching it. It made me feel connected with people I
couldn't see. People I was never going to see."

Hannah's apple lay forgotten in her cupped hands.

"All through the years since I…since I lost you, Hannah,
I've looked at the sky and imagined you somewhere looking
at the same sky, the same stars at night."

A sheen sprang into her eyes. "I understand," she said very
quietly.

"I used to tell myself that you were out there somewhere,
and maybe you were thinking about me. As long as I could
think you might be, it seemed possible we'd be together
again."

Absently Hannah put the half-eaten apple into her pocket
and joined him on his log. She threaded her hands around his
forearm. "I'm a lousy liar, so I'm not going to try. There
were a lot of times when I worked real hard to forget you."
She rested her head on his shoulder. Soft hair brushed his
jaw. Her cold nose pressed against his neck. "I never made
a very good job of that."

He smiled into her hair. "And here we are. Under the same spot of sky again. I do love you, Hannah."

She raised her face and put a finger on his lips. "Don't talk about that now, please. When I think of how much stuff is piled up in the way of us finding anything together… Roman, it's going to take a miracle to pull it off."

His smile probably didn't camouflage the anxiety that must have shown in his eyes. "We're coming up to that season of miracles, sweetheart. It's already begun. Two months ago I couldn't have dreamed we'd be here today—cutting Christmas trees and making plans."

Hannah put inches between them. "We aren't making plans, Roman. Not yet."

Caution told him to go slowly. "I think it's time we *did* make plans." Caution had never been one of his dominant skills.

"I'm going to start getting the trees ready to load." Hannah got up. "It's going to take time. Then we're supposed to stop by and check on that cabin belonging to Reverend Grady's friend."

"What will it take to get you to talk about a future with me?"

"Mrs. Grady sent soup and some other goodies. She said to light the cabin stove and make sure everything's working okay. We'd better move it if we're going to get loaded, find the cabin, eat, and—"

"Okay, Hannah," he said softly. "Point taken. You don't want to discuss us yet."

Her response was to start rolling a tree over and over on top of a length of twine and trussing branches close to the trunk to protect them from breaking in the wind on the homeward drive.

"OH, ROMAN!" On tiptoe, Hannah walked to the middle of the one-room cabin. "It's wonderful. It's like something out of a fairytale. It's a dream."

"Whew. Now I *am* cold." Roman came in behind her and shut the door. They were promptly plunged into darkness.

"Roman!"

He muttered something she thought she'd probably prefer not to hear and opened the door again. "I'll go get a flashlight from the truck."

"No need. There's a kerosene lamp and matches on the table. Let's hope there's some fuel left." She lifted the glass chimney, adjusted the wick and struck a match. Immediately a warm yellow glow flickered over the inside of the cabin.

"Unbelievable," Roman said. "Why would someone go to all the trouble of outfitting a place like this in the middle of nowhere?"

"There's no electricity."

"What does that have to do with the question?"

Hannah made a slow tour of the cozy room. "I meant that they didn't exactly make it civilized. Not completely." There was a sink with a thick wooden draining board. Below, a bright print curtain draped to the floor. "Did you see a water pump outside?"

"I wasn't looking for one."

She eyed him sharply. "What's the matter with you? Don't you like rustic? Or are you just plain grouchy?"

Roman leaned against the door, his hands thrust into the pockets of jeans that were now dirty as well as ancient. The red plaid coat he wore resembled an old horse blanket. The toes of his boots bore deep scuff marks.

He was staring straight back at her. "I'm not grouchy," he mumbled.

Hannah crossed her arms and advanced on him. "So you don't like this place. We can leave without eating if you like." He might have donned his shabby worst, but he looked wonderful. Roman would look wonderful in anything...or nothing. She parted her lips, sucked in a short breath and felt heat rush to her face.

"You okay?" His dark brows drew together. The blue of Roman's eyes had been something she had no difficulty remembering from the day they first met. And his mouth… wide, sensual, expressive…

"Hannah?"

"I'm fine. We'd better just lock up and go."

"Uh-uh. You promised me soup." His grin transformed the serious set of his features into boyish charm. "I'll just sit in the rocking chair and watch you perform miracles."

She relaxed a little. "You light the stove and find some water, and I will perform miracles. Then we'll both clean up."

He slapped a hand to his brow. "You've turned into one of those roaring feminist types."

Hannah feigned amazement. "Roaring feminist? Because I'm not into the doormat position? I'm going to get the supplies from the truck. You fix the stove."

When she returned with the basket of food Mrs. Grady had sent, Roman had already stuffed paper and kindling into the black stove. He lighted the paper, waited a few moments and added small lengths of wood from a box on the stone hearth.

"You do that like a pro," Hannah told him, unpacking canned soup, bread, cheese, homemade cookies and fruit. "Now water."

Grumbling, not too convincingly, Roman left, a pail in hand.

The fire in the stove quickly started heating the cabin. A small table and two chairs stood against a wall beneath shelves holding dishes and staples. Rag rugs were scattered on the wooden floor. On the far wall, beneath a window covered with a curtain made of the same chintz as the one below the sink, stood a bed covered with a puffy patchwork quilt.

Hannah found a can opener, put the soup on to heat and set the table. When Roman opened the door, bringing with him a cold rush of clean-smelling air, she was rocking in one of the two chairs close to the stove.

"I almost forgot how to use a hand pump," he said. "Do you want some of this heated for coffee?"

When she nodded, he poured water into a big black metal kettle and plunked it on top of the stove.

He tossed his gloves beside Hannah's on the draining board and walked behind her. "I don't want to go back."

Startled at the toughness in his voice, Hannah craned around to see him.

Roman kissed her temple, turned her face forward and began to massage her shoulders. "It's just a dream, but I sure would like to forget everything in Clarkesville and hole up here with you."

A delicious shiver ran through her. His strong fingers worked stiff muscles in her neck, gentled and moved up to caress her jaw. He gathered her hair in one hand and bent to press his lips to her ear.

Hannah closed her eyes. Her heartbeat jittered. She stirred unwillingly and stood up. "You'd soon miss Penny," she told him, not wanting to break the spell but not prepared to torment herself by losing her hold on reality. "We should eat and get on the road."

Hannah excused herself and ventured to find the outhouse. Chilled, she scurried back again and finished putting their meal together.

Physical labor had produced hearty appetites for both of them. The soup was soon demolished together with most of the rest of the food Mrs. Grady had sent.

"We'd better hurry," Roman said when they had sunk into companionable silence for what felt like a long, lovely time. He reached across the table and wound his fingers with Hannah's. "I'm glad we had today. I want more todays."

She smiled and pulled her hand away. "I hope we get what we both want...without hurting anyone else." But Roman wouldn't get what he wanted at the expense of too much compromise on her part. Certainly not at the cost of completely swallowing her pride.

By the time the dishes were washed and stowed away, a peek through the drapes showed total darkness outside. "Will we have any trouble finding our way out of here?" Hannah began to feel anxious.

"Nope. Stay inside while I get the engine warmed up and some heat going in the cab."

She did wait. The glow from the lamp seemed more golden, cozier than ever. It flickered over dark, rough-hewn log walls and glimmered on the brass wood box. Yes, she knew what Roman had meant about not wanting to leave.

The door opened and he came in, stamping his feet. He didn't say a word, just stayed by the door stamping his feet.

"Are we set?" she asked. "The stove will be okay. I'll blow out the lamp."

"Don't do that." Not looking at her, he went to the stove, used the wooden-handled holder to lift the fire-box lid and shoved more wood inside.

Hannah frowned at him. "Roman?"

"There are actually flakes of snow coming down out there. When's the last time you saw snow?"

She snorted. "The day I left Chicago."

"Yeah, yeah. But here?"

Hannah had zipped up her jacket. She slowly undid it again. "I don't remember seeing it in Georgia more than once or twice. More than a dusting that is. But we're higher here."

"It shouldn't be snowing." He crossed to lean over the bed and draw back the curtains. Swirling out of the darkness, snowflakes softly batted the panes.

"It won't bother us," Hannah said. "Jed's tires are bound to be fine. He's good about keeping equipment up."

Roman muttered something unintelligible and went to wedge still more pieces of wood into the stove.

"We should go," Hannah said, genuinely becoming nervous. The track out of the area was overgrown and difficult to follow in daylight. At night, with snow falling, it would be a true challenge. "What's eating you, Roman? Come on. Spit it out. Then let's get out of here."

He raised his chin. "That damn truck has a flat tire. I mean *flat*. Pancake flat."

After digesting what he'd said, Hannah rubbed her hands together. "I'll help you change it."

''No you won't. There isn't a spare.''

''No spare?'' She made for the door but Roman blocked her path. ''There has to be a spare. Jed wouldn't send us off without one.''

''He did. And I know what happened. We cleared the bed out to make sure we had as much room as possible for trees. The spare must have been set aside, then we forgot to put it back.''

''There isn't some sort of patch kit?''

''We didn't come up here on bicycles.''

Hannah smarted at the sarcasm. ''Sorry. Just trying to find an answer. We'd better start walking.''

Roman ran his hands over his face. ''It's dark, and we're miles from anywhere. I'm afraid we're stuck here till morning.''

''We've got extra batteries for the flashlight,'' Hannah said stoutly. ''We could make it out.''

''I probably could,'' Roman said, his nostrils flaring. ''No way am I going to risk you breaking an ankle. And we could run into something we'd rather not come up against day or night.''

Hannah shuddered and wrapped her arms around her middle. ''They'll worry about us.''

Roman looked at her speculatively. ''Didn't you tell Mrs. Grady to lock up when she left the shop?''

''Yes.'' She swallowed.

''She had a spare key Jane had given her?''

''Yes.''

''So she won't know if you aren't back?''

''No...I don't suppose anyone will.''

''Adam went to see a friend in Atlanta.'' He watched her so intently she had to struggle not to look away. ''Gil doesn't live in, and he's off for the holiday weekend, anyway.''

''Oh.''

''And Mom and Jed are too busy to keep tabs.''

''Oh.'' Her brain refused to work.

''We'll hole up here and keep the stove going. Once it's

light enough I'll walk out and get someone to drive me back with a spare.''

Hannah rallied. "I'll go with you." She waved an arm. "I'm not having you out there on your own. Even in daylight."

He smiled. "You care what happens to me?"

"Don't fish." She grinned back. "Yes, I care. If you don't come back I'll have to get out of here on my own."

"Ah, I see." Roman took off his jacket and hung it on the back of the door. "Worrying about your own hide, not mine. Charming."

Suddenly she didn't trust herself to say anything.

He sat down and bent to pull off a boot. The black wool of his shirt stretched across broad shoulders. "You might as well get comfortable. This could be a long night." He glanced up at her, and this time she had to turn her eyes away.

"You'll be warm enough in the bed," he told her. "I'll keep the stove going." The boot wasn't coming off easily.

"I don't mind sleeping sitting up," she lied. "There's an afghan. You take the bed."

"*You'll* take it. And there won't be any more argument."

"Oh, let me do that." Hannah turned her back to Roman and stood astride his leg to yank the boot off. "Give me your other foot."

He stuck his foot between her knees and she began to pull.

Roman's broad hands, settling on her hips, electrified Hannah. She stood where she was, bent over, her hands supporting his foot. Slowly he passed his fingers around to her stomach and down her thighs.

Hannah closed her eyes. Her head felt light. Weakness rushed into her limbs.

She tried to concentrate on pulling.

Roman rested his forehead on her back and stroked all the way to her knees. He pressed her belly and moved gradually upward, crossing his arms to ease her onto his lap.

"Roman?"

He kissed the nape of her neck, covered her breasts, held

their weight through the loose sweater she wore. "You don't have a bra on," he said against her neck.

She could scarcely think, only feel. Hannah could feel very well, and she burned beneath Roman's hands. He moved his thigh subtly where it pressed into the vulnerable place between her legs. Hannah dropped her head back. Breath hissed through her teeth.

"We... Roman, I don't want to regret anything between us. I've had enough of that."

"Mmm." The low words he uttered were thick and unintelligible.

He crossed his legs, pressing against her more urgently. Hannah felt the breath rush from her lungs. She ached, deeply, erotically. In seconds there would be no drawing back.

Roman leaned back in the chair, pulled her with him to lie against his hard chest, her face turned into his neck. He pushed his hands beneath her sweater until he cupped her naked breasts. Dimly she heard him groan. His body stirred and stiffened beneath her bottom.

Stroking rhythmically, passing the roughened tips of his fingers over her nipples, he destroyed any shred of remaining reason.

Almost unconsciously, Hannah squeezed the unyielding muscle on the insides of his thighs and worked upward until she kneaded and supported the heavy heat of his arousal.

He gave a broken groan, and his grip on her tightened. With feverish intensity, he clamped her to him and worked the waistband of her jeans undone. The zip slid loudly down and Roman pushed his fingers inside the stiff fabric to touch her through silken panties.

"Roman?" She didn't know what she wanted to ask. He was tugging at her sweater, and she raised her arms above her head. Sensation seared into her from the probing of his touch. The sweater dropped to the floor.

Hannah gasped, twisting in his arms, swinging her leg over to sit sideways where she could see his face. She had to see his face.

Roman's eyes met hers with burning intensity. He grasped her shoulders and looked at her. "Hannah," he murmured. "Why did we wait? We shouldn't have done that." He fastened his mouth on her breast, and she felt as if she would scream.

She began to shake, to hang on to him.

Roman lifted his face and gathered her convulsively against him. "I'm sorry. I'm sorry, Hannah. I didn't... I never intended this. Not this way."

"We both wanted to wait." Although her body begged for fulfillment, part of her clung to the reality that the moment and the situation were sweeping them on.

"We didn't want to wait for years," Roman said hoarsely. "I wanted... I didn't want you to..."

She became very still. "You didn't want me to be with anyone else?"

Torment darkened his eyes. "I guess that's what I mean."

"I see." Hannah felt quiet and chilled. "Seven years is a long time, Roman. And it wasn't any of my doing."

"Nor mine."

Hannah twined her arms around his neck. His shirt was rough against her breasts. "I know. But you didn't exactly live like a monk." She felt hurt and embarrassed. "And I didn't live on the wild side, either. I don't want to talk about this."

His hand slid beneath her hair, and he made long strokes up and down her spine. "I'm sorry. My timing's lousy. I'm so sorry, Hannah. Could we just go to bed and keep each other warm?"

She reached for her sweater and pulled it on. Awkwardly she rezipped her jeans. "We need to keep the fire going or it'll get too cold. I'll take the first shift." Inside she ached. She wanted to lie with him, to hold him, but everything had to be right between them first.

Roman got up and took the piece of wood she'd picked up. "Get into bed and go to sleep."

"I'd rather sit—"

"That's an order, Hannah. *Please.*"

Utterly miserable, she gave up the argument, took off her tennis shoes and slid beneath the covers. The bed was cool but incredibly soft. Wriggling, she worked off her jeans, stuck a hand out and threw them on top of the quilt.

For minutes she watched Roman moving around the cabin until he settled in a chair, his back to her, and pulled the afghan around him.

She felt dazed, unreal. A few more moments and they'd have made love. It seemed impossible now that they hadn't. She wasn't even sure what had stopped them.

Around and around her mind wound until exhaustion made her eyelids heavy. The sweater scratched. She peered at Roman's back. His head rested against the chair back and he breathed quietly. Hannah pulled the sweater off and tossed it on top of her jeans before feeling herself drift into sleep.

A SCRAPING NOISE roused Hannah. She began to sit up, then remembered she wore only her panties and pulled the covers beneath her chin instead. The lamp still glowed, but there was no sign of Roman.

"Roman," she whispered.

He wasn't in the cabin.

She looked at her watch. Only two in the morning. The scratching sounded again, and she clutched the covers to her chin.

The door opened. Her heart leaped to her throat before she made out Roman's shape coming in. Hannah pushed back down into the bed, almost covering her head.

Rustling and clinking ensued...and the creaking of floorboards beneath stealthily placed feet. He'd probably been to the outhouse.

Hannah could see the wooden beams and planks of the ceiling above her head. She screwed up her eyes. Wavering blobs of color shivered on the dark surfaces.

Moving carefully, she inched the blanket and quilt down just enough to see the room.

Roman knelt in front of a small pine tree. She wiggled a little higher. The trunk of the tree was supported in a bucket of earth. He was carefully hanging colored glass ornaments, and it was these that cast a reflection on the ceiling.

Hannah's eyes filled with tears. "Where did you get those?"

He leaped to his feet, rubbing his hands on his jeans like a kid caught doing something wrong. "The ornaments? They were right there on that shelf."

She frowned. "I didn't see them."

"Neither did I. But they were. I woke up feeling cold. They were the first thing I noticed." He looked at his handiwork. "Do you like it? I wanted to surprise you."

"I love it. And I am surprised."

In the shadows, she saw his tentative smile and her heart turned.

"I'm sorry about the way I came on to you, Hannah. I guess I'm more human than I realized. Too human."

Everything within Hannah softened, and seared at the same instant. "Come here, Roman."

He did as she asked until he stood over her, looking down.

"It's a beautiful tree. Come to bed and watch it with me."

She saw his throat move sharply. Without a word, he took off his shirt.

Hannah stopped breathing. His body was perfect, broad at the shoulder and across the chest, tapered to the point where dark hair narrowed into a line down his flat belly. Lamplight cast a shimmering aura around his physique.

He sat on the edge of the bed and made to lie on top. Hannah caught the waistband of his jeans. "Take these off."

His brows rose in question, but he stood up.

"Please, Roman." She pushed back the covers and he stood very still, looking at her. And he swallowed again. "Come to me. We've waited long enough." Without taking her eyes off him, she knelt and reached to pull open the curtains. "Later we can watch the snow fall."

Roman skimmed off the rest of his clothes and sat beside

Hannah. She remained on her knees while he kissed her brow, her jaw, her lips...her breasts.

It was Hannah who pushed him to his back and sat astride his hips. In the soft glow of the lamp, she passed her lips and hands over every inch of him, holding him off until he groaned for release.

And when she knew his need was more than he could bear, and that her own was beyond endurance, she took him into her and watched the wildness etch his face in tough, passionate lines.

They were together. Finally.

At last, lying wrapped in the heat they'd made, they gazed at the colored shapes bobbing overhead.

"I can't let you go, Hannah," Roman said.

She heard his desperation, and his doubt. They didn't matter, not for now. "Hold me, Roman. Make love to me again."

Beyond the window, delicate white snowflakes drifted down.

"WHAT'S THAT?" Hannah shot up in bed and shook Roman.

He groaned and rolled onto his stomach, then groped to throw an arm around her waist. "Lie down," he mumbled. "We're staying here. Never going back."

"Roman! Someone's outside." She shook him again, more roughly. "Get up!"

Evading his reaching hand, Hannah slid from bed and began frantically tugging on her clothes. Still grumbling, Roman followed. The light that poured through still-open drapes suggested the morning was growing very mature.

Hannah located a comb and yanked it through her tangled hair.

Roman put on his clothes at a more leisurely pace, leaning to see through the window at the same time. "I'm damned," he said. "I don't believe it."

"You don't believe what?" Hannah said crossly. A cool head was one thing. Hard-headed refusal to respond in the face of potential complete mortification was another.

"Reverend Grady."

"What," she squeaked, aghast. "Here? Reverend Grady's here?"

"That's what I said." Roman put on his boots and held out a hand for Hannah's comb. He used it on his own hair with very little sign of improvement.

Without being prompted, he jerked the bed away from the wall and quickly untangled the twisted sheets and blankets. In an admirably short space of time the quilt was smoothed into place, and he regarded the result of his efforts with satisfaction.

Hannah shifted anxiously from foot to foot. "Ready?"

"Now or never," Roman said, grinning wickedly.

She made a face at him and opened the door…just in time to see Reverend Grady standing up and brushing his hands together. "Morning," he called. "I do hope you both managed to get some sleep. Most upsetting for you to be stranded like this. Most upsetting."

Hannah gaped.

The Reverend wore a long, heavy wool coat. The coat and his trilby were vaguely reminiscent of male garb in thirties films. Not for the first time, Hannah decided the Gradys were permanently arrested in some earlier time…at least as far as their wardrobes went.

"Reverend," Roman said. "Boy, are we glad to see you. We were getting ready to walk out and find help."

A shiny red Chevrolet truck, evidently right off the assembly line, stood beside Jed's green monster.

"Mrs. Grady and I had a chat this morning. We decided you had almost undoubtedly suffered vehicle problems. I came up to make sure you could get home safely. You shouldn't have any trouble now."

Hannah stared at the wheels. The flat tire might never have existed. "How did you manage to change it without waking us up?" she asked, then blushed. "I mean… You were certainly quiet about the whole thing." A retired minister might take a grim view of what had happened inside his friend's cabin.

"It wasn't anything," Reverend Grady said, beaming and backing toward the Chevrolet. "One does whatever the situation calls for."

"I guess so." Roman sounded as puzzled as Hannah felt.

The older man crammed the outmoded hat more firmly onto his head and got behind his steering wheel. "Mrs. Grady would probably say that the end justifies the means. See you back in Clarkesville." He drove away, waving.

"The end justifies the means," Hannah said slowly. "What did he mean by that?"

Roman's attention was wholly on Hannah. "I can't say I care." He swept her from the ground and swung her around before kissing her soundly. "Do you?"

"No. Roman, what happened to the snow?" The ground was dry, the bushes bare.

He set her down. "Damned if I know. Must have melted fast, I guess."

Hannah smiled up at him. "Maybe we dreamed it."

"Sure," Roman said, laughing. "We dreamed it."

Chapter Twelve

Hannah tucked two Santa-shaped, glass tree ornaments into a tissue-lined box and closed the lid. "There you go, Donna. They'll look lovely on your tree." She slid the box into a green-and-gold bag and handed the postmistress her change.

"That's the loveliest tree we've ever had," Donna said. "Mother thinks so, too."

"Roman and I had fun cutting it," Hannah said. Instantly her mind wanted to snap back two weeks and dwell within the walls of a cabin in the woods with Roman.

"It's hard to think of this shop without you in it," Donna said. "What do you hear from Jane?"

Hannah picked up a pencil and the order pad she'd been using before Donna came in. "Jane's cousin is still ill." The latest bulletin from Jane had been that her cousin would need her for at least another week or so. Jane hoped that Hannah would be able to stay as long as possible.

"It's certainly lucky you came when you did," Donna said.

Lucky? Hannah supposed that would do. But surely the hours she'd spent with Roman since her arrival in Clarkesville, the several calls he made to her each day, and the ways he engineered meetings, couldn't be tossed off as "just luck."

"It was so nice having you put up the paper chains again." Donna had already thanked Hannah profusely for helping to decorate the post office for Christmas. "Just like old times."

"I enjoyed it." Hannah closed the till drawer.

"And on Saturday you'll be at the Christmas Fair?"

"I'm planning on it." She was almost afraid to trust the happiness she felt.

"Roman will bring you?"

Hannah didn't miss the hint of anxiety around Donna's eyes. "That's the arrangement. We've got a game to run, remember?" She wasn't the only one afraid that something might come between her and Roman again.

The door opened. Right on cue, a possible source of trouble had arrived. With a sinking heart, Hannah saw Mary-Lee come in and begin to browse.

Donna rolled the top of the bag tightly. At the sight of Mary-Lee her mouth had thinned. "I'll see you both there, then."

"Yes." Hastily Hannah walked Donna to the door. "Give my love to your mother."

"I will." Donna hesitated, angling her head significantly in Mary-Lee's direction.

Hannah shook her head slightly. "I wouldn't worry about a thing," she said, turning up the corners of her mouth. "Saturday will be a smashing success."

The door closed behind Donna, and Hannah turned around. She clasped her hands behind her back. In the past days, every time she'd been with Roman she'd expected Mary-Lee to materialize. "Morning, Mary-Lee. Is this your first visit to the shop?"

"Never had a reason to come before." This morning Mary-Lee wore a shaggy fur coat that ended just above the knee. Her legs were encased in tight black pants.

"Are you looking for something specific?" Hannah asked, determinedly polite. "It's hard not to get sidetracked in here. I find I want one of everything."

"Why?" Mary-Lee faced Hannah. She didn't smile. "You don't have a home to put anything in, do you?"

Hannah pressed her lips together and breathed through her nose. "No, Mary-Lee. I was just making conversation."

Devoid of makeup, the other woman looked younger, like

an overdeveloped child wearing flashy, grown-up clothes. "What's going to be such a success on Saturday? The silly fair?"

Suddenly angry, Hannah ignored the question and straightened a row of hand-painted felt elves along the edge of a shelf.

"I know you were talking about the fair. I suppose you're going with Roman."

The elves would look better in groups than in a line.

"Don't ignore me!" Mary-Lee's voice rose. "You think you can walk back in here when you feel like it and take Roman."

"I'm not in the habit of *taking* anyone. I don't think of people as things to be manipulated."

Mary-Lee waggled her head. "You don't think of people as things to be manipulated," she mimicked. "You always did think you were a cut above everyone else around here."

Hannah sighed. She glanced at the door, praying for another customer to appear.

"Why don't you just move on?" Mary-Lee's eyes narrowed, and her brows drew down. "You don't fit in. We've got a good life going. All of us. I'm not going to let you ruin any of it for me."

"What are you talking about?" Hannah bristled. She could remain polite for only so long. "Why does it matter to you whether or not Roman and I are still friends?"

"Don't give me that. Still friends? You want to be more than his friend. It's written all over you every time you're near him…every time someone even mentions his name. It's enough to make you sick. He doesn't want you, Hannah. He's got a life now, and you aren't part of it."

"And you are?" Hannah asked quietly.

Mary-Lee's face flamed. "Never mind me. It's Penny who's a part of Roman's life. The most important part."

"Roman loves Penny very much. That's never going to change."

"You don't have to tell me that," Mary-Lee shouted. "I

already know. And I won't let you try to interfere in what's best for our little girl.''

Hannah was bemused. ''Why would I want to interfere? I like Penny. Roman loves her.''

''You don't know *anything* about the Hunters, do you?''

This was already out of hand.

''*Do* you?'' Mary-Lee repeated.

''I think you should leave,'' Hannah said.

''I'll go when I've said everything I came to say, and when you give me your word you'll get out of Clarkesville.''

Hannah slammed a hand on the counter, spread her fingers and waited.

''Did your mother tell you what really happened between your father and Roman's?''

''What do you mean?'' Hannah's head snapped up. ''My father and Matthew Hunter barely knew each other.''

''That's what you think.'' Mary-Lee put a fist on her hip beneath her coat and swaggered close to Hannah. ''Your father and Matthew Hunter were in college together.''

Hannah's mind blanked.

''Surprised? I'll just bet you are. Afterward, Will—your dad—and Matthew went into partnership.''

''They did not,'' Hannah said hotly. ''You don't know what you're talking about.''

''Don't I?'' Mary-Lee tipped back her head and laughed. ''Ask Roman. He knows. Will and Matthew decided to resurrect the *Clarkesville Echo* together.''

Hannah shook her head. She began to feel sick.

''Then Matthew got tired of working long hours for no profit.'' Mary-Lee admired her bright pink fingernails. ''After all, Matthew was the one with the money when they went into the business. Will had the newspaper know-how, I guess.''

''I don't believe a word of this.''

''Ask Roman.'' Mary-Lee slid her coat off her shoulders. She wore a figure-hugging black turtleneck with the tight pants. ''Ask him what happened when his daddy pulled out and left your daddy to run a business without enough capital. Ask him if his daddy ever felt a teensy bit guilty about enjoying his farm while Will Bradshaw worked all day and all night—when he wasn't too drunk to work at all.''

Hannah flinched. "Please go."

"Oh, but I haven't finished yet." She tutted. "I can hardly believe that your good *friend* Roman hasn't admitted all this to you. After all, this is what eventually killed your daddy. The anger—and the booze. The Hunters ruined the Bradshaws.''

"Mary-Lee, stop this." Hannah couldn't keep tears from filling her eyes.

"The Hunters are people who don't keep their word. You already know that, and so do I. And so does your poor mother. Lord, how that woman worked to try and keep things together. And in the end she lost about everything, anyway. I'll bet she was glad you gave her an excuse to get away from this town." Mary-Lee brought her face close. "You should have stayed away. Go, Hannah. Go quickly."

Hannah couldn't answer. Pieces began to slip into place; the way her mother had never wanted to talk about the paper after they lost it, and her refusal to mix with anyone in Clarkesville. And then there had been Emily's coolness toward Roman. She'd never actually told Hannah she didn't approve of him, but neither had she encouraged the relationship. *"There's a lot you don't know about the Hunters and the Bradshaws."* Hannah could hear her mother's voice saying the words on Thanksgiving Day.

Mary-Lee put her hand beside Hannah's on the counter. "Don't you forget that Penny is Roman's child. He'll put her first, and she doesn't want another woman in her daddy's life."

Reeling, Hannah worked to clear her mind. "We both know the truth about Penny." Whether or not Roman had told Mary-Lee that Hannah now knew the truth about the child no longer seemed to matter.

"The birth certificate says she is." Mary-Lee spat out the words. "That's legal. That's what counts."

"You should be having this conversation with Roman." And she would have her own talk with him as soon as possible.

"Are you so sure what he told you about Penny is the truth?" Mary-Lee's blue eyes flashed. "The Hunters have a history of doing and saying whatever it takes to get what they want."

Would Roman lie to get Hannah?

"Think it over," Mary-Lee said. "But don't take long. You need to get out of here and get on with your life. The Hunters are selfish, and they've already done the Bradshaws enough damage."

"Please go away." Hannah's heart ached.

"With pleasure. I've done what I came to do. All I wanted was to save you from being hurt the way Roman hurt me. This may not be what you want to hear, but I've lost count of the times Roman's made advances to me since I've been married to Davis."

"I don't believe you."

"Don't you? Hannah, on Thanksgiving Day, when I dropped Penny off at his house, he tried to get me into bed. You can ask him if you like. But he'll only lie."

Before Hannah could think of another response, Mary-Lee had swept from the shop and slammed the door.

Hannah realized she was shaking. She wanted Roman, and she had no doubt he wanted her, too. But they couldn't build a life on lies.

THE GARDEN WAS DARK. Although it was only seven in the evening, night felt settled. Roman swung the beam of his flashlight along the path in front of his feet, then ahead.

Something pale moved. "Hannah?"

No response. He was almost at the ring of dogwoods surrounding the little graveyard. Why had she sounded so distant on the phone? And why had she chosen to meet here? Roman wished he could feel excited, that he could believe she wanted to see him here because of all the good times it represented for them together.

He couldn't.

The fence around the single grave shone white. So did the beam trained on Esther Ashley's headstone.

"Hello, Hannah."

"Hello, Roman."

Only her hand and arm and the suggestion of trousered legs showed.

"I came straight here, but you were faster."

"I didn't have far to come."

Roman opened the gate and entered the enclosure. When he stood side by side with Hannah, he looked down at the headstone. "You feel a kind of kinship with her, don't you?"

"Yes. I wish I could have met her. We'd have been friends. I'm not sure why, but I'm sure of that."

"If she was as nice as I think she was, you're right." He put an arm around her shoulders. At first she resisted, but then she allowed him to draw her near. "What's up, Hannah? Why here?"

"Here?" She sounded puzzled by the question. "I...I don't know. It just seemed...right."

"Okay." Roman waited, sensing that he should let her be the one to talk.

"This is where we always felt so close. The first time we kissed was in this garden." In the darkness, she turned her face up to his, but he knew there was no invitation in the comment. "This is an honest place, Roman. I think it would be hard to lie with Seth and Esther hanging out."

"Hanging out!" He laughed. "I wonder what they'd make of that lingo."

"Let's sit on the bench." Without waiting for him to agree, she left the burial plot and started back along the path. By the time Roman had closed the gate and caught up, she was already seated on a wooden bench overhung by the naked branches of a willow.

He sat beside her and reached for her hand. Hannah let him lace their fingers together. Her skin was cold, and he put both their hands into his parka pocket. "I was going to take you out to the farm tonight. Mary-Lee called to say Penny wasn't feeling well and wouldn't be able to come over after school, so I thought I'd expose you to a dose of my home-cooking."

"Couldn't I have come even if Penny was there?"

Whatever was on her mind, Roman was sure he wasn't going to like it. "You could have. I just hadn't thought about it."

"Does Mary-Lee bring Penny to the farm?"

"Sometimes I pick her up. Sometimes Mary-Lee brings her."

"I see."

He didn't. "What's all this about?"

"When you... When we met all those years ago and you helped me—was that because you felt guilty?"

"You tell me."

He turned to Hannah, but she averted her face. "I'm not going to fool around like this, Hannah. Something's bugging you. Just tell me what it is."

"Someone told me an interesting story today."

He'd been waiting for something like this. Hoping it wouldn't happen.

"Roman, did you feel bad about what your father did to mine? Is that why you found a way to help me out when we were kids?"

Having half guessed what she would ask didn't inspire his reflexes. Roman pinched the bridge of his nose and scrambled for a response.

Nothing came.

"Did you feel bad because your dad backed out of the deal he'd made?"

"Who talked to you about this?" He had a good idea, but he wanted to hear Hannah tell him.

"It doesn't matter. And don't push me on it, because I won't tell you."

He ordered his thoughts more slowly. "I had no reason to feel bad...or guilty. What happened between our parents had nothing to do with you and me." If he proceeded cautiously, he might find she knew less than he feared.

Hannah turned her face up to his. "I used to feel we could tell each other anything here." Her eyes glittered moistly.

"As far as I was concerned, we could," he told her. "We still can. Tell me who talked to you and what was said."

"Your dad left mine to cope with a struggling operation."

He couldn't deny what she said. "That was a long time ago. Neither of us was born."

"But you knew, Roman." Her voice fell lower. "And you didn't talk to me about it." Neither had her mother. Something else that would be hard to forgive.

Roman had been warned not to tell Hannah. "No." His parents had said Emily Bradshaw never wanted the incident discussed. They told Roman he was not to interfere with a mother's right to decide what she wanted her daughter to know about her father's business.

"You lied to me."

"No, I didn't."

A sudden rush of wind lifted her hair and threw it across her face. Hannah brushed it back. "When you decided not to tell me, you lied. Telling a lie. Thinking a lie. There's no difference."

Hopelessness settled on Roman. Unless he was prepared to hurt her more than she already had been, there was probably no way out. "All of that was years ago. It's part of other people's lives, not ours."

"My father *was* part of my life and he still is. Just because he's dead, it doesn't mean he wasn't my father."

"I'm sorry about what happened."

Leaves swirled up from the ground. Hannah huddled into her coat and crossed her arms. "Why didn't you tell me? Why did I have to hear it from...from someone else. You should have told me."

The wind rose to a howl. Roman thought of holding Hannah but changed his mind. She wasn't ready.

"Roman?"

"I'm sorry it all happened. I don't want to talk about it." He knew he sounded stubborn. There was no alternative unless he was willing to open doors that had been rightfully shut a long time ago.

"Have you given any thought to telling Penny the truth?"

The sudden change of topics caught him by surprise. "No." He had thought about it. But he didn't have any answers.

"I don't believe you."

"Hannah. What I decide is best for Penny isn't your business."

Her chin came up. "This wasn't a good idea. I'm sorry I brought you out here in the cold."

"I like being in the cold with you." He touched her arm, but she jerked away. "Most of all I like being here in this garden with you, Hannah. I always dreamed of this being our garden. Our house." Only yesterday he'd asked a real estate agent to trace the Ashley heirs and find out if they would consider selling the place. His plan was to see if it might be possible to buy Harmony for Hannah. If the asking price wasn't too high they could live there and still run the farm. Adam would probably enjoy having the farmhouse to himself. He might even be more productive.

"How can I be sure Penny isn't yours?"

Roman opened his mouth. He half rose, then sat down again. "You can be sure because I said so." Anger surged. As quickly, it ebbed. His mind felt clear and sharp-edged. "I don't lie. I've told you that enough times."

"And I don't have any reason to doubt you?"

A shiver traveled over Roman's skin. He glanced around with the sense that something other than the wind moved through the trees. "You have no reason to doubt me," he murmured. Now a soft, silvery whine sang faintly in his ears.

"What was that?"

Hannah hunched her shoulders. "Don't try to change the subject. When are you going to tell Penny, Roman?"

"I don't know."

"The older she gets, the harder it's going to be."

"You can't be sure of that. What do you think it would do to a seven-year-old? Have you thought about that?"

"Yes."

He barely heard her. What he saw in her face wasn't self-ishness, but concern for Penny. The sound grew louder. "That's not the wind."

Hannah ignored him. "This has been a game for you, hasn't it? For a while you wanted to enjoy playing at being who we used to be."

"We're lovers now, Hannah. That's not what we used to be." Concentration became harder.

She stood up and looked down on him. "If we can't go forward from here without any secrets, we can't go on together."

Tell Penny—and tell Hannah everything. Roman braced his weight on his hands. The thought amazed him. He couldn't risk breaking the silence now.

"I know you'll have to be very careful how you do it, but Penny is going to have to be told the truth about herself."

"No." Beyond the reaching, naked limbs of trees, the sky shone silver.

"If you wait too long, someone else will start making suggestions. Penny's smart. She'll come to you for a denial. If you insist she's yours, you'll lose her eventually for sure. If you admit the truth, you may still lose her because you'll have broken her faith in you by allowing her to be hurt by others."

She's right. "No." He must not allow desire for Hannah to sway his logic. "Why are you pushing for this now?"

"Because I have to."

"Why?" He hadn't been honest with Penny. Hannah needed proof that he hadn't lied to her, too.

"I'm not going to say any more. Good night, Roman."

"This wasn't bothering you when we were at the cabin."

The instant the words were said he longed to snatch them back.

Her white teeth dug into her bottom lip. "That was before... That was before I began to really think about what all this means to Penny...and me." She turned away.

Roman caught her hand. "Don't go without working this out."

"I've tried. You won't budge."

"You don't believe what I told you about Mary-Lee and me, do you?"

"I don't know."

Maybe it *was* time to talk to Penny. "No!" He stood up, held Hannah's elbow and propelled her along the pathway. "You were quick enough to leave town without giving me a chance to defend myself before. Why did I think you'd changed?"

"Roman!" Hannah spun toward him so sharply he grabbed her shoulders. "Don't play with me."

He stared at her. "What's the matter with you?" Through the wind came a tinkling noise. Roman gritted his teeth. Next he'd be hearing voices. He and Hannah were both under too much stress.

She had bowed her head. "Okay. You're right. We're both too upset. I think going home would be a great idea. I can wait until you're ready to talk about it."

"Hannah?"

"Yes. Yes, that's what we'll do."

With her hand tucked through his arm, they walked through the gardens to the road. Roman opened the driver's door of the van and Hannah got in.

She started the engine. "I'll see you on Saturday."

Calm drifted in around him. "Yes. On Saturday."

Hannah waved and drove away.

He smiled, and as quickly frowned. Why did he feel calm, and warm...?

The taillights on Hannah's van dimmed, then faded away. Roman wandered up the driveway until he could see the old house. Its bulk loomed black against the pewter sky. Even cloaked in empty night slumber, Harmony was inviting rather than ominous.

He made to leave. A light? Roman turned slowly back. Yes, surely a light. In the little sitting room. He took a step closer and saw nothing. Probably moonlight touching the window.

It wasn't until he was in his truck and halfway home that Roman wondered about the swift change in Hannah. What had he said to make her suddenly so pliable and reasonable?

He ducked to see the sky.

There was no moon tonight.

Chapter Thirteen

Stars cut from colored construction paper and strands of over-sized flashing lights decorated the giant tree in the middle of the gym. On the topmost branch a plastic angel with blond hair nudged the ceiling with her tinsel crown. The scent of pine didn't quite mask the lingering aromas of radiator-heated dust, pencil-shavings, old chalk and used athletic shoes.

Clarkesville had turned out in force to throng the school-house. Chatter and laughter ebbed and flowed behind the shrieks of stampeding children.

Hannah found herself smiling at Roman, who was across the room, then quickly managed a frown. Two days of puz-zling over what had happened in the garden at Harmony hadn't produced any answers. The fight had simply gone out of her. She'd looked at Roman's worried face and wanted nothing more than to make him happy again.

Either she'd become too tired to keep fighting, or her in-fatuation with him had taken over reason. That was at Har-mony House. This was now...and their differences hadn't dis-appeared.

"Feeling any better?"

She jumped. Roman had moved beside her without Hannah noticing. He wore a ridiculous reindeer suit made with an oval hole in the neck for the wearer's face. The fake animal's shiny black nose stuck up on top of his head. Antlers rested at the back of his neck.

"Hannah? Do you feel better?" he asked again.

"I haven't been ill." With every hour her irritation grew, and her confusion. "We've got customers."

Libby Miller approached, a twin attached to each hand. "Hi, Hannah... I mean, Hi, Santa's reindeer's helper." She chuckled. "Children, doesn't the reindeer's helper look cute in her little green lederhosen and fishnet tights? And that hat? Ooh, don't you wish you had a red hat with a green feather?"

Roman laughed.

Hannah laughed, too. "Would these two good children like to help Santa find his nose?"

Side by side, the fingers of one hand firmly in their mouths, Libby's dark-haired little girls sidled forward. Santa's nose-less profile, glued to a board, sat on an old-fashioned school-room easel. Roman moved the pegs and dropped the board until it was low enough for the children.

"I think you should do this together," Roman said in a booming voice.

The girls took a step backward, but nodded.

"Helper," Roman said loudly. "The blindfold, please."

Grinning, Hannah covered one girl's eyes with a scarf.

Flourishing a lacquered hoof, Roman pranced. "And now, the *nose!*" He took the red lump of papier mâché, mounted on a tack, from Hannah and gave it to the child without the blindfold. "This is hard. Very hard. Now, with only one of you able to see, put that nose where it belongs!"

The girls shuffled forward, hand in hand, giggling. Hesitantly, looking at Libby, then Roman and Hannah, the child with the nose duly pinned it in place.

"A winner," Roman roared, cavorting. "Move those gorgeous legs of yours, Helper, and give these children a prize!"

Tears squeezed from Libby's screwed-up eyes. Hannah aimed a scowl at Roman, a smile at the beaming girls, and dug two brightly wrapped packages from a sack. "Here you are. Get Mommy to take you for juice and cookies next. And you can have your fortunes told and toss rings for goldfish—

Christmas goldfish, of course. And don't forget Santa's promised to come on his sleigh soon."

Roman and Hannah waved at the departing trio. "How much longer?" Roman muttered from the corner of his mouth. "This thing is roasting me alive."

"This thing's freezing my... I'm cold in this."

"Mmm. There really is something about black fishnet tights."

Hannah glared at Roman, and he returned the look with a mock leer. "Are they tights? Or are they stockings?"

"Tights," Hannah muttered. The Gradys were approaching with Penny.

Roman sighed. "Too bad. There's something about garter belts. But the garters would probably show, wouldn't they? On the other hand, that might be—"

"Roman!" Hannah warned him into silence. "Hello, Reverend. Hello, Mrs. Grady. I suppose Penny's using you as an excuse to play our game again...and see her daddy."

Penny leaned against Roman and wrinkled her nose at him. "You look silly, Daddy."

"And that's all the thanks I get for going through this." He hauled her up, planted a kiss on her forehead and set her down again.

Placing a small hand on Hannah's arm, Mrs. Grady smiled. "Isn't this lovely?"

"Yes," Hannah said. "I'd almost forgotten how wonderful Christmas is in a small place where people really know one another."

"Good people," Mrs. Grady murmured, her face suddenly reflective. "This town always had its share of special people."

Hannah relaxed. Despite her fluttering manner, this silvery little woman had a calming effect. So did her husband. And already they felt to Hannah like special friends, almost as if she'd known them a very long time rather than only weeks.

"Mrs. Grady," the Reverend said, bending over his wife,

"we had a mission. Oh, dear me, we do get sidetracked easily these days."

Penny, blindfolded and moving forward with outstretched hands, made contact with the blackboard and squealed. "Did I do it?"

Moving with speed that amazed Hannah, Reverend Grady whipped the nose Santa now wore in the region of his chin and plopped it quickly where it belonged.

"A winner!" Roman shouted and pulled off the blindfold while Hannah found a shiny package.

Mrs. Grady spoke quietly to Hannah: "Everyone's expecting Santa to come onto the stage. But he's going to come in this way instead as a surprise." They were located near a door to the long hallway. "They want you to put your equipment away to make room. Leave the packages, and Santa will hand them out with the ones he's got. Tell Roman. Try not to draw attention to yourselves."

Within minutes, the Gradys moved on with Penny. Evidently Mary-Lee, having left already, had arranged for Penny to be taken home by the Gradys when the fair was over.

As unobtrusively as possible, Roman and Hannah gathered their props and slipped from the gym. Once at the end of the hall, they broke into a run, clattering down an echoing flight of concrete stairs to a basement storage area.

"What's the hurry?" Roman carried the easel under his arm and a wooden bar scraped each step on the way down.

"I don't want to miss Santa."

Roman laughed. "Still a kid at heart."

Hannah pushed her way into the crowded room where their game equipment had languished during the years since the last appearance of the reindeer and his helper. She stashed what she carried in a corner and stood back, waiting for Roman.

Thunderous banging sounded overhead.

"Hurry up! He's here."

Muttering, Roman shoved the easel away and yanked off the reindeer head. He began to unzip the body of the suit.

"Hey! That's not fair. Why should you change if I can't."

Roman smirked. "Go ahead and take off the costume. We've got time."

"Very funny." She crossed her arms. "Unfortunately I'm not wearing anything underneath."

"Not anything?" Roman held up his hands in phony horror.

"You know what I mean. Hurry, or I'll go without you." She walked to the door and turned the handle.

She turned it the other way and pulled.

"Roman. Why did you close this door? It's stuck."

Half out of his reindeer suit, he shuffled across the room. "I didn't. It swung shut. Boy, Hannah, I think living in the city must have sapped your strength. You sure seem to be having difficulty with simple tasks these days."

He turned the handle, turned it the other way, pulled, grabbed with both hands and tugged. "Holy... Oh, come on! This is ridiculous." Using his whole weight, he leaned against the door, straining hard enough to raise veins at his temples. "I'm damned. I think it locked on us."

Hannah stared at him with disbelief. "It can't have."

"Okay." He waved her forward. "*You* open the thing."

She tried. "It's locked."

"Perceptive of you."

"Well, get it *unlocked*. I want to see Santa."

Roman looked heavenward. "Good grief. She wants to see Santa. Not, she wants to get out of here because she doesn't like being locked in or because there might be a fire—" he brought his face close "—and we might get sizzled like barbecued meat. Or—"

"Stop it!"

He shrugged and eyed the door, hands on hips. The suit trailed from his waist, and the front of his wrinkled navy-blue shirt hung open. "They'll come down to put other things away."

"They'd better." She paced. "And they'd better make it quick. I've had it with this routine."

Roman cleared his throat and waited until he got her attention. "What routine is that, Hannah?"

"Getting locked into places. With you. Or marooned in the..." She coughed and closed her mouth. This wasn't the time or the place to talk about interludes in mountain cabins.

"And is it my fault?" Roman asked, more quietly than Hannah found comfortable. "Don't you think I've got better things to do than hang around drafty rooms with ornery females?"

Hannah crossed her arms and leaned against a wall. "Someone will come."

"Exactly."

"I didn't mean to suggest this was your fault."

"Of course not."

"And when we were in the mountains, that wasn't... It wasn't..."

"It wasn't what?" His clearly defined brows rose.

"The same," Hannah said in a small voice.

He smiled, a slow, deeply sensual smile. "No, my love, it wasn't."

She felt hot, very, very hot. Meeting his eyes was more than she could handle right now. "Bang on the ceiling with something. There's a broom."

"Pointless."

Hannah picked up the broom, listened to the cacophony from above, and set the broom aside again. "They'll quiet down in a minute."

Half an hour later, peering at his watch in the sickly overhead glow of a naked, low-wattage bulb, Roman announced: "They aren't any quieter."

"I'm missing Santa."

Roman shook his head. He'd rolled up the reindeer suit and put it away. "Is it getting colder in here or is that just my imagination?" He jiggled his Reeboks by their laces and curled up his bare toes.

"Colder," Hannah said. She bowed her head and ran her

knuckles along her jawline. "I don't want to panic. But what if no one does come down?"

"They'll come." He sounded confident enough to almost convince Hannah.

"What's that?" Her heart began to thud. "That? They're all moving along the hallway."

Roman sat on a pile of threadbare cushions and pulled on socks. "Probably going out to the parking lot to wave jolly old Santa off." He shaded his eyes and pretended to gaze skyward. "Up, up and away. There's Dancer and Prancer and…"

Under Hannah's hard gaze he let his words trail away.

"What do you suppose everyone's doing now?" She went to the door and pressed an ear to a panel. "I can't hear a thing."

"Your legs are turning blue."

She ignored the comment. "Roman, I'm getting nervous."

"So am I."

Hannah rounded on him. "You can't. You're not supposed to." She puffed up her cheeks and expelled the air slowly. "Listen to me. I'm turning into a helpless little woman. Sickening."

"Mmm. I kind of like it. We macho types thrive on the adoration of the weaker sex."

"Oh, spare me. I think I'm going to be sick."

"You could always throw yourself into my strong arms and let me protect you." Stretching out, he locked his hands behind his neck.

Hannah was too anxious to remain amused. "Roman. It's quiet up there. Do you hear anything?"

He cocked his head. "Cars." The sudden serious set about his mouth did nothing for Hannah's confidence. "Geez. I wonder if they decided not to clean up until tomorrow."

"It is cars. Roman, what are we going to do?"

"Relax," he said. "Somebody's bound to come looking for us."

"Are they?" She thought it perfectly possible that anyone

interested would decide they'd chosen to go off together. "Roman! Your truck. It'll be seen in the parking lot, and then they'll wonder why it's still there. The lot's locked at night."

He gnawed his lip and his eyes slid away. "No good, I'm afraid. The truck's not in the lot. It's on the other side of the square. I had some crazy notion that we'd managed to bury the hatchet the other night. So I came to the shop to ask if I could walk you over. Remember that?"

"Mmm." And she'd told him she'd come when she was ready...alone.

"But then I saw your face. That was enough to put anyone off."

"Thanks."

They fell silent. Above, there was no sound. The occasional engine still roared to life in the parking lot, then faded into the distance.

"Roman," Hannah said finally. "Everyone's left. I mean *everyone*. What are we going to do? Can we jimmy the lock or something?"

He swung his feet to the ground and unfolded his length from the low scatter of pillows. "I thought of that. I doubt it, somehow. These places were built like jails."

Hannah shuddered. "Don't use that word."

"Sorry." Roman located a rusted screwdriver and went to work on the door.

Twenty minutes later he dropped to sit on the floor. "Any idea what time the janitor comes in tomorrow?"

"What time...?" She searched around, frantic. "In the morning?"

"It's beginning to look as if we've got a long night ahead of us, Hannah. Panicking won't help a thing."

She tugged a lock of hair repeatedly. "Obviously they'll come back to clean up in the morning. The local women's institute has got a Christmas table decoration workshop and lunch tomorrow. There's a poster about it upstairs."

"Well. I guess that's what we've got to look forward to. It's going to get damned cold in here."

Another hour passed before Hannah finally gave up hope. By that time Roman had spread his cushions and lay watching Hannah roam the room. The tiny attached bathroom was the only consolation.

She wished she hadn't chosen to come dressed in costume with only a coat on top. *Her coat.* Hannah located the bundle she'd stuffed into a cardboard box and pulled the ugly brown woolen garment on.

"I left my jacket in the truck," Roman said, sounding forlorn. "Geez, I'm cold."

Hannah wrapped the coat firmly around her and paced. "Move around and you'll keep warm. And put your arms down. You lose heat through your armpits."

"Thanks, doc." He left his arms where they were. "Heat rises."

"So?"

"So it's *really* going to get cold down here."

She stopped beside him. Even in repose he looked powerful, ready to spring. "I've had this old thing for years." She indicated the coat. "Almost threw it out. I'm glad I didn't now."

"I'll bet."

"You could always put your reindeer suit back on."

"I could." He extended a hand. "Or we could hold each other under that coat of yours."

Hannah fidgeted, rocking slightly. Under "that coat of hers" she wasn't exactly well-covered.

"Afraid of me?"

"No," she said honestly. "Afraid of myself, maybe." Her face flamed.

"Nothing to fear, my dear. We're both too tired to be a threat." Roman scooted close to the wall and patted the pillows beside him.

"Roman, I feel stupid asking this." She glanced at his wide mouth with its full lower lip. "The other night in the garden. Did we really solve everything?"

He turned on his side and propped his head. "I thought maybe we'd agreed to disagree about Penny."

"But we didn't really. I just... You looked so unhappy."

"Frustrated and unhappy. I hated you thinking I'd only spent time with you when we were kids out of some warped sort of guilt complex."

Hannah dwelled on the slight cleft in his chin, his square jaw, the narrow straight bridge of his nose. A faint line ran from each nostril to the corners of his mouth, and a dimple showed there whenever he spoke or laughed. "I don't think I do believe that, Roman. But I still wish you'd told me what you knew."

"My folks said it would be interfering in what your mother preferred be kept secret. She didn't want it talked about. Now I wish I'd ignored them. But I can't change what I did."

He was right. "No. And it doesn't matter anymore."

"Thank you," he said quietly. "But something tells me the thing with Penny really does."

"It's going to be hard for us—" He'd said he loved her. He'd said he wanted her. "Close relationships tend to get bent out of shape when something as big as this is in the way."

"I do have to be the one to decide what's best for Penny."

She nodded slowly. How could she argue?

"Come lie with me, my friend." Roman smiled, a disarming, boyish smile.

For a few more seconds Hannah held out. Then she sighed and took off the coat. Sitting down, she arranged her legs primly on the lumpy makeshift bed and spread the coat. She dropped carefully to her back and pulled the substitute blanket over both of them.

Now her ankles stuck out. Hannah kicked off her shoes and bent her knees. Lying very still, her arm and hip touching Roman, she stared at the light bulb until glaring brown spots danced before her eyes.

Roman breathed evenly, deeply.

Hannah's skin prickled. She wiggled, trying to get comfortable, and her leg collided with Roman's. Quickly she moved away.

He was looking at her. She could feel it.

"We do seem to be making a habit of this," Roman said thoughtfully.

"It's weird."

"Do you want the light out? We might manage to get some sleep."

Hannah doubted if she would. "If you like."

"You're on the outside."

She groaned and sat up.

"I was only joking." He got to his knees and swung a leg over her. "Unless you really want to be the one to go."

Hannah shook her head, staring up into his eyes. With the light behind him, they were black rather than blue.

Roman stayed where he was, one knee on either side of her body, looking down into her face. Carefully he put a hand under her head and moved her to the middle of the cushions. Hannah's heart tripped. Deep in her belly, heat flared.

"Would it be okay if I kissed you…before I put the light out?"

She parted her lips.

"Then I'll be good. I'll lie quietly and let you get some sleep."

When she nodded, the muscles in his jaw jumped. The concentration in his eyes turned to searching.

"Does that mean I can kiss you?"

"Yes, Roman."

Stretching out slowly beside her, he studied her face. "I never get tired of looking at you." He centered on her mouth. "I want you, Hannah. But you know that, don't you?"

She knew. And she knew she wanted him. The rest, the uncertainties about other things, receded. Her breathing became shallow.

Roman closed his eyes tightly. Without warning, he pressed his face into her neck and gathered her in his arms. Hannah hesitated, then stroked his hair with a shaky hand. He kissed her neck and held her more tightly.

Hannah let her own eyes close. "It feels right. Being with you."

"It is right."

At this moment she couldn't argue. Turning, she faced him and held on, stroking his back. She pulled up his shirt and smoothed his broad shoulders.

Roman groaned. "I don't think you'd better do that."

"I want to."

Roman lifted his head and regarded her. "I think you do." He tilted his face and brought his mouth slowly down over hers. "And you can take responsibility for whatever happens." His teeth closed on her bottom lip and he nibbled gently.

She wound her arms around his neck and closed her eyes. Holding him, kissing and being kissed by Roman, still felt like something stolen from a dream. He was warm and solid— he was the only man she had ever loved.

His hand ran from her shoulder to her waist, over suede leather shorts, to her legs. He teased her mouth open with his tongue and kissed her deeply.

Hannah hugged him more tightly.

Roman's fingers closed over her thigh.

His mouth moved with whispering softness to her cheek, to her ear. Hannah bent to brush her mouth along the tendon in his neck, then she felt him pause.

They were both holding their breath.

Hannah opened her eyes. Beneath her hands, Roman had become rigid.

He sneezed.

She bit her lip, suppressing a laugh.

Roman sneezed again…and then he laughed.

Hannah leaned away until she could see his face. "Roman?"

"I'm sorry," he said, pushing her down and burying his

head in her shoulder. "The feather." Laughter rocked his body.

Pursing her lips, Hannah caught a handful of his hair and tugged his head up. "What are you laughing about? What do you mean, the feather?"

"Your...your..." He gritted his teeth. "Hannah, I'm making love to a woman in bib-overalls and a hat with a feather in it."

"Lederhosen," Hannah said. Her own laughter bubbled out of control. "Shorts with straps. Some men might think they were sexy."

"They are!" He rolled to his back, taking her with him. "I'm sorry. The damn feather made me sneeze, then I thought about the pants, and—" With a strangled noise, he cradled her head against his quaking chest.

"And?" Hannah asked, as threateningly as she could manage.

"And... You don't want to know."

"Tell me."

He coughed and cleared his throat. "And the tights made me think of turkey roasts."

"What?" She struggled until she sat, glowering down into his face.

Roman shrugged, a chuckle rumbling in his throat. "Turkey roasts. They wrap them in...in that stretchy net stuff."

"That does it." But even as she mercilessly poked his ribs and watched him writhe, Hannah giggled. "Passion purged, or quenched...or murdered. Move. I want to get comfortable."

He tried to take her back into his arms. Hannah resisted, determinedly plunked herself down, and stared at the water-stained plaster ceiling.

"You're mad at me."

"No, I'm not." She pried out the pins that held the hat on and tossed it over Roman and onto the floor. "Just because you wound my pride and make me feel undesirable? Would that make me mad?"

"Never."

They lay, side by side, gazing upward.

Hannah felt the stealthy creeping of Roman's hand over hers until he could wind their fingers together. "Is this awful? Do you hate every second of it?"

Sighing, she turned her head to kiss his shoulder. "I'm loving every minute of it. Something else just happened, didn't it?"

Roman was quiet for a long time before he said, "Yes. I want to do things properly with you. *We* need to do things properly. Does that make any sense?"

"Yes." A great deal of sense.

"On our own time."

"Yes. With our own timing."

Roman rubbed his stubbly chin on her forehead. "Not because some accident—or disaster—throws us together."

Hannah frowned. "Exactly. Not like a couple of puppets getting the appropriate strings pulled."

Rolling her gently away from him, Roman drew up his knees behind Hannah and curled her against his body. "We're making a stand here, my love. The next time we make love it's going to be because I decide when and where."

"What?" She wriggled, but he held her fast.

"I'll plot and plan and sneak up on you, if necessary. But there will be no question of any accident. Right?"

"*You'll* decide?" she squeaked.

"Talking uses too much hot air. Be quiet and let me use you to keep me warm."

Hannah opened her mouth, but decided against any more argument. She sighed and snuggled, folding her arms over his.

"Mmm," Roman murmured. "This taking charge thing is a great idea. I'm beginning to like it already."

Chapter Fourteen

"I'm telling you for your own good, Hannah." Beaulah Cassidy rocked her head back on her neck like a sanctimonious python letting its lunch know how fortunate it was about to become.

A restless night spent on lumpy cushions atop a concrete floor had left Hannah cranky. "Couldn't this have waited until tomorrow? When the shop opens?"

Beaulah settled herself at the kitchen table. "If I waited until tomorrow it would be all over the town."

"What would be all over the town?"

Buttoned to the neck in a thick gray woolen coat, Beaulah folded her hands on the table. "I'm glad it's Sunday. I told Maury Sleps he had no right gossiping on a Sunday. That closed his mouth. And it gave me time to tell you before someone else does."

Wrapped in her fluffy yellow bathrobe, Hannah scuffed around the kitchen, putting water on to boil and getting a cup ready for the tea that always made her feel more human. She wouldn't give Beaulah the satisfaction of feeding her the questions she obviously wanted.

"I don't know what my Mary-Lee's going to say about this."

With a tea bag suspended by its string, Hannah stopped. She turned slowly around. "Spit it out, Beaulah. I'm tired." Very tired, incredibly tired of the Cassidys' venom.

"You don't have to be rude," Beaulah said, sounding huffy. "Be grateful I was the one who went over to the schoolhouse this morning. That Maury was aching to tell someone his story. Better me than some people."

"Maury told you that he rescued Roman and me from the basement of the schoolhouse." Irritation had a way of escalating into fury. Hannah had passed the point of irritation minutes earlier. "He told you we'd been locked in the storage room all night. So what?"

Beaulah made a noise reminiscent of a pug dog with sinusitis.

Hannah bent over the other woman. "Roman and I are grown-up people, Beaulah. I'm not going to make any announcements about what did or didn't happen last night. And I really don't care what any small-minded people think about me. I doubt if Roman does, either. Not that I make a habit of guessing what other people do or don't think."

"Well—"

"And I don't appreciate you ringing the doorbell on a Sunday morning when I'm trying to get the sleep I need." Hannah paused. "The sleep I need because I didn't get much last night." She closed her mouth. *The devil made her say it!*

"Well!" Beaulah wiggled inside her coat. "This is what comes of a girl not having a proper family to guide her."

Hannah felt bone-weary. "If you've said what you came to say, would you mind going? Please?"

"I certainly will go." Beaulah got up. "And I won't bear any grudge. That's not my way. But I know you haven't been told about Matthew Hunter."

"Please, Beaulah—"

"No." Beaulah stood her ground. "You don't know what Matthew did to your folks. And you should. I wouldn't be doing my duty if I didn't tell you."

The kettle whistled. Hannah swept it to a cold burner. "This is going to hurt, Beaulah, but I do already know. Mary-Lee told me, and I'm surprised she didn't report back to you."

"She did, I mean—" Beaulah turned red. "My Mary-Lee was too kind to tell you everything."

"But you aren't," Hannah muttered under her breath.

"Your mother and Matthew Hunter were engaged to be married."

Hannah blinked. She ran her tongue over her lips. "No, they weren't."

"Yes, they were. And if the Hunters hadn't always had so much influence in this town, what happened back then wouldn't have been hushed up." Her bosom swelled. "Matthew was partners with Will Bradshaw and engaged to your mother. Then Lenore came along."

Hannah breathed through her mouth. "You're making this up."

"Matthew Hunter and Lenore got together. Matthew was already leaving Will Bradshaw to manage a business without the money Matthew had promised him. But that wasn't enough. Then he took up with Lenore."

"What did—" Without thinking what she was doing, Hannah slid the kettle back over the heat. "What did Lenore have to do with my father?"

"She was engaged to him, of course," Beaulah announced triumphantly. "After Lenore got involved with Matthew, Will and Emily got together for a mite of comfort and ended up married. Matthew had already married Lenore. In more of a hurry than some thought seemly. Rightly so. Lenore was pregnant with Adam before Matthew Hunter married her!"

Hannah looked into the woman's flushed face. "I don't believe you."

"You'd better. And you'd better stay away from Roman. He's Hunter stock. You think you can trust him? You can't. And he's already got responsibilities."

"He's divorced," Hannah said weakly.

"He's got a little girl who doesn't want another woman in his life. He knows that. And Mary-Lee needs him. There's no place for you here."

"Mary-Lee's married to someone else."

"Don't interfere," Beaulah said. She marched to the door. "Things are settled. Leave well enough alone. If you don't, Lenore will be the one to suffer. Jed Thomas can't know everything about his wife. He isn't a man who'd cotton to the kind of tricks she got up to. You remember that."

Beaulah left, slamming a blast of cold air into the kitchen.

Goose bumps raced over Hannah's skin. A loud meow startled her and she reached for Blossom's can of food.

Her father and Lenore? Her mother and Roman's father? Hannah spooned out food for Blossom, trudged to the sink and dropped the spoon.

The kettle screamed again.

"Like father, like son," she said to the ceiling. "That's what she's saying. That's what my mother was saying."

FOR THE FIRST TIME since her return to Clarkesville, Hannah drove the winding road to the Hunter farm. Leafless trees stood before the miles of wire fencing that edged fallow fields. Somehow she couldn't believe Beaulah had made up the story about her parents…and Roman's. The woman didn't have that much imagination. She also couldn't believe Roman would have kept that from her, too. She didn't want to. Her mother hadn't told the true story because she'd wanted to protect Hannah. Surely Roman's parents might have chosen to keep quiet for the same reason?

Did it matter?

Lies, and more lies. *They* mattered.

Hannah reached the wide track into Hunters'. A wooden sign swung between tall posts. She drove in and pressed the accelerator, spewing damp gravel in her wake.

In front of the white, two-story farmhouse, she slewed to a stop and wrapped her arms around the steering wheel. What was she going to say? *"I won't marry you if you've been keeping even more secrets from me. I won't marry you if you're still emotionally attached to Mary-Lee as well as Penny."* He *hadn't* asked her to marry him.

A movement caught her eye, and she saw Adam Hunter

stroll from the outbuilding that housed his studio. He sighted her and waved.

Driving away was out of the question. Hannah got out of the van and walked toward Adam.

"Hi, there, Hannah. Good to see you."

Hedging would be pointless. "I'm looking for Roman."

Adam reached her, his blond hair attractively ruffled. "Not here. But I'll do, won't I?"

She couldn't summon a smile. "Where is he?"

Adam turned the corners of his mouth down. "Is my little brother in hot water?" He wore a baggy, paint-spattered blue shirt and white, draw-string pants. The latter were rolled up past bare ankles.

Hannah's nerves jiggled. "I need to talk to Roman. Tell him I was here, please."

"Not so fast." He caught her hand. "I was just going into the house for some coffee. You look as if you could use some, too."

Already he was pulling her behind him. "Adam, not now. Okay?"

"Nope. I was coming to see you. You've saved me the trouble."

Hannah dug the heels of her tennis shoes into the gravel. "Adam—"

He was too strong for her. A firm pull and he had her traveling in his wake. "I can't have a serious conversation without sustenance. Coffee and spaghetti. Then I'll tell you whatever you want to know."

"Spaghetti? Is this lunch?"

"Breakfast." They entered the pleasant old house and tramped along a red-tiled hall with big, comfortably untidy rooms open on either side. "Cold spaghetti is my favorite breakfast. Roman's, too. Didn't you know that?"

She shook her head. That was the least of the facts she hadn't known—about a great many things.

"Sit down and don't move." In the kitchen, Adam guided her into an oak rocking chair worn by age to a dark and beautiful patina. "This is fate. Give me a second and I'll have the coffee on. You want spaghetti?"

Hannah's stomach rolled. "No, thanks." She hadn't eaten since last night and the thought of any food sickened her.

"There." He slid the plug on the coffee maker into an outlet beneath a cabinet. "Now we're going to talk. First I'm going to talk and you're going to listen."

"Adam. I want to—"

"You want to see Roman. I've already seen Roman, and I know a few things that need to be said. Please let me say them. Then you can go looking for him."

Hannah slumped and rocked. She and Adam had never really known each other. He'd always been pleasant, but she couldn't say she'd ever thought of him as a friend.

"Trust me, will you?"

She jerked her head up. He must have read her thoughts in her face. "Please be quick, Adam. I need to talk to Roman."

"He loves you."

She stopped rocking.

"Don't look shocked. You knew that. And you love him."

Hannah felt hot all over.

"I'm worried about him, Hannah. It's time he had what he wants for himself. As long as I can remember, Roman's been doing what he thought was best for other people. Never for himself."

"Roman is a very kind man," Hannah said faintly.

"Kind can get old." Adam crouched and rested a hand on Hannah's knee. "He doesn't want to stay in Clarkesville."

Hannah opened her mouth, then couldn't decide what she wanted to say.

"He stays here because he knows how much this farm means to me. Roman knows he can't pull out unless I go, too. We own the place jointly. He knows I can't afford to buy him out. And I'm not capable of running the place, anyway. If he goes, so do I."

"Roman would never cause you to have to leave your home." Hannah sat straighter. "He wouldn't do that."

"You don't have to convince me. What you have to do is

convince him that I'll get over having to move.'' Adam took
her chin between his thumb and finger and made her look at
him. ''Roman needs and wants to get away from here. There
are too many memories and too many stories whispering
around under the surface.

''And there's something else. He thinks you're set on staying here.''

''I never said that.'' Even though she did wish she never
had to leave again.

''That's not the point. It's what he thinks. And I can't be
the one to persuade him otherwise. Help him, Hannah. Tell
him you'd rather live somewhere else where you don't have
to deal with the past at every turn. Roman's a peanut farmer
at heart. He always will be. The last few years have been
financially good. With his share of the proceeds from this
place he could buy another farm. It would have to be smaller,
but he knows what he's doing. He could work any spread into
a profitable concern in half the time any other man would
take.''

His earnest intensity mesmerized Hannah.

''Help him, Hannah. Persuade him. Tell him you're sure
I'll be happier without the pile of guilt I'm carrying around
because I feel responsible for holding him where he doesn't
want to be.''

''Adam. I don't think Roman will listen to me.''

He stood up and offered her his hand. ''And I know he
will.''

''I really doubt—''

''Please,'' Adam said when she stood beside him. ''If you
love him as much as I think you do, get him out of Clarkesville.''

''Adam—''

''Roman loves you, Hannah.''

THE SUN MADE a dandelion-colored wash behind a thin cloud
bank. Roman felt great. Hannah hadn't said she would see
him tonight. But she also hadn't said she wouldn't.

He drove over the hard and bumpy track from the outer reaches of the farm where he'd been repairing fences since he got back from town.

Roman grinned and shoved his Stetson to the back of his head. When Maury Sleps, the schoolhouse janitor, had opened the storage room door that morning, his face had been worth a photograph. Hannah had been worth a photograph this morning, too. For different reasons. When Roman had watched her sleeping, he'd felt a euphoria like nothing he'd ever experienced before. Somehow he would find a way to work the kinks out between them.

He topped a rise and started the last downhill run to the house. Smoke rose from the chimney. Adam had been half asleep when Roman told him he'd be out dealing with fences until early afternoon. Gil's truck was no longer parked behind the chicken sheds, which meant the old man had headed home early as Roman had told him to do. Gil had probably thought to go into the house and light the kitchen woodstove before he left. Roman appreciated that.

Once parked, he hauled toolboxes out of the truck bed and stashed them in the brick workshop his father had built behind the house. Stamping dried mud from his boots, Roman climbed the steps to the back porch and swung open the screen door to the kitchen.

"Hello, brother."

Warmth blasted Roman. "Hi, Adam. Sure you've got enough wood in the stove?"

"Sarcasm doesn't do a thing for you, kid. There's probably some coffee left. Take a pew and get warm."

"Can't stay long. Pops Wilburn said he'd be by to help check some of the irrigation equipment. These months can get by fast, and we've got to use them, Adam."

Adam set his mug on top of the stove and hauled a chair beside his own. "Get some coffee and sit. I've been waiting to talk to you."

Talk. Adam would talk about anything but the actual business. Living here was perfect for an artist, his brother had told him numerous times, but he showed no interest in the stuff that kept them afloat financially.

Roman worked off his thick jacket and hung it on a peg with his hat on top. With coffee in hand, he sat near the stove. "Okay," he said. "Let's have it."

"Hannah."

Roman choked on his coffee, coughed, and set his mug beside Adam's. "What about her?"

"We talked this morning." He held up a hand. "Don't ask questions. We talked. That's all you need to know. She didn't want me to tell you about it."

Roman gripped his thighs. "What's wrong?" He could feel trouble coming and he didn't like the sensation.

"If I didn't care so much about the two of you I'd do what I told Hannah—keep my mouth shut."

"Someone's giving her a hard time." Roman got up. "Who is it?"

"Sit down," Adam said. "I'm out of line. I shouldn't have said anything."

Roman didn't sit. "Either you finish what you've started or I'll drive over and ask Hannah myself."

"*Don't* do that." Adam rose slowly and faced Roman. "She's trying to cope, Roman. Hannah only talked to me because she needed someone, and she thought she could trust me. She's suffering here. You and I don't talk about it much, but we know how much gossip there is floating around this town. Hannah's sensitive. She wants to be with you, but she's not happy in Clarkesville."

"She's never told me that."

"Did she say she *was* happy?"

Roman rotated his shoulders, trying to relax. "I guess not. But she hasn't mentioned moving on for a couple of weeks, not since she settled in to care for the shop."

"Hannah's kind," Adam said. "She won't say anything

until Jane gets back. Even then, I've got a feeling she'll keep on swallowing her feelings for your sake.''

"I want her to be happy." Thanks to him she'd already suffered more than any woman should.

"I know," Adam said quietly. "That's why I decided I had a duty. It's up to me to let you know what she's going through.''

"What am I supposed to do?" Disappointment and indecision squeezed his gut. He'd never wanted to be anything but a farmer, and he'd never wanted to be a farmer anywhere but in Clarkesville.

Adam draped an arm around Roman's shoulders. "Listen to her, Roman. Really listen. Don't make the mistakes I did.''

Roman looked sharply at his brother. Adam's early and failed marriage was never mentioned. Incompatibility had been his young wife's grounds for divorce. Adam hadn't contested the suit.

"Just listen to her," Adam repeated, his mouth set. "When she's ready, she'll start letting you in on what's worrying her. Then it'll be time to make up your mind about how much you really want her. Do you, Roman…want her, that is?''

"You know I do." Leave Clarkesville? Sell the farm and start somewhere else?

"I'm sorry," Adam said. "I know this isn't going to be an easy decision. But you lost her once and you were miserable for years. Don't let it happen again.''

No ONE SEEMED TO KNOW where Roman was. Hannah tipped her head to gaze at the dearly familiar facade of Harmony House. The gray sky had thickened, blotting out the last traces of sun. She walked slowly to the steps leading up to the wide front porch. The white wrought-iron glider had been dragged close to the house to protect it from bad weather. Hannah tugged it away from the wall and sat down, pulling her jacket sleeves over her hands to shut out the cold.

If Roman decided he needed a place to think he might come here. She could hope.

Slowly, one foot on the ground, the other beneath her, Hannah rocked. If this were her house, her glider, she'd put yellow-and-white striped pillows on the metal seat and backs and have other furniture with matching pillows. She'd grow wisteria in tubs and let it climb pillars. And in deep winter, when Christmas was in the air as it was today, there would be evergreen wreaths on the double front doors and red bows fluttering, and bunches of holly in pots, and...

This wasn't her house.

"Hello, Miss Hannah!"

She heard the gardener's voice and saw him walk toward her across the lawn. "Hello," she called back. "How are you?"

"Well," he said. "Always well." His garb was the same as always. No coat covered his overalls and shirt, and his straw hat was firmly in place.

"I was driving..." Hannah watched him climb the steps. In his hand he carried several long sprigs of holly. She couldn't lie to him and say she'd come here without planning to. "This seems the right place to come when I'm upset about something."

"Quite right," he agreed. "A peaceful place helps when there's something important on your mind."

Hannah kept rocking, and he kept watching her. Beyond his shoulder, the sky darkened to late-afternoon silver streaked through with navy-blue.

The gardener smiled and placed the holly on her lap. "You take that back to the shop and put it somewhere you can see. It'll cheer you up."

Heavy clusters of blood-red berries nestled beneath spined and shiny leaves of the darkest green. Hannah ran a finger over a glossy surface. "Roman and I used to come and cut holly for Christmas."

"Oh, my, you certainly did. The two of you made such a picture. So full of high spirits together. Enough to make a man feel good."

Of course he'd remember. He'd been the one to tell them they could have the holly.

He put his hands into the pockets of the loose overalls. "I don't believe in interfering in other people's business, but if I can ever help you—just by listening, of course—you feel free to come and talk to me."

Hannah smiled. "I could use some help. Roman and I have been through so many things, and now... Well, now I'm not sure what to do."

"Is that a fact?"

He didn't move. Hannah found his solid, motionless presence soothing.

"I expect you know what happened. Why we didn't get engaged and married the way we were going to. I almost think we might be getting a second chance, but I'm afraid." She looked into the man's eyes. "I'm just afraid there are too many troubles from the past—and complications in the present—for us to get together."

"Maybe," he said. "Maybe not."

And then she was telling him everything. The flight to Chicago, the months of hoping she'd somehow find herself back with Roman, the gradual hopeless giving up and the dull years of coping. And now. She told the gardener about Penny and what the Cassidys had revealed about Roman and Hannah's parents.

In the end, Hannah studied her hands in her lap and sighed. "Roman didn't tell me about it all. I don't even know if he knew everything. But if he did, he should have told me." Peace, warm and soothing, crept into her limbs, and she swung more slowly. The gardener made her feel safe. He didn't judge; he only listened. "I don't know what to do."

The crowns of trees swayed. A prickle of chill traveled on the air and brushed Hannah's cheeks. There was a sound...singing? Now she was becoming fanciful. Wind in the trees made a high, silvered chorus like a million crystal bells.

"Christmas is coming," the gardener said.

She breathed deeply of the pine-scented air. "Yes."

"A good time, Hannah. A time to trust your heart."

She looked up. He smiled down, his gray eyes crinkled at the corners. Such kind eyes.

"I'll try to trust my heart." His quiet assurance gave her hope.

The trees bent and rustled. The tinkling sound ebbed and flowed. Hannah closed her eyes.

"Can't you feel it?" A firm, gentle hand settled on her shoulder.

She nodded.

"Good. Christmas is coming, Hannah. A time for miracles."

Chapter Fifteen

"Nobody but you, Hannah," Jane had said on the phone the previous evening. Her voice, its lightness, the soft but unmistakably Georgian accent, rang clear in Hannah's mind.

Seated beside Roman in one of his trucks, she sank lower in the seat and tucked her chin inside the neck of a black, down-filled parka he'd made her wear.

"You're quiet," Roman said. He glanced at her, unsmiling. He hadn't smiled since picking her up just after six, less than half an hour after Hannah got up.

"Still tired," Hannah said. She didn't feel like smiling, either. Adam had sworn her to secrecy about their conversation, but that didn't stop her mind from constantly churning over what he'd told her.

Roman turned up the heater. "I was glad when you called last night." He hadn't sounded glad. And he didn't look glad now.

"Good. Thank you for agreeing to come and do this."

"All in a good cause."

Adam had been right. Roman was definitely morose and anxious. At least she knew why.

Hannah looked out at the early-morning landscape: a study in shades of gray. She had always loved this time of year when the world was eerily soft. Plumes of mist rimed the ground, shifting, disappearing where the track rose, then reappearing in each dip.

Again she had to decide how to approach Roman about their parents' tangled pasts. Yesterday she'd been prepared to confront the subject head-on. Today she wasn't sure what to say. She hated thinking that what Beaulah had said was true, and that she'd grown up in Clarkesville with everybody but her being aware of what had happened.

"Reverend Grady's full of good ideas, huh?"

Hannah frowned at Roman. Inside the turned-up collar of the coat, her breath warmed her. "What idea did he have now?"

"Going out to Harmony to cut holly, then selling it in the shop."

"That wasn't his idea."

"No?" Roman's eyes were indigo in the shadow of his black Stetson. "I thought...well, I assumed it was. You did say the money will go to charity?"

"Yes. It was the gardener's idea. He said the bushes could use some thinning. And he pointed out that if people are going to want it at all it'll be now—not when it's too late to enjoy."

Roman tilted his head so that she couldn't see his face and sank into silence.

Jane wasn't coming back to Clarkesville.

Hannah gnawed at her bottom lip. The cousin needed Jane and would continue to need her for some time to come. Jane wanted to sell the business to Hannah, and only to Hannah. If she didn't want it, the place could just sit, because Jane couldn't bear to have it sold to someone she didn't know and trust.

"Almost there," Roman said.

"Mmm."

Part of Hannah had leaped, excited at the prospect of owning her own business, something she'd never considered before last night. To Jane, she had poured out plans that had been formulating, virtually unacknowledged, since she'd been running the Christmas Shop. A Shop For All Seasons. A specialty shop with special stock for each season. Almost without knowing it, Hannah had been mulling over the possibilities for such a business.

"Hannah, I knew you were the perfect one," Jane had said when Hannah shared her ideas. *"Don't worry about money. We'll work out something you can manage."*

And Hannah hadn't said yes, but she hadn't said no. Jane would call again a day or so before Christmas.

The apartment in Chicago had already sold, and soon there would be a sizable chunk of money in Hannah's bank account. She could consider Jane's proposition. She wanted to. She wanted to stay in Clarkesville—with Roman.

Only Roman didn't want to stay in Clarkesville.

"What's on your mind?"

She turned to him, met that dark, observant stare. "Did you know the old Echo building's for sale?" She had intended to pass this information on to him. Now was the perfect time. "Reverend Grady mentioned it to me yesterday."

"I knew the last people who bought it never put the paper into production." His profile was clear-cut against the lightening sky beyond the truck windows. A shadow defined the flat plane beneath his cheekbone.

"They put in new equipment. Evidently top-of-the-line stuff, then changed their minds about the project," Hannah told him.

He glanced at her. "They'll never recoup their investment. I can't understand anyone tying up that kind of money in the first place—not in a small town like this."

"No?" Was she being selfless, or selfish? "I wonder if someone who wanted to start up an independent press might be interested."

She scarcely breathed while she waited for his response.

"I wonder how much something like that goes for."

His mind had to be running exactly along the lines she'd planned. "Word is, it'll go for much less than it's worth." She wouldn't do or say anymore. Adam wanted to stay in Clarkesville. He also wanted his own press. If Roman decided to sell and move on, surely there'd be enough capital for

Adam to buy the Echo. Roman would then have to decide what he really wanted for himself and Hannah.

Hannah might be forced to decide between going away with Roman and staying here...without Roman.

She slanted a look at him. His mouth was pulled back from his teeth. The deep dimple showed in his cheek. His white-knuckled hands squeaked back and forth over the steering wheel. Hannah could almost hear him making decisions. If Adam could have the Echo and start his own press right here in Clarkesville, he'd be happy. And Roman could do what he wanted to do: move on.

Was there a choice for Hannah? If Roman asked her, would she go with him? *Like father like son?* Hannah's stomach clenched. Roman must have known about their parents. He should have told her instead of treating her like a child...and so should her mother.

"It's cold," he said absently.

Hannah unzipped the collar on the jacket. "I think it's too hot."

"I meant outside. Don't forget to take your gloves."

She hid a smile. From that first day, on a dusty track dried by Georgia sunshine, Roman Hunter had been trying to look after her. "Thanks. I won't forget." A small sadness spoiled the moment—sadness for the time they'd lost. She should dwell on today, forget yesterday and stop worrying about the future. Today she was with Roman. The right time would come for what must be dealt with between them.

They'd reached the long stone wall enclosing Harmony. Roman drove through the gates and along the driveway to the house and parked.

Side by side, silent, they trudged through overgrown vegetable gardens and into the woods that stretched to the far reaches of the estate.

Within an hour they'd cut more holly than Hannah ever hoped to sell...and they'd relaxed together.

"Watch your hands," Roman told Hannah yet again.

She shook her head. "Will you stop worrying about my hands? They're fine."

Roman tied the holly into big bunches and they set off, dragging their loads behind them.

Their breath made pale clouds. Hannah puffed deliberately and watched the vapor rise. Roman's boots thudded on hard ground.

"That didn't take so long," Hannah said. Scrabbling in an overgrown boxwood hedge sent her hand to her mouth. "What's that?"

A speckled bird zipped upward, dipped and disappeared into the trees. "Whippoorwill. He's late getting home," Roman said and laughed.

They reached the paths between vegetable frames. "This won't go on forever," Hannah murmured. "I try not to think about not being able to come here."

"Why shouldn't we be able to?"

Ridiculous tears prickled. "Sooner or later the house will be sold. I've never been able to figure out why it hasn't been already."

Roman didn't reply.

"When someone comes to live here, they won't want strangers tramping around." She couldn't keep her thoughts from straying to the future. They hadn't made any promises, or any plans.

"I can't imagine being considered a stranger at Harmony."

Hannah stomped to warm her feet. "The gardener told me the Ashleys still own the place. They arrange for him to come, and for the house to be kept clean inside."

"You asked him?" Roman looked surprised. "Somehow I never had the nerve."

"I didn't. He told me."

"Did he tell you whether they ever plan to live here again? Who are they, anyway? Where do they live?"

So, despite his disenchantment with Clarkesville, Roman had some of the same thoughts as Hannah about the possible future of Harmony.

"He didn't say." Near the sundial on the back lawn, Hannah paused to catch her breath. "Only a week to Christmas. The days seem to be flying by."

A step in front, Roman stopped. "You will still be here at Christmas?" He didn't turn around.

Hannah's heart pounded. "I think so...probably."

"You won't be going to your mother's?"

"No." She had to say it, had to ask. "I was told that your father and my mother were once engaged. Did you know that?"

Slowly he faced her. "Mary-Lee?"

She shook her head. "Beaulah." It was true then. "She said that Lenore was supposed to marry my father, but... In the end your father chose Lenore. My mother and father only got together because they were both hurting."

Roman opened his mouth as if to speak, but bowed his head instead.

Hannah waited.

He looked at her with narrowed eyes. A muscle flicked in his jaw. "Your father was engaged to my mother. My father was engaged to your mother. They all changed their minds. End of story. Forget it."

He had known. Not being open was a natural state for Roman Hunter.

"Can we just put aside all the things that are past, Hannah? There's nothing we can do about them, anyway."

And there was nothing she could say to him at that moment.

Roman unwound the string from her fingers and pulled her load of holly together with his. "It's not late," he said. "Could we take a look inside the house?"

Hannah's chest expanded, and her heart. "As long as we keep it short. I don't want to be late opening the shop." But she couldn't say no to Roman. And she was too confused to know if she was making a mistake with every second she spent with him.

"You stay here." Roman pried up the stone at the base of

the sundial and gave her the key. "I'll load up and be back in a couple of minutes."

She watched him go, a tall, striking man. He glanced back and she saw him grin. The teenage Roman was in that grin, and she had to turn away. They were balanced on the edge of their future now, about to tip together or apart. Afterward, there would be no more chances.

Roman was true to his word; almost as soon as he'd passed from sight, he bounded back. "Come on. Run." He caught Hannah around the waist and hustled her to the porch. "Your nose is red."

"Thanks," she said, hopping from foot to foot while he unlocked the door. "When it starts to warm up it'll probably run."

"Spare me the details, kid."

Then they were inside the kitchen.

"Geez." Roman took off his hat and raked at his hair. "Would you look at this? Nothing changes in here, does it?"

"I came inside the first day I got back in town. That's what I thought then."

Roman led the way into the hall, past closed doors and the foot of the staircase and into the sitting room. He went to the window and pulled aside the left drape. "Remember this?"

She didn't have to look at the glass. "Yes. Seth and Esther."

Without looking at her, he held out an arm. Hannah took in a shaky breath and went to him.

Their coats swished together. "Go away, world," Roman said. He stared straight ahead. Pallid rays of early sun had begun to pierce the gray morning.

Hannah popped to her toes and kissed his jaw quickly. "So serious, Roman. The world only has to be as complicated as we make it."

"We can't control everything."

They were both learning that lesson fast. "Not everything. Just some of the most important stuff." Like decisions to be truthful and take the consequences. Hannah's eyes met his and her concentration slipped.

"Saturday night was wonderful," he said.

She laughed and pressed her face into his jacket.

"It really was." Roman shook her gently and eased her chin up. "You were ornery, but cute."

"Ornery?" She laid a finger on the dimple beside his mouth. "You made me miss Santa. I didn't even cry."

Roman held his bottom lip in his teeth and reached into his pocket. "Bravery should be rewarded. I almost forgot." He pushed a small black velvet box into her hands.

Hannah turned hot. Her vision blurred.

"Open it," Roman said.

She lifted the lid and swallowed. "It's beautiful." Inside lay a pin, a crystal angel that caught colored light in every facet. Keeping her face down, Hannah touched the cool glass. What had she expected? A ring?

"You really like it?" As he spoke, Roman took the box from her and removed the pin. "I bought it last week...for Christmas."

"You should have made me wait," she said quietly.

Roman glanced at her sharply and frowned. "We've done enough waiting. Both of us." His gaze moved over her face, her hair. Slipping two fingers beneath the neck of her sweatshirt, he attached the pin.

Hannah heard him breathe, felt his breath on her cheek. "How does it look?"

"Better now," he said. With one hand he held her shoulder, with the other, he touched the crystal. "It needed you to make it beautiful."

Hannah heard her own laugh: false, self-conscious. "You sound like a failed poet."

"Do I?" Roman studied her face again. He didn't smile. "I'm only saying what's true."

Seconds passed.

"We're making our own timing now, Hannah."

She sighed and turned her head to kiss his wrist.

Roman's lips found her temple, her cheek, the side of her neck. He slid her jacket off and let it drop. Hannah pushed her hands beneath his coat and circled his body with her arms. She held on tightly.

"I want to be with you, Hannah." He linked his hands loosely around her neck. "My decision. No one else's. I don't think I can wait much longer."

Nor can I, she wanted to tell him. Instead, she reached up and brushed her mouth slowly back and forth over his. Roman became very still. He closed his eyes. Hannah slipped the tip of her tongue just inside his lips and heard him groan.

Raw tingling passed from deep inside, all the way to her toes. Roman stroked downward, then upward under the sweatshirt to support the soft weight of her breasts. Her hips leaned into him.

"Hannah, Hannah," he whispered, opening their mouths wider, rocking their faces together.

She couldn't get close enough. Roman backed her to a wall. His thumbs rubbed over the lace that covered her nipples. Hannah sagged, clung to him, trembling.

He found the front fastening of her bra and worked it undone. She moaned and foraged deeper with her tongue. There would never be any getting too much of Roman.

Then his mouth left hers, and he kissed her breasts with slow reverence. Hannah rested her head back, offered herself voluptuously, reveled in the arousal that bore her on.

"Roman," she murmured. "Roman, we can't."

His answer was to cover her breasts with caressing fingers and kiss his way to the dip at her navel. The air on her naked skin did nothing to cool her flesh…or her desire.

Urgently Hannah plucked at Roman's shoulders until he lifted his face. She ran her tongue over her lips, watched his mouth open, his eyes turn even darker. She jutted her hips, not caring that she was wanton.

Roman studied her a second longer, then claimed the kiss she offered. His thigh ground between Hannah's and she trapped it, felt his body harden and leap against her.

"There are beds upstairs," he said against her ear.

"And a carpet on this floor," Hannah gasped, running her fingers into his hair.

Roman groaned again. "God, I want you. We don't know who's likely to come."

"Or when." Hannah panted. She pulled up his shirt and arched her breasts to his bare chest.

"Hannah! Oh, my God." Almost roughly, he pushed himself away, held her shoulders while he struggled for breath. "When can I be with you?"

Her mind didn't want to focus.

"You're alone at the shop. We could be there together."

Hannah gritted her teeth, fighting for control.

"Tell me that'll work. Please, Hannah."

She breathed through her mouth. "We need to get back. We'll talk later." Her legs threatened to fold.

"Yes," Roman said. He smiled, jerkily smoothed her face and pressed her to the wall once more. Concentrating hard, he refastened her bra, lingering over the pale flesh that swelled above white lace. He pulled her sweatshirt back into place and patted the shining angel. "Merry Christmas early," he said.

"Thank you, Roman."

He smiled and kissed her again, very softly.

Trembling, Hannah rested her brow on his chest. "I'm going to be late." She straightened and looked around the room. Fresh holly decorated the mantel, and more had been added over the brackets that held candle sconces to the walls.

Roman followed her glance. "You do love this house, don't you?" His expression was somber.

The warm safety of the moment fled. He was asking her far more than a simple question. Hannah made herself smile and shrug. "Yes." The testing had begun. "But it's just a house. It'll be something special to remember. I can be happy somewhere else...away from Clarkesville."

HER MESSAGE HAD BEEN subtle but unmistakable. Roman sat in his den with Adam, morosely watching wood burn in the fireplace. Hannah didn't want to stay here.

He got up and went to stare through the window toward the road. Stepping away, not taking her right there on the carpet she'd been the one to mention, had left him semi-aroused all day. And she hadn't agreed to making another definite date.

"You're restless," Adam said from his chair. "Aren't you going to see Hannah tonight?"

"Stay out of my life!" Roman closed his eyes.

"Sorry. I didn't mean to step on your toes."

"You didn't." He drove his hands into his pockets. "Just don't talk about Hannah right now, okay?"

"Okay, okay." Adam was sketching. "I just wondered if you two had gotten anything sorted out. But forget I asked."

Roman prowled. This had been a day from hell…and heaven. Heaven with Hannah. Hell after the most amazing event to come his way except for Hannah.

Harmony was for sale. The real estate agent had contacted him at the request of the owners. The price was ridiculously low. The place "needed work" these faceless people said. Therefore they were making allowances in the asking price.

Roman, his stomach in his throat, had calculated his financial position. He could just afford to buy Harmony and keep the farm running. There wasn't that much work to be done immediately to the old house. The grounds would take time to whip entirely into shape, but he and Hannah would have time. Eventually they'd be able to move into the house and he could run the farm from there. Adam could keep his home.

But Hannah didn't want to stay in Clarkesville.

"Roman," Adam said tentatively. He waited until Roman faced him. "I don't want to interfere, but what's eating you? Can I help?"

"No." He was going to have to help himself. "But thanks, Adam. Anything new with you these days? I guess I've been too tied up with myself to ask."

"Uh-uh." Adam let his sketch pad trail. "Nobody's beating on my door."

"Do you still think about opening your own press?"

Adam started to draw again. "Not much point. That kind of thing costs money, which I don't have." He smiled suddenly and brilliantly. "But don't sweat it. At least I'm living where I want to be."

Thoughtfully Roman looked at the top of his brother's blond hair as he bent over the pad. "Yeah. I think everyone should live where they want to live." Or at least, not where they didn't want to live. Compromise was the name of the game. Roman knew what he had to do.

Chapter Sixteen

Hannah felt herself turn red. Every time she glanced at Roman, he was staring at her. Everyone else in the room must have noticed, too.

"We're glad you could come, Hannah," Lenore Thomas said in her gentle voice. "We thought you'd make our Christmas party complete."

"Thank you." Hannah found it hard to meet the woman's eyes. In the four days since she'd been with Roman at Harmony, Hannah had avoided him. If she'd said what he wanted to hear that day, told him to come to her, then he might have asked her to leave Clarkesville with him. She wasn't sure she could do that. But she was less sure she could do without Roman.

"We're going to Hawaii on Christmas Eve," Penny announced suddenly. She sat on the floor near the fireplace, one arm wrapped around Roman's leg.

Hannah gave the child her full, surprised attention. "You are? How nice. I didn't know that."

"Davis takes us every year...since Mommy and Daddy didn't want to live together anymore. And Daddy likes to take a trip, too. He went skiing last year."

Hannah met Roman's eyes yet again. "Did he?"

"Yes," Roman said. "But not this year. I'm going to be right here."

There was a small, awkward silence. Hannah gazed at the

beautiful, glittering tree with its scatter of brightly wrapped packages at the base. The room smelled of pine and the lingering aromas from the huge dinner they'd just eaten.

"Dinner was lovely, as usual, Lenore." Ellie Sumpter, for unclear reasons, was evidently a fixture at the Thomas's annual family Christmas party. Roman had said something about her being a special favorite of Lenore's.

Jed Thomas, his feet stretched contentedly out in front of him, smiled benevolently at Ellie. "One of these years you'll figure out we're taking advantage of you. How else would we get the best pies in Clarkesville for our dinner?"

Ellie chuckled delightedly. "Oh, go on with you, Jed. You know Lenore's a better cook than I am." Her white hair was rolled into tight sausage-shaped curls, and she wore a red brocade dress that reminded Hannah of formal draperies.

"Roman," Lenore said, leaning forward. "Take Hannah to see the skylight Jed put in over the stairs. Adam can entertain Penny awhile till we're ready to open presents." To Hannah, she said, "All I had to say was that the staircase was a bit dark. The next thing I knew—there was a hole in the roof. It's lovely, though. Roman will show you."

Adam got up, swept Penny, squealing, onto his shoulders and capered around the room. "You'd better be good," he sang in an off-key tenor. "You better not whine. Because, if you do, your presents will—" He stopped, frowned and bounced up and down until Penny yelled. "Because, if you do, your presents won't *shine!*"

A collective boo went up.

Roman went to Hannah, caught her hand and led her from the room. She followed him upstairs to a broad landing.

He turned out the light and pointed upward. "One skylight. Forgive my mother. I think she sees herself as a matchmaker."

"She's happy," Hannah told him. "And she wants everyone around her to be happy, too."

Beyond a bubble skylight, stars loaded a black sky.

"Are we going to be happy, Hannah?"

She stared at the stars until they blurred. "Cold stars," she said, afraid of what might come next. "Have you noticed how hard and bright they are in winter?"

"Yes. Hannah, I'm going to do something tonight. You need to know about it first."

She looked at Roman, and waited.

"I'm going to give Adam a gift. It'll change his life...and mine."

She held her breath.

Roman smiled, sadly, she thought. He framed her face and drew her close. "I've decided it's time for a new beginning."

In the dark, warm hallway, beneath a star-catching bubble, he kissed her brow, her closing eyelids and finally, softly, her mouth.

Hannah nestled against him. "What are you going to give Adam?"

"His own press. I'm giving him my promise that I'll sell the farm and help him buy the old Echo. He's talented. He just hasn't had the right breaks. Lately he's seemed to lose hope."

Roman was a good man. Hannah had to smile and hug him for his goodness. "He's going to be so happy." And Roman was giving her notice that he intended to move on. She could settle somewhere else, as long as it was with him.

"Hannah—"

Footsteps sounded on the stairs. "Daddy! Grandma says we're going to open presents."

"Tell her we're coming," Roman called back. He switched on the light again. His chest rose with a deep breath. "I guess it's time. We do have to talk, Hannah."

"We will."

He stopped her from turning away. "Tonight, Hannah. This time I won't be waiting for you to call me. We'll talk tonight."

"Daddy!"

Hannah rested a hand on Roman's chest for an instant, then turned to run downstairs. "Lead the way," she told Penny, who swung back and forth on the newel post. "Let's see if Santa's brought you anything."

Penny made a face. "I know who brings the presents. I've known for *ages*."

"In that case, young lady—" Roman caught up with them "—I hope you've been good. I know, too, and Santa told me he wasn't at all sure about you this year."

Giggling, Penny ran ahead into the living room and plopped down near the tree.

Within minutes she was exclaiming over a doll Ellie Sumpter had given her. Dressed in a green crinoline and sporting a straw bonnet over glossy, dark curls, its pink face smiled blankly up at Penny.

"D'you know who she is?" Ellie asked, basking in Penny's approval. "She's—"

"Why, Scarlett, of course," Penny said with a mock simper.

Everyone laughed. Roman leaned to poke the girl's ribs. "You're entirely too grown-up, m'dear," he drawled, bringing more laughter.

One by one, they opened a gift. Hannah smoothed the beautiful silk scarf Lenore had given her and found herself viewing the room through tear-filled eyes. "Thank you," she mumbled. Roman had been right. What had happened between their parents all those years ago didn't matter. She looked at him. His head was bent while he unwrapped a gift himself. The old stuff didn't matter, but nothing less than complete openness could be the foundation for her future. She'd already taken too much of the other.

"Thanks, Adam." Roman got up and thumped his brother's back. "A pair of red flannel sleepers with a drop seat. Just what I always wanted."

"Hey," Adam said, grinning. "They'll keep you warm on cold, *lonely* nights." His gaze slid to Hannah.

She felt warmer again.

"This is for you," Roman said to Adam, almost abruptly.

He took an envelope from his hip pocket and pushed it into the other man's hands.

As if the import of the moment was expected, everyone fell silent.

Adam looked into Roman's face, then at the envelope. "What is it? A bill for the labor I don't do at the farm?"

"Open it."

Still Adam hesitated, turning the envelope over and over.

The phone rang in the hall, and Jed got up to answer. "Wait till I get back," he said. "I don't want to miss anything."

In only moments he returned. "For you, Adam. Someone in New York."

Adam shifted to the edge of his chair. Hannah noted his sudden pallor. "Why would anyone in New York call me?"

"Go find out!" Roman pulled Adam to his feet and shoved him toward the door. "Move it, will you. We've got important stuff to do here." But when Adam had left the room, Roman's face settled into an anxious mold, and he clasped his hands behind his back.

"Sit down, Roman," Lenore said quietly. "They wouldn't call to tell him more bad news at this time of night, would they?"

So Adam had been getting a lot of rejections. Hannah picked up her cup of hot buttered rum and sipped. He seemed to keep such a good face on things. She admired him for that. Anyway, thanks to Roman, Adam's life was about to change.

Minutes dragged. Penny played happily with her doll. Ellie smiled comfortably at the child. Lenore and Jed, and Roman and Hannah, carefully avoided one another's eyes. Hannah's head began to ache.

At last Adam came back into the room. His arms hung at his sides. A dazed expression filmed his eyes. "The damnedest thing," he muttered. "I don't believe it."

Silence prevailed until he flopped into his chair once more.

"What?" Roman asked explosively. "What was it?"

"I don't believe it."

"Tell us," Lenore said, leaning toward him. "What's happened?"

Adam raised unseeing eyes. "My layouts. They want them."

"What layouts?" Roman shot to his feet and stood over Adam. "Who was that? What are you telling us?"

"That was my agent," Adam said, an almost foolish smile in place. "I sent illustration layouts for a book of opera librettos written for young people. Geez. Everyone sent layouts for it. The thing's expected to be a hot number."

Roman waved his arms. "So tell *us*, Adam. Tell us what your agent said."

"With this generation of older parents…" He pushed back his hair. "They have one kid, one point two kids, maybe, and they want them all grown-up by the time they're potty trained. A potty-trained kid's gotta know his opera. But fun, he's gotta have fun learning about it."

Roman lifted his face to the ceiling and closed his eyes. "You, Adam. Where do you come into this?"

"The fun pictures," Adam said. He leaped to his feet and swept Roman into a bear hug. "I'm going to do the fun pictures. They want my layout. *My* layout. I'm absolutely bloody brilliant, brother. That's what old Fedsker said. That's what the publisher told him. This is big. Really big."

Jed, silent until now, got up and caught Adam's arm. "How big is big, Adam? Will you get any say on what they use?"

"I get *all* the say. Almost all. Fedsker says I've got to get my—" he glanced at Penny and winked. "—Fedsker wants my nether regions in New York. And he wants them now. Tomorrow."

Roman's face glowed. "Fantastic, Adam. I knew it would happen to you one day. And you're never going to have to worry again." He dodged to pick up the envelope Adam had dropped when he went to answer the phone. "Open this."

Keeping his eyes on Roman, Adam did as he was told. He slipped a piece of paper from the envelope and read.

"Well," Roman said. His body tensed.

Adam raised his face. "Fedsker told me this is just the start. I'm really going places, Roman." Swallowing, he put the paper back in the envelope and clenched it in his fist. "He says I should plan on moving to New York. There'll be a studio available to me. The advance they're offering sounds like nothing I ever dared dream about."

"Adam, that's—"

Before Roman could finish, Adam brushed past him and strode from the room. They heard the front door open and close.

Hannah saw Penny lay her doll down carefully and fold her hands in her lap. No one else moved.

"Well," Lenore said at last. "I thought he was happy."

Ellie Sumpter surprised Hannah by saying, "He is. Bit mixed up is all, I expect."

"Yes," Hannah said, more to Roman than the others. "I think someone should go to him."

Roman stood with his back to her. "Come with me," he said.

Without a word, she got up and followed him into the hall and outside.

"He was upset," Roman said when they stood in front of the house. "Not by the offer. By my gift. I don't get it."

Neither did Hannah. "His car's still here. Where would he go?" She wore a soft scarlet sweater with black silk slacks, and the evening's bite cut into her flesh.

Roman fumbled for Hannah's hand and held her still. "I thought he'd given that up," he said in a low voice.

Peering into the darkness, Hannah saw what he was talking about. In the region of the lawn, the tip of a cigarette glowed briefly.

They moved on without a word. Arms crossed, Adam stood on the cold and crunchy grass staring at nothing.

"Hey, Adam," Roman said when they stood a few feet from him. "The news is really terrific."

"Yes," Hannah said. "I bet it doesn't feel real."

"I'm a son of a bitch," Adam muttered. "I don't deserve what I'm getting."

Roman's hand tightened on Hannah's. "Sure you do. This is all a bit of a shock. You're reacting to that. Come back inside. It's freezing out here."

"You think I'm a nice guy," Adam said to Roman. "I'm not. I'm a liar and a cheat. And I don't deserve any luck. But I guess tonight proves all those sayings about bad guys finishing first, or whatever."

Hannah shivered and hugged her body. "Come inside, Adam. You deserve any breaks you get. You're the one who's worked for them."

"I can't go back in there. Let's go to Jed's workshop. There's a heater."

He turned away. Roman put his arm around Hannah and they followed.

The shop was situated in a row of outbuildings behind the house. Inside, Adam pulled a string to light a single bulb hanging from a beam and turned on a heater beneath the workbench. He faced Roman and Hannah.

"What is it?" Hannah asked, genuinely alarmed by the gray tinge to his skin and the drawn-down lines around his eyes and mouth. "Adam—"

"He'll tell us in his own time," Roman said in a low, measured voice. "Isn't that right, Adam?"

"I hate Clarkesville."

Roman stopped chafing Hannah's arm. She didn't dare look at him.

"I've hated Clarkesville since the day some kid at school called me a bastard and a bigger kid told me what that was."

"Adam—"

"No!" Adam shouted Roman down. "It was never openly talked about. Roman, Mom was already pregnant with me when Dad married her."

"Maybe I shouldn't be here," Hannah said.

"Yes, you should," Adam said.

"Yes," Roman agreed. "I didn't know you knew about it, Adam."

"You knew, but you didn't think I did?"

Roman shrugged. He went to crouch in front of the heater and warm his hands. "I figured out the birth and marriage dates and asked Mom. I was only about nine. She told me I must never do anything to hurt my brother. She didn't care about herself, but she couldn't stand the idea of you feeling bad. And you aren't a bastard, Adam. Mom and Dad got married."

"In a town this size, with the kind of morals they like to think they espouse, the marriage date's incidental if the baby's a nine-pound, *premature* miracle."

Hannah rubbed her hands together and stood, staring through the window at nothing. She didn't know what to say, what to do.

"What does all this have to do with getting great news from New York?" Roman asked.

"I resented you."

Hannah closed her eyes.

"There was no slur against you," Adam continued. "I always felt the folks liked you better because you weren't the kid that forced them to get married."

"Neither did you," Roman said sharply. "They loved each other. You know that."

"Yeah." Adam let out a long sigh. "Yeah. At a logical level I do know that. But I'm like anyone else. I'm not always logical. I lied to you. And I lied to Hannah. I wanted to use the two of you to get what I wanted. What I wanted if I couldn't have what I really wanted."

Hannah turned and looked from Adam to Roman. Roman had stood up. His hands hung at his sides.

"How many times did I apologize to you for not being involved with the farm?" Adam asked Roman.

"Plenty."

"Do you remember me suggesting it would be fairer to sell

and for you to get a smaller spread that didn't have to support my dead weight?''

Roman bowed his head. "Yes. I remember. But you always said you loved it here, and I knew you needed a place to live. I thought you liked being where you grew up. The arrangement was fine with me. More than fine. You knew that.''

"Yes, I did. And that only frustrated me more. I *wanted* you to resent doing all the work for half the proceeds. I *wanted* you to sell out! For my sake!''

Stunned, Hannah pressed a fist into her stomach. She felt numb.

A nerve flickered beside Roman's eye. "Why?''

"Do I need to spell it out?'' Adam picked up a chisel and pointed it at Roman. "I needed money. As long as every penny I owned was tied up in a damn goober farm, I had no way of getting that money. I *needed* us to sell.''

"We're going to sell,'' Roman said quietly. "That's what I just gave you—my intention to sell. You told me that having your own press would make you feel successful. You said it would give you the creative outlet you need. And you're getting it.''

"You're *not* getting it.'' Adam jabbed the chisel savagely into the workbench. "I set you and Hannah up. I told her you wanted to leave Clarkesville. I told you she wanted to leave Clarkesville. I hoped you'd end up deciding to sell the farm and go. Then I could have my money.''

"Oh, Adam,'' Hannah whispered.

He laughed. "Roman doesn't want to leave. He lives and breathes damn Clarkesville and his stinking *peanuts*. I don't know what you want and I don't...I didn't care.''

"This is where I want to be,'' Hannah said. She looked not at Adam but at Roman.

His haunted eyes stared back. "Why are you saying this now?''

"You couldn't be human, could you, Roman?'' Blood swept into Adam's taut face. "You had to be so noble.''

Roman straightened his spine visibly. "We're going back

inside. This is Mom and Jed's night.'' He offered Hannah his hand.

"I'm sorry. Hell, I'm sorry."

"I don't understand you," Roman said, closing cold fingers around Hannah's.

"I said I'm sorry." Adam sank to sit on a crate and buried his head in his hands. "You did what I'd worked for. And then you gave me what I wanted as a Christmas present, for God's sake. Only when I opened it, I'd already gotten what I'd wanted most of all."

Roman paused. "Yeah. New York. You wanted New York and a string of people telling you how brilliant you are. And you've got it. But if you hadn't, you'd have watched Hannah and me walk away from the place we're perfectly happy in, the place we'd *rather* be. Just—" He shook his head. "Why confess, Adam? Why not just say you'd changed your mind about a press here?"

"Because you make me feel dirty. You could take less than you already had just to give me a shot at something you thought I wanted—even though I never worked for any of it. Then I get a chance of a lifetime, anyway. I'm sorry, Roman. Right now, you don't give a damn, but I'm sorry, anyway." He got up and made for the door. "Does Mom know what you were going to do about the farm?"

Roman shook his head.

"Do you have to tell her?"

"You know I don't."

"Thanks. Why don't you two take some time here on your own. I'll go back in." He grimaced. "Maybe I'm in the wrong profession. What do you suppose a talented liar like me should be doing?"

The door closed behind him. Arctic air shivered across the floor.

Hannah looked at Roman. He looked away. Pulling her with him, he moved close to the heater again. "One day I'll see the funny side of this."

"Will you?"

"Sure. When I can laugh at myself for being such a fool. Boy, did he take me for a ride."

"You should have heard the routine he worked up for me. Poor Adam."

"Poor Adam?"

Hannah stood in front of Roman. "He must have been an unhappy little boy."

"I'm sorry about that. I wish he'd talked to me."

"You could have talked to him." She braced herself. Some things had to be said. "Roman, I don't know how to cope with that part of you... The part that isn't very honest."

His chin came up. "What does that mean?"

"You tell yourself you're being kind to others by not telling the truth. That doesn't cut it. Not telling Penny someone else is her real father—not telling me how unhappy your father made my mother. You did those things for you, not for anyone else."

Roman looked at her a moment, then averted his face. For an instant she was certain he'd walk out. Instead, he pinned her with a hard stare, advanced until he towered over her. "Noble. Wasn't that what my brother called me?"

Hannah swallowed.

"Well, I think I'm sick of being noble. Let's leave Penny out of this for a moment. My father didn't make your mother unhappy. If I didn't believe it was wrong to sour someone's opinion of a parent, I'd have told you this the first time the subject came up."

Hannah backed up, but he only followed.

"Your mother broke her engagement to my father because she wanted your father. She wanted my mother's fiancé. Will Bradshaw's ego loved having a chance to score on my dad."

"Roman—"

"No, Hannah. Just listen. Your dad and mine met in college. Your dad was making his own way. Mine came from a certain amount of money. Not a lot, but enough. Will visited Clarkesville, saw the old Echo going begging and persuaded my dad to help him buy it. Dad did that. Will set about squandering Dad's investment, then complained when Dad pulled out. It didn't matter that he continued to get financial help long after my father should have told him to jump in the lake. Your mother never told you that, did she?"

"No," Hannah whispered.

"No. But I'm a liar. So I'm probably making it up."

"I believe you." She felt sick.

"Emily was going to marry Dad in June. That May she announced she was in love with Will. That was it. Your father dumped my mother and married Emily. It was then, Hannah, *then,* when my mom and dad were lonely and hurting, that they got together. The rest, as they say, is history. And they were very happy, together, thank God. *That's* the true story. I don't lie. The day we met, really met, I told you that. It's always been true."

"I know," Hannah whispered. She ached. She ached for the loss of the intimacy she'd thought her mother gave her. "My father was a very unhappy man. My mother, too. Not that I can expect you to care."

"I care because it matters to you."

She let him pull her into his arms. "I'm going to have to confront my mother, aren't I?"

"Not until you're really ready. And not unless you want to. We've got other things to deal with."

Hannah looked up at him. "Penny."

"Penny," Roman murmured. He let his head loll back. "What the hell am I going to do about my little Penny? I love her. Did you hear what Adam just said about being a bastard? Can I tell Penny... Can I? Can I take away the security she has in thinking I'm her real father?"

Hannah smoothed her hands over his chest and around his neck. "Penny will find out the truth. If she finds it out the way Adam did—and she will if you don't stop it—she's likely to carry around the kind of hate he has."

"Penny couldn't hate anyone or anything."

"She's human. Give her a gift, Roman. Make a Christmas present of the truth."

"Make a gift of taking something away?" He rested his forehead on Hannah's.

She kissed the corner of his mouth and whispered, "Make her a gift of telling her the truth. Tell her that she is your daughter. Tell her she wasn't a child who came into your life as an accident, or a duty. You chose her."

HE COULD STILL CHANGE his mind.

No, he couldn't.

Roman stood before the impressive fireplace in Davis Murray's restored antebellum house. A portrait above the fireplace, a pale likeness of some long-forgotten girl in a yellow dress, was reproduced in a mirror that faced him. Stiff, heavily carved furniture gave the room a forbidding air.

"They'll be right down," Davis said, clinking ice cubes in his Scotch. A tall man already going to fat, his complexion was even more florid than usual. "Bit of a difficult time, Roman."

"Yes." Davis wasn't the enemy. He'd simply been available and suitable when Mary-Lee was ready to move on, to move on from a marriage both partners found intolerable.

Roman looked at Hannah. She smiled steadily back. He would do anything for this woman. He hoped to God nothing would stop him from getting the chance.

Beaulah Cassidy was also present, but Roman avoided her furious glare.

"I think you're doing the right thing," Davis said. "Penny's a sharp little girl. About time she knew the truth, and you should be the one to tell her."

Roman shot him a grateful glance. "I think so, too. Now. It took me long enough to decide, though."

"Some folks know to let sleeping dogs lie," Beaulah announced. "Selfish, I call it. Two days before Christmas. Ruining everything. But then, we all know about the Hunters."

"Do we?" Hannah said before Roman could respond. "Don't push that, Beaulah. You and Mary-Lee didn't tell me the truth about my parents. Now I know what it was. That doesn't make me feel good, but I can live with it.''

"His father—"

"Drop it," Hannah said. "You're despicable. Work on that.''

The expression on Beaulah's face almost made Roman laugh.

He heard approaching footsteps and arranged a smile in time for Penny to come into the room. Mary-Lee followed some distance behind. He frowned. Her eyes were red and puffy.

Penny eyed each one of them solemnly. "Mommy says we have to talk.''

He'd wanted to see Penny with only Hannah present. This felt too much like a staged production. Mary-Lee had put forward the cast and insisted he accept them. "Yes, sweetie. Don't look so sad. It'll be okay.''

Davis cleared his throat. He smoothed back his sandy hair and darted a glance around the room. "Beaulah, I don't believe I showed you the new range we had put in. Now would be a good time.''

Beaulah gaped.

"We'll be in the kitchen," he said. With a firm hand, he helped Beaulah from her chair. To Mary-Lee he said, "It'll be all right, darlin'. Leave it to Roman…and Penny.''

With more admiration than he'd ever expected to feel, Roman returned Davis's nod and watched while he escorted a purple-faced Beaulah Cassidy from the room.

Hannah motioned to suggest she should also leave. Roman shook his head no. He needed her, would always need her.

"Roman," Mary-Lee said. "I've told Penny.''

He felt his mouth open. His solar plexus contracted as if he'd been punched. "You—"

"Mommy says you're not my daddy.''

He heard a small, choked noise come from Hannah. "Sweetie, I really love you.''

Penny lifted her chin. Her eyes filled with tears, and the corners of her mouth jerked down.

"Penny," he said, knowing that he was begging her to understand. "Penny, sweetheart, don't cry. Nothing's going to change. You're still my little girl."

The tears coursed down Penny's face. "That's what Mommy said. But I don't understand."

"You will," he told her. "And it won't matter, because we've always had each other and we always will. It's just that I realized it was time to tell you the truth. I was afraid if I waited too long, someone else would tell you and then you'd be angry with me."

"That's what I told her," Mary-Lee said. She'd begun to cry silently. "This is my fault."

"No," Hannah said, so loudly Roman jumped. "There's no fault. We're all just human, aren't we? We cope the best way we can at the time."

"Yes," Mary-Lee said, but she continued to cry.

"Penny," Roman said. "Your mommy and I knew each other from when we were kids. When—" Hell, she *was* too young for some things. "I'm glad I got to marry her and be your daddy. I'm never going to be sorry about that."

He reached for her. In the seconds that followed, while she avoided looking at him, he thought she might reject him. Then she raised her face and let him hold her.

Across the room, he met Hannah's eyes. He loved her so much. Despite all this, they had a chance. They must have a chance.

"Tomorrow you'll be on the beach in Hawaii," he told Penny. "Use that underwater camera Davis gave you and bring me some fish pictures."

"I did that last year," Penny mumbled into his sweater.

"Do it again."

She sighed hugely. "Okay."

"Will you bring me one, too?" Hannah asked.

"Yes." Penny turned from him. "Who is my real daddy?"

Mary-Lee covered her mouth. He could see that she shook.

Roman took a deep, deep breath. "He had to leave before he knew about you. We don't know where he is, but maybe we will one day." He sought Hannah's gaze again. "I wanted you, Penny. I *chose* you for my little girl. Is that okay?"

"You chose me?" Penny pursed her mouth. "That's okay, I guess."

Roman saw Hannah smile at Mary-Lee, and he saw the answering flicker the smile coaxed.

They'd taken the first small step with Penny. For now he'd try not to think about how many steps and falls lay ahead.

Chapter Seventeen

If Hannah didn't know better, she'd expect snow at any moment. Tree limbs jostled faintly in the darkness. Dusky banks of cloud shifted over a veiled moon. An edge of ice laced the light wind.

"We could be somewhere warm," she told Roman.

"No, we couldn't. Not right now."

"You love this, don't you?" Puffing, Hannah trotted to keep up with his rapid strides.

"Yes," he said emphatically. "Yes, I do."

Hannah willed her leaping heart to be still. "You always did enjoy being in charge, Roman Hunter. Do this. Do that."

"Absolutely. Move it, will you? I've got places to be. Things to be dealt with."

Places to be? They were already in the only place Hannah wanted to be: in the gardens at Harmony with Roman by her side. *Things to be dealt with?* Yes, they both had things to deal with.

"Won't Lenore and Jed be expecting you?"

"No. Watch for potholes here. You'll twist your ankles in those shoes." He shone the flashlight beam on the pathway in front of her feet. "They've always made Christmas Eve their time alone together. I'm not usually here. Remember?"

"What about..." The past few days had been so packed with events. There hadn't been opportunities to really talk through what had happened. Hannah tightened her grip on Roman's hand. "Is Adam already in New York?"

"He flew out yesterday," Roman said shortly.

"Poor Adam," Hannah murmured.

"Yes. Poor Adam. I hope we get a chance to build some sort of relationship again."

Hannah shivered inside the red woolen coat she wore over a silk dress. "It won't be your fault if you don't. Be patient. Give him time to forgive himself."

Ahead lay the door to the walled garden. Roman pushed it open and they moved inside.

"Some might think we were mad, coming out here in the cold and dark on Christmas Eve," Hannah said.

He stopped abruptly and faced her. His eyes glinted, as did his teeth when he smiled faintly. "They would be people who don't know our history, Hannah. We're keeping a date. A seven-year-old date."

Her heart wasn't obeying orders not to jump around, nor her squirrelly stomach. "In that case, lead on. Let's get this show on the road." She hoped she sounded as flip as the words suggested. Doubtful.

"Now, you didn't ever know what I had in mind when I set up that date."

Her breath came in short bursts that sent white vapor into the air. "No, of course not." And she was a liar. At least, she'd had a very good idea what he'd intended.

Past the bench to the circle of dogwoods they went. Roman's flashlight picked out bending, sweeping branches—like the skeletons of crinoline skirts ducking and bobbing in the breeze.

They reached the fence around Esther Ashley's grave. Roman draped an arm over Hannah's shoulders and shone his flashlight on the pink headstone.

"Merry Christmas, Esther," Hannah said softly.

Roman hugged her tightly. "Yes, merry Christmas."

Quiet seconds passed before Hannah slipped her hands inside his jacket and around his middle. She turned her face up to his, and he looked steadily back into her eyes.

"Have we done what we came to do?" she asked him, a pulse pounding in her throat. "Can we go home now?"

"I don't think so."

He continued to watch her until she had to glance away.

"I've waited a long time for this night, Hannah."

She buried her face in his neck.

"Don't—" he gathered her hair behind her head "—don't distract me."

"How would I do that?"

He rested a cold, firm hand on her throat. "By making any move that interrupts my cool, calm, collected reasoning."

Hannah laughed. "I won't stir a muscle, sir." Immediately she found a way beneath his sweater to his shirt and ran her fingers up and down his spine.

Roman groaned. "This is serious, Hannah. Very important things have to be said here."

"Mmm." He smelled clean. She kissed his jaw. "Nice." The slight roughness of his skin against hers began to excite Hannah, and the almost imperceptible jut of his hips.

Roman stiffened his back and captured her face. "Be still," he said, his eyes narrowed. "I'm going to say my piece. Concentrate."

She smiled sweetly at him. "I am concentrating."

His chest expanded. "Yes. But concentrate on what I'm saying, please. I did show up here for that other date, y'know. Just in case."

Hannah's smile wavered. "I'm sorry, Roman. I don't like to think about that now. It makes me angry and sad. My mother… I can't blame it all on her. I should have waited until I could talk to you before leaving. But I'm still angry with her. So angry."

"You'll work that through in time. I wanted to talk to you here on Christmas Eve because it felt right. There was something I wanted to ask you, and I'd sort of decided Seth and

Esther might like to be in on it. I still want to ask you that question, Hannah. And this has to be the place to do it.''

Roman stepped back.

"What are you doing?'' Hannah covered her mouth. "Roman! Get up, you idiot!''

Ignoring her, he went down on one knee, wincing as he made contact with gravel.

"Roman!'' She giggled, looking around.

"Exactly,'' he said. "Check for audience reaction. When you put on a performance, you'd better make sure the people you put it on for approve. Do you think Esther would have taken Seth seriously if he hadn't stuck with the formalities?''

"You're a nut!''

Roman sighed. "In that case, I guess I might as well give this up. You're too discerning a woman to marry a nut.''

Hannah stood very still, her hand still hovering over her mouth. Fine shiny droplets of moisture swirled in the flashlight beam. The wind blew a little harder, and colder, and swept Roman's hair this way and that. He frowned slightly, turning his mouth down slightly.

"Roman…'' She closed her eyes, unsure what she wanted to say.

"I'd be very honored if you'd consent to becoming my bride,'' Roman said clearly.

Hannah squeezed her eyes even more tightly shut. This wasn't a joke anymore. He meant it.

"My knee hurts.''

Her eyes flew open. "What?''

"Will you?''

"Will I…''

"Will you marry me?'' he almost shouted.

"Get up.'' She felt giddy. "Up!''

Roman didn't budge. "Hannah, answer me.''

"Yes, oh yes, I will marry you.''

Roman's whoop made Hannah jump. He bobbed to his feet and swept her into his arms. "Great. Wonderful.'' He kissed her gently. "Oh, Hannah, it's finally going to happen for us.''

"Yes." She seemed to have lost the ability to think clearly. "When?"

"I..." When she'd had a chance to really realize what she'd just agreed to. "I don't know."

"Tonight?"

Roman had asked her to marry him and she'd said yes. "Tonight? That's silly, Roman. You know we can't get married tonight."

"Tomorrow, then?" His grin made his eyes glitter.

"Oh, yes, I'm quite sure we can arrange to be married tomorrow...on Christmas Day. Roman, there must be all kinds of things we'll have to do first."

Roman crossed his arms and frowned. "You leave this to me. But be ready. The minute everything's arranged, I'll snatch you away. You won't know when I'll be arriving with the ladder."

Hannah hunched her shoulders. "I'll be ready."

He trailed a finger down the side of her face and moved close. "I want to make love to you."

Her knees weakened.

"I want to do it slowly." His arm went around her and he smoothed his mouth across her brow. "I want to watch your eyes when I touch you. I want—"

Hannah pressed her fingers to his lips. "Not in front of Seth and Esther."

Roman cleared his throat. "Of course not. Let's go. I want to leap about...and shout. I want to tell people."

Grabbing her hand, he spun Hannah around and set off at a pace that forced her to scramble in the high heels she hadn't thought to change before leaving the shop. He didn't slow down until they'd crossed the back lawns, skirted the house and arrived in the driveway.

"We'll go and tell Mom and Jed." He hugged her to him.

"No. I want you all to myself."

"Roman, look!" Hannah pulled away and pointed. "Look at the house. The trees."

A soft glow showed at every window. In trees and bushes along the veranda, tiny colored lights twinkled and shivered.

"I don't get it," Roman said, almost to himself. "They weren't there when we got here."

"They must have been. They just weren't turned on." She clutched his sleeve. "Someone must have moved in."

Roman didn't move, or answer.

"Oh, Roman, that means—"

"Come on," he said, cutting her off. "Come with me."

His tone baffled her. He sounded...eager?

At the foot of the front steps he stopped, and Hannah clung to his arm. "The door's open," she whispered.

She could see the sparkle of light on myriad crystal prisms in the beautiful hall chandelier.

Then she heard the music. Tinkling bells and the sweet tone of flutes. "How beautiful it is," she told Roman. "Christmas music."

"It's—" He stared straight ahead.

Hannah followed the direction of his stare and smiled. Ambling through the front door came the gardener. Smiling, he walked down the steps toward them.

"Hello," Hannah called.

"Hello, Hannah. Hello, Roman. I was hoping the two of you might be out tonight."

She wondered why, but didn't ask.

Roman moved forward, his hand outstretched, but the gardener didn't appear to notice. He pointed back to the house. "Got a message from the owners. Asked me to open the place up a bit. Warm it through. Thought I was going to have to sit here all night till I saw you two coming."

"Did you put up the Christmas lights?" Hannah asked and chuckled. "Of course you did. Who else? They look lovely." With every fresh gust of wind, branches swayed and colored rays trembled.

Roman was silent. Hannah glanced up at him. "What's wrong?"

He stirred. "Nothing. Absolutely nothing."

"Are you two in a hurry?" the gardener asked. "Could you stay awhile, then put the lights out when you leave? The fire's alight in the sitting room. Won't hurt to leave it. There's a little something to drink and a bite to eat there, too. That was just in case you came."

"Roman," Hannah said urgently. "Can we stay?"

He turned a brilliant smile on her. "You bet we can."

"We'll make sure everything's all right," Hannah said.

"I left what you'll need," the gardener said. "Take good care of it all."

"Thank you," Roman said. "I expect you need to get home to your family."

The man stood at the foot of the steps. "Yes," he said, his face oddly remote, Hannah thought. "Yes, it's time to go now."

He walked past them.

Hannah slipped her hand into Roman's and they walked, side by side, up the steps. In the doorway, Roman paused, glanced at Hannah. "This is very strange, but I'm not complaining."

"Neither am I." She turned and called, "Thank you."

"Yes," Roman said. "Merry Christmas to— He's gone."

"Must be in a hurry," Hannah said. "His wife's probably waiting for him."

"He makes a habit of that. Hurrying away while you aren't looking. I wonder where he lives."

"I've never thought to ask." She pulled Roman inside and closed the door. "It's warm in here. Wonderful."

As if they shared one mind, Roman and Hannah made their way to the sitting room. On the threshold they stopped and drew in a simultaneous breath. A fire leaped in the fireplace, throwing dancing shadows over the walls. More colored lights had been tucked into the holly lining the mantel.

On a low gilt table before the fire stood a gleaming silver tray. A bottle of champagne, a white cloth wrapped around its neck, nestled in an ice bucket flanked by hollow-stemmed glasses.

"I don't get this," Roman muttered.

Hannah shook her head. "Neither do I. But sometimes it's better not to ask questions." She picked up a small crystal platter of canapés and offered it to him.

"I'm not hungry." He walked to the windows, drew the drapes shut and stood with his back to her.

Hannah watched him. His broad shoulders were hunched beneath his leather jacket. "Maybe we should just see to the lights and get back to town," she said.

Roman's answer was to take off the jacket and turn toward her. The dark, set lines of his face startled Hannah. She stared into his eyes and drew in a sharp breath. The passion she saw there was raw and demanding.

"Champagne?" Without waiting for her response, he picked up the bottle and popped the cork. Foam bubbled over, but he'd already swept a glass beneath the neck. He poured once, twice, and set the bottle down. "What shall we drink to?"

He held himself erect. His fingers, when they touched hers against a glass, were still cold.

"To us?" she suggested. Tender, singing heat sprang to life in her belly. "Roman?"

"To us," he said, raising his own glass.

Hannah drank.

Roman regarded her steadily over the rim of his glass, before setting it down and going to put another log on the fire. He stared at the flames and showers of sparks shooting up the chimney.

"I meant what I said to you out there," he said. "I want to make love to you. And now I know I want to do it here. It's right."

Hannah drank her champagne more quickly than she should and set down the glass. Inside her head, her body, a dull heavy throbbing began.

"Aren't you going to say anything?"

Hannah swallowed and touched the top button on her coat.

"I'll do it," Roman said. But when his fingers sought the

button they were clumsy. He worked it free and moved to the next one.

Hannah looked at the way his dark, well-cut hair grew in waves. The wind had tousled it across his puckered forehead. Lowered in concentration, his eyelashes were thick, the angles of his face sharply defined. Sensuality showed in the clear contours of his wide mouth.

He finished undoing her coat and pushed it back from the black silk dress. "God, you look wonderful." Splaying his fingers over her sides, he brought his thumbs to rest against her breasts.

"Are...Roman..." She wanted to ask about the wildness she felt in him. It thrilled and frightened her—excited her until her lungs felt crushed.

As if she hadn't spoken, he slipped his hands to her waist, over her hips. Gathering the dress fabric, he hiked it up until warm air slipped around Hannah's legs and she closed her eyes.

"Hannah, Hannah," Roman murmured. His mouth found hers, teased and tasted, brushed and opened. She felt him drawing her inside him with tongue and teeth—sometimes gentle, sometimes desperate. He grasped her thighs, urged her hips against his and ground them together.

"Take off the coat," he said, breathless.

She arched her back, shrugging the heavy wool away.

Her arms were behind her back when Roman slipped his hands inside the crossover bodice of her dress. She moaned, struggling to free her hands. But she saw Roman's smile, his eyes hot with desire, and then he worked the scanty lace of her bra down and covered her breasts, smoothing, rubbing her nipples with his palms, cupping pulsing flesh while her strength ebbed.

The coat fell, but Hannah didn't touch Roman. Tipping her head back, she offered herself to him—and he bent to kiss the sensitive skin. Hannah ran her fingers into his hair and pressed him to her.

"God." Roman straightened. His chest rose and fell rapidly. "You are so beautiful, my love." Carefully, strain showing in every feature, he found the front hook on her bra and brushed aside the black lace. He caressed the naked swell of her breasts.

Roman backed her to the chaise, eased her to sit and, taking the bra straps with it, slid the bodice of her dress down until it settled at her elbows.

He didn't want her to move. He wanted to do this. Hannah grew hot, and the heat brought molten pressure to hidden places. She opened her mouth to breathe.

"Stay where you are," Roman said quietly. He pulled his sweater over his head and tossed it aside. His white shirt, thin enough to show the shadow of dark hair beneath, fitted his wide chest and shoulders perfectly.

"Are you thirsty?" he asked. "I am." He took up the champagne and drank from the bottle before tipping it to Hannah's lips. She coughed and laughed, then let out a small shriek when cold droplets sprayed her skin.

Roman held her still. A tiny river of champagne coursed down her chest. He watched it, caught the trickle with a thumb and rubbed it on a nipple, made slow, maddening circles over the hardening flesh. Hannah writhed. His features swam before her blurred vision. She felt him sweep up another drop of champagne and lavish attention on her other breast. Then his hands were gone, replaced by his gently sucking mouth.

Without taking his face from her, he struggled out of his shirt. Hannah heard the buckle on his belt clink, and the sharp sound of a zipper being pulled down. She kicked off her shoes.

Only two buttons at the waist fastened her dress. Roman sat on his heels. He studied her face, her body, before parting the skirt. His eyes closed for an instant before he smoothed trembling hands over her stockings and bent to kiss the bare skin at the lacy edge of her panties. Heat flooded Hannah and she moaned. Roman undid the buttons and pulled her to her feet, tugging the dress away.

While she stood before him, Roman took off the rest of his

clothes. His waist was narrow, his belly flat. Hannah let her eyes travel over him: long, strongly muscled legs, sprinkled with dark hair, hard and narrow hips—a thrusting arousal. She quivered.

Roman took Hannah into his arms. He kissed her lips, her jaw, her neck, crushing her breasts to his chest, driving his insistent hardness into her belly. This was what the waiting years had been for. This was why there had never been, could never be, another man for her. She'd been waiting to find this passion with Roman.

He parted from her for an instant, spinning her around so that the fire's heat warmed her face, pulling her back against him and skimming her panties from her hips and letting them drop. Hannah toed them aside the instant before Roman knelt behind her, pulling her onto his lap.

Hannah didn't know what she said. Roman's murmurs were incoherent. He caressed her back, stroked her sides, covered and supported her breasts until his weight drove her forward onto her hands.

In a hot, dark second she registered what they were doing. The next second brought molten oblivion, except to the searing of nerve and soft moist skin. They joined, and behind her closed eyelids, Hannah saw heated gold.

CAUTIOUSLY, TRYING NOT to disturb Hannah, Roman stirred the fire and added more wood. He'd wrapped her in her coat, but the room had grown chilly.

Dressed in his slacks, with his shirt hanging loose, he sat by the hearth and watched her. She snuggled, not really asleep, he knew, but hanging on to the luxurious drowsiness they'd created together. They were going to be married. Sighing, he tilted his head and let the warmth the thought brought fill him.

Her thick russet hair fanned in a tangled mass on the carpet. The sprinkle of freckles showed clearly across her nose. Roman got up and lifted a drape. It had to be almost midnight.

"I'll be… Good grief." He peered closer, his breath clouding the glass.

"What is it?" He heard Hannah moving around behind him.

"Come and see."

Wrapped in her coat but still shivering, she came to stand beside him. "It isn't," she said, squinting. "It can't be."

"It sure is snow."

"Snow doesn't fall here. Not ever." She looked at him. "Almost never."

"Well, this is the almost never."

"Snow for Christmas," she said quietly, her eyes bright. "Perfect."

"You're perfect." He left her to take an envelope from his pocket. "This is for you. For us, if you agree."

She turned the envelope over.

"Open it."

Looking apprehensive, she did as he asked and pulled out a sheet of paper Hannah read, and reread. "Roman! Why didn't you tell me?"

"Because I wanted the moment to be right. I only got that this afternoon."

"You're buying Harmony?"

"We're buying Harmony. If you want to. I can live here and run the farm with tenants in the house there. You can live here and run the shop. You did make up your mind about that?" She'd told him that Jane had offered to sell.

"Yes. I definitely want the shop. And I want Harmony."

Hannah read again, aloud: *"In accordance with our clients' wishes we request that you add the name Seth Ashley to his wife's headstone."* She looked up. "Roman, I wonder why they didn't do it themselves years ago."

"Never got around to it, I guess. But we will." Roman took the envelope and stuffed it in his back pocket. "One more thing. Is this okay?" From another pocket he pulled a ring. "I took it out of the box. It was too bulky."

Open-mouthed, Hannah stared at the diamond solitaire he

offered. "Roman! Loose in your pocket? You could have lost it."

He grinned wryly. "Not if I'd done what I planned and given it to you properly."

She eyed him quizzically.

He shrugged. "I should have offered you the ring *before* I ravished you. Is it okay? We can get something else if you don't like it."

Wrinkling her nose, Hannah held out her hand. "I'll give it a trial period."

The exultation he felt wavered. "Really. We don't have to keep this one."

"Yes, we do." She grinned and helped him put the ring on her finger. "It's absolutely beautiful. I'll be crazy about it forever. And *I* ravished you."

"Great," he said. "I wasn't sure. I just hoped you'd... What did you say?"

"I ravished you," she said with evident satisfaction. "Led you on, then took advantage when passion overcame you."

"Hannah!" Roman grabbed her and started to unwrap the coat she clutched over her breasts. "We'll see who does the ravishing around here."

"Stop." She forgot the coat. "Oh, Roman. You are such a romantic."

He turned, still holding her in one arm. "What do you mean?"

"You know very well. What a lovely idea."

Etched in the window, beside Seth and Esther Ashley's heart, was another. In the middle, it bore the inscription: Roman Loves Hannah. Hannah Loves Roman.

"When did you do that?" Roman asked.

Hannah dug his ribs. "I thought you were the one who never fibbed." Her smile grew even broader. "Never mind. It must have been one of those Christmas angels we talked about."

"Sure." Roman rested his chin atop her head and closed his eyes. "An angel with perfect timing." If she wanted to call herself an angel, it was okay with him. Anything Hannah wanted was okay with him.

Epilogue

"Be nice," Hannah whispered. "Donna almost lives at that post office. This historical society stuff makes a good break for her. And it's her pride and joy."

Roman gave a phony smile. "I'm nice. Don't I look nice? Aren't I *always* nice?"

"You're impossible. Behave. Here come Donna and Penny."

Penny trailed behind Donna Jackson, her arms stretched around a heavy book. She grinned importantly. "Miss Jackson says I'm a great helper."

"She is, indeed," Donna said. She straightened the brown canvas apron she wore over her inevitable blouse and skirt. "I'm glad you newlyweds decided you could share yourselves for an afternoon."

Hannah looked at her shoes. Immediately Roman's hand settled possessively at her waist.

"Wasn't it nice of the Gradys to leave this lovely house to the historical society?" Donna said. "We were all sorry to see them go, of course. But this is still wonderful to have."

The Gradys had left two months earlier, a day or so after Christmas, evidently. Hannah hadn't seen them herself since the Christmas Fair.

"I never did get to see it before the Gradys went away," Hannah said. "Jane told me it was beautiful. Now I believe it." Generously proportioned, with a wide entrance hall and sweeping curved staircase, the house had been lovingly renovated. Carved oak moldings gleamed around William Morris panels in shades of green and gold. Wooden floors glowed like dark satin.

"Daddy," Penny said. She stood in front of Donna and made a face. "Donna wants you to look at some old photographs. She says you and Hannah will be interested in them."

Hannah didn't dare look at Roman. "Show us where they are, Donna." So far things seemed to be going very well between Penny and Roman. The child definitely liked Hannah. If there were troubles ahead, they'd face them when they arrived.

"Very old photographs, they are," Donna said, sounding proud. "Daguerreotypes and ambrotypes mostly. We found them in the basement here. Imagine that. Reverend and Mrs. Grady must never have gone down there. The display's in the dining room."

Twelve places were set at the dining table. Very old silver shone dully around Spode china edged with gold. Blood-red crystal reflected in the light of an intricately enameled chandelier.

"On the sideboard," Donna said. "We didn't want them too close to windows. Penny, give Hannah that leather album."

Dutifully Penny handed over her burden. "Can I go back to the kitchen?" she asked. "We baked some cookies."

Hannah scarcely heard Roman agree. She'd opened the album and begun to turn thick pages of photographs.

"People used to have pictures taken and mounted on cards to give away to their families and friends," Donna said in a tone that suggested reverence. "*Cartes de visite,* they called them. That's what those are. The albums were specially designed."

Hannah read the inscription inside the front page. "Roman!" He'd wandered to the silver-framed collection on the sideboard. "Look at this."

"I'd better go and see what Penny's up to," Donna said. "Come and have cookies when you're ready."

Too excited to stand still, Hannah nodded vigorously and sat on a tufted, red velvet sofa. "Seth and Esther Ashley," she told Roman. "This is *theirs*. Most of these were taken outside Harmony."

"You're kidding." He sat beside her. "How do we know if any of the pictures are of them?"

"We'll know." Of course, they'd know.

"How?"

"We just will. Look at the gardens, Roman. They're beautiful." In shot after shot, Harmony's grounds bloomed with lush flowers. There was the sundial flanked by rose bushes. Another picture showed clematis dripping from a trellis along the front porch.

Roman laughed and rested his chin on her shoulder to watch as she slowly turned pages. "Wait right there!" He got up and went to the sideboard to pick up a frame. Returning slowly, he studied the photograph. "This must be them."

When he sat again he showed Hannah a wedding picture. She looked from the faces picked out in the gold tones of a daguerreotype, to the shots in the album. The same faces appeared again and again.

"Yes," Hannah said softly. "Seth and Esther. Look how tiny she was, and how fair."

"Well, they've finally got what they wanted," Roman said. He lifted Hannah's hand and kissed her fingertips. "Lovers to carry on at Harmony. I hope they approve of us."

"I'm sure they do." Hannah realized she felt shaky. Her hands trembled. "Such good-looking people. His eyes are so kind. And she looks as if she's trying not to laugh. Her dress in this one—" she turned the album toward Roman "—it reminds me of Jane's dresses. She used to dress in old-fashioned costume for the shop."

Roman leaned closer. "Do you know, they look a lot like the Gradys."

"Yes, you're right. But Esther still looks more like Jane to me.'' Hannah took the wedding picture from him. Esther's wedding gown appeared to have been made of fine cotton lawn with bands of lace joining tiers on a billowing skirt. "I wonder if she made the dress. Don't you think she looks a bit like Jane?''

"I don't know. I only met her briefly.''

"That's right,'' Hannah said with regret. "I'd forgotten. I'm sorry she doesn't intend to come back here.''

"It's great you're enjoying the shop,'' Roman told her. "Hannah, we shouldn't be too long here today. Jed's coming to Harmony to help me haul away some of the bushes I cleared.''

"It's too bad the gardener suddenly dropped out of sight.'' Hannah sighed. Since Christmas Eve there had been no sign of the man. "Did you make any more enquiries about him?''

"Nobody seems to know anything about him. I can't even find someone who met him apart from us.''

"Jane did,'' Hannah said, frowning.

"He'd have fitted right in here, wouldn't he?'' Roman tapped a picture of Seth Ashley on the back lawn in front of what was now a giant sycamore. "Could almost be the same man.''

"I suppose,'' Hannah said. "Let's talk to Donna and take Penny home with us. We can look at these some more later.'' Roman put the wedding picture in its place on the sideboard and Hannah closed the album. "Go and be nice to Donna. I'll be right there.''

As soon as she was alone, Hannah opened the album to the last page and found what she was looking for: a picture of Seth as an older man. Bearded, dressed in a layered cloak and a light-colored Stetson, he stood in front of Harmony with one booted foot braced on a step. She'd only glanced at it before closing the album for the first time.

He looked like…? Hannah shook her head and stood. The cloak was familiar, that's all. The old man who'd brought Roman's lost letter to her door in Chicago had worn a cloak similar to this, or so it seemed in her memory. Her memory was obviously overloaded. Any likeness between the two men was coincidental.

She set the album on the sofa. She never had found the letter again after leaving Chicago. Not that she cared anymore. One day she must remember to tell Roman exactly what had happened to it.

"HOLD MY HAND, Esther."

"I love you, Seth."

"I know. And I love you. Do you smell Christmas?"

"Oh, yes. Cinnamon and cloves."

"And pine, Esther. And frost on holly berries."

"A magic time. Give love. Gather love."

"And make love grow forever, my angel."

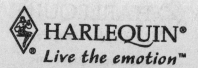

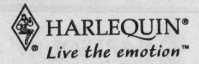

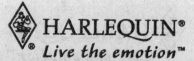

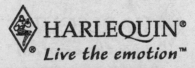

A night she would never forget...

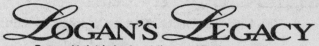

Because birthright has its privileges and family ties run deep.

THE BACHELOR

**by national
bestselling author**

MARIE FERRARELLA

With a full-time job and a son to care for, event planner
Jenny Hall didn't have time for men. So when her friends
pooled their money at a bachelor auction to buy her a date
with Eric Logan, she was shocked—especially when she
found herself falling into bed with the billionaire playboy!

Coming in October 2004.

Where love comes alive™